Thunderbird Trail

**Center Point
Large Print**

Also by William Cold MacDonald and available from Center Point Large Print:

The Battle at Three-cross
Master of the Mesa
Ranger Man
The Singing Scorpion
Powdersmoke Justice

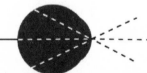

**This Large Print Book carries the
Seal of Approval of N.A.V.H.**

Thunderbird
Trail

William
Colt
MacDonald

CENTER POINT PUBLISHING
THORNDIKE, MAINE

This Center Point Large Print edition
is published in the year 2011 by arrangement with
Golden West Literary Agency.

The text of this Large Print edition is unabridged.
In other aspects, this book may vary
from the original edition.
Printed in the United States of America
on permanent paper.
Set in 16-point Times New Roman type.

ISBN: 978-1-61173-104-0

Library of Congress Cataloging-in-Publication Data

MacDonald, William Colt, 1891–1968.
Thunderbird Trail / William Colt MacDonald.
p. cm.
ISBN 978-1-61173-104-0 (library binding : alk. paper)
1. Large type books. I. Title.
PS3525.A2122T47 2011
813′.52—dc22
                                    2011004816

1. Trail to Destiny

After the sun lifted above the Sangre de Esteban Mountains and penetrated the thicket of brush, much of the chill departed from the atmosphere, which all through the previous night had held more than a touch of frost. To the hidden man— and to the gray horse as well—the advent of the warmer morning light was more than welcome. There'd been a certain stiffening of muscles where they'd waited, close to the damp earth, shielded from view in a tall clump of aspens, already commencing to turn yellow, and hedged about with a growth of stunted cedar, tall grass, and other wild vegetation.

And then, at long last, the staccato beating of hoofs heralded the approach of a rider, the rider for whom the man with the gray horse had maintained the long vigil of the dark hours. The hidden man had quickly seized his saddle blanket and held it over the head of the gray animal, that no whinnied greeting might betray their concealed nearness. By then the rapidly pounding hoofs had drummed nearer and a chestnut gelding swept into view in the clear morning sunlight, its rider seated, arrow-straight, in the saddle and unaware of the man and gray horse lurking not twenty-five yards distant behind the curtain of tangled brush. The chestnut gelding drove on past, and within a

5

few minutes its running hoofbeats commenced to recede in the distance.

Even then the man with the gray horse appeared in no hurry to follow. Perhaps he required time in which to control the hot wave of insensate rage that engulfed his frame. He peered, tight-lipped, through the screening leaves until the rider on the chestnut gelding had passed from sight around the shoulder of a high outcropping of eroded granite. Only then had he tensely commenced saddling up the gray horse. There was no use, he grimly told himself, trailing too closely behind that chestnut animal.

Eventually he climbed on his mount. Once he'd taken up the trail, he found it easy to follow. Two days previously it had rained hard; hoofmarks showed clearly in the soft, still-moist earth as they led the way not far distant from the west bank of a willow- and cottonwood-bordered stream of water. As the river traced a leisurely winding course, so ran the tracks of the chestnut horse.

An hour passed while the rider on the gray horse moved steadily forward, his narrowed eyes picking up the hoofprints left by the chestnut gelding ahead. And then the tracks of another horse, coming from the west, met and joined those made by the chestnut. The two, then, had halted a moment before proceeding, side by side.

Now the rider on the gray mount had a definite confirmation of his suspicions, though it brought no relaxation in his movements. If anything, the tight lines about his mouth became even more relentless as he leaned from the saddle to gaze on the parallel lines of hoofprints two horses had chopped in the soft earth. Involuntarily one hand crept toward the gun, holstered at his right hip. He checked the movement just as his fingers were closing about the walnut butt, and an angry, low-toned oath burst from his stiff lips.

"Plenty time yet for that," he fiercely told himself, and jammed savage spurs against the gray horse's ribs. Just as savagely he halted the beast's sudden tendency to bolt, and checked it once more to a slower pace. He rode on, muttering angrily something that had to do with "wiping out a double-crosser," his narrowed eyes seldom lifting from the double set of hoofprints he was following.

After a time the trail swung directly toward the narrow river, known as the Rio Esteban, and the hoofprints disappeared in the cool, limpid waters. The gray horse followed and, when knee-deep, halted to drink, but the man on its back impatiently urged it on across the gravel-littered bottom. As the stream's depth increased, the man drew his feet from stirrups and held them high, until the water once again became shallow. A moment later the gray was scrambling up the slightly sloping opposite bank, only a few feet from the point at which the pair of horses had emerged earlier.

Now the trail commenced to climb into the foothills, wending its way through brilliant, sun-lighted groves of yellow aspens, the early morning breeze transforming the leaves to shimmering gold which cast an ever-moving aureolin- and shadow-dappled patter over gray horse and rider. A sudden break in the trees showed a clearing ahead, and the gray was at once pulled to a halt while its rider dismounted, dropping his reins to the earth. At the far edge of the clearing stood a roughly built cabin of peeled logs, in the front wall of which was an open doorway and a paneless window.

Hidden among the trees, the man paused, scrutinizing the cabin with narrowed, angry eyes. If he was disappointed in not seeing the two horses he'd been following, there was nothing in his features to indicate such state of mind. The horses might well be screened from view in the trees and brush beyond the rear of the cabin. For a moment, just the briefest moment, the thought crossed his mind that the riders might have gone on, that the cabin was unoccupied; then an abrupt bit of movement against the window's darker rectangle dispelled the idea.

The man wondered if he had been observed and waited, with bated breath, for someone to appear in the cabin doorway. Minutes ticked off; the doorway was as empty as before. The waiting man breathed a trifle easier. Gradually a frown appeared on his forehead, as he endeavored to plan his next move. Would it be best to walk boldly in, or should he take a roundabout course, sneak up on the cabin before the occupants could become aware of his presence? He leaned against the saddle of the gray horse, contemplating the best procedure, lines of thought deepening in his weathered features.

Overhead, gamboge-tinted treetops formed moving patterns against the turquoise sky. Beyond the cabin of peeled logs the foothills swelled until they blended with the towering heights of the Sangre de Estebans. Grass waved lazily in the morning breeze before the cabin, and not far from the doorway a clump of opuntias raised clusters of ovate heads, their last summer's blooms now sere and withered.

All this the hidden man took in abstractedly. A pair of buzzards winging, dipping, soaring, like vagrant bits of paper caught in the wind, momentarily held his attention and brought to mind the old question as to whether the birds could scent death before it actually transpired, or if it were but mere chance that drew them to spots where life had but recently ended.

The man stirred himself impatiently. "Time's awasting," he muttered, his upper lip lifting in a half snarl. "This showdown can't be postponed. No man living is going to be able to boast he robbed me and got away with it. Thunderbird luck! Bah!" He paused a moment more, mentally arranging words, accusations, the phrases that would make clear his position and justify the thing he planned to do.

Abruptly he left the shelter of the trees and walked boldly into the clearing toward the cabin. His arms swung freely at his sides, each stride through the thick grass attesting his unswerving, indomitable purpose. As he neared the log structure the six-shooter was drawn from holster, nor did he hail whoever was within the cabin to give warning of his approach.

Still there was no movement to be seen there, and when he pushed through the open doorway of the cabin only a sharp exclamation greeted his appearance. Then followed quick, hot words, the tones heightened, blurred, confused, by the clash of angry wills. The voices suddenly died away, to be replaced by the sounds of rapid, scuffling steps. The jarring report of a heavy weapon shook the cabin rafters, to be followed, an instant later, by a second explosion. Black powder smoke drifted through the paneless window.

Overhead the floating buzzards circled nearer the cabin roof.

2. Special Investigator

The owlish eyes of the clerk at the reception desk of the Cenotaph House bulged behind his spectacles. Never in all his years of hotel management had he heard anything quite like this. Of course, you could never tell about these western people; they lacked the refinements of folks back East in, say, Kansas City. There ladies—genuine ladies, that is—didn't make such requests or propose such . . . Gracious! What ever was the world coming to? And for *this* to come on top of all this other business, with the freight wreck down the line, and passengers from the Limited, which couldn't go through, being dumped off at Cenotaph to fill the hotel to overflowing, not to mention the way he'd had to find rooms all over town, even to the extent of sending some of the passengers to that terrible dive of a place, the Cowmen's Rest, over west of Cochise Street, and that Mexican boardinghouse. . . . His mind went off at a tangent again. Some women, yes, but not the wife of one of the most prosperous ranchers in the country—

"Toby Nixon! Have you lost your mind?" The feminine tones were tart.

Looking at her, and he felt his eyes almost glazing, the hotel clerk wasn't certain whether his mind was just slipping or if he had already lost it.

He glanced quickly about the small lobby to see if anyone else was listening. He noted that at least two of the drummers, seated near the window, had dropped their boredom and were eying the slim feminine figure at the desk with definite approval and admiration.

As had a good many men before them. The girl—she was probably in the neighborhood of twenty-five, though she looked much younger—was fairly glowing with health and vitality. Dark, lustrous eyes, a straight nose, a determined chin, and full red lips. Despite the well-worn high-heeled boots, divided riding skirt and fawn-colored, dusty sombrero that covered her thick glossy black hair, she had a certain poise, a definite sureness of bearing that was unusual. The quirt hung at her left wrist slapped impatiently at her skirt. She commenced again, "Toby! I want you—"

Toby Nixon found his voice: "But if he's not in the dining room, at supper, Mrs. Harmon, I don't—"

"Fiddlesticks!" There was a bit of edge in the throaty contralto tones. "You asked once before if he was in the dining room and I told you I'd already looked there. Now I want his room number."

The clerk gulped and replied in a horrified whisper, "Mrs. Harmon, please! Perhaps, he isn't here—may not have arrived—I scarcely know where I'm at, with all this rush. The wreck, you know, has caused considerable fuss and bother. I don't know where I'm at from one minute to the next. Only that the railroad people keep one room reserved all the time, I'd never been able—"

"You'd never have been able to give Mr. Quist a room." Mrs. Harmon's voice was scornful as she finished the sentence Nixon had unwittingly commenced. "All right, Toby. I'll admit you're right when you say you don't where you're at. One instant you say he may not have arrived; the next you're telling me if the railroad hadn't had a room reserved—"

The clerk swallowed hard. "You'll pardon me, Mrs. Harmon, but you wouldn't think of going up there—a lady visiting a gentleman's hotel room . . ." The words dwindled weakly away, but the eyes continued their abject pleading.

"Toby! You're acting ridiculously. If you're so concerned about my good name, just send up word I'd like to see him, if he can spare a few minutes for me."

"I wouldn't dare, Mrs. Harmon. He gave strict orders he wasn't to be bothered—had to get some sleep—had a long trip to get here—I really couldn't—"

Mrs. Harmon started away from the desk. For an instant the clerk looked relieved, but the relief on his features was quickly changed to consternation as he saw she was heading in the direction of the stairs leading from the lobby to the second floor. Voicing a weak protest that brought the girl back to the desk, he asked, "What—what—where are you going?"

"Unless you give me that room number," the girl threatened tersely, "I intend to knock at every door upstairs until I find the right one—"

"Mrs. Harmon—"

"It's important, Toby, darned important! What's the number?" she concluded relentlessly.

Nixon wilted. "Number Seventeen," he said feebly. "It's the room overlooking the corner of Main and Lincoln Street."

"Thank you, Toby. We could both have saved considerable time if you'd been sensible in the first place, couldn't we?" And she bestowed such a bewitching smile on the dazed Toby that he began to think she'd been in the right all along. Before he realized it she had disappeared in the direction of the second floor.

One of the drummers sauntered over to the desk and leered at Toby. "Who's the peach?" he asked, shifting a fat cigar from one cheek to the other.

Nixon came out of his daze. "The *lady*," he said pointedly, "is the wife of one of our best-known cattlemen. She won't be interested in seeing your stock of liquor, or cigars, or dress goods, or anything else you're selling." Which was about as near as the clerk ever came to insulting one of his patrons.

Lighted kerosene lamps in the halls on the second floor enabled the girl quickly to locate Room Seventeen. The door was closed, but light showed through the crack at the bottom. She hesitated a moment, drew a deep breath, then knocked a trifle faintly. Now that she was here . . .

"Who is it?" The voice from beyond the door was deep with an almost musical quality, like a tone welling from a bass viol.

Without replying, she knocked again, this time more firmly.

A certain resignation showed in the voice now: "Hell's bells! If you can't talk, you might as well come in. It's unlocked."

Mrs. Harmon turned the knob. The door opened easily under her hand, giving her an instant view of the room furnished with dresser, washstand, double bed. There were a couple of straight-backed chairs A rag rug partially covered the bare wooden floor, and there were windows, with shades drawn, in two of the walls. There was also a table, on top of which were several sheets of paper, a lead pencil, a shaded oil lamp and—could she be sure?—perhaps, an instant before, a holstered gun, now swiftly covered with a flat-topped sombrero, as the tawny-haired man who had been sitting at the table came to his feet in a half-lazy, half-catlike movement.

"Well," he said, and again, "well," with just a

touch of surprise in the deep tones. "I think you must have the wrong room, lady."

The girl found her voice: "Not if you're Mr. Gregory Quist."

"That's the name." He waited, puzzled.

She closed the door and came farther into the room. "I'm Lilith Harmon."

He bowed slightly and waited again; then, seeing she was a bit flustered, nervous, he crossed and started to reopen the door, giving her an opportunity to regain her composure, but she stopped him with a gesture. "Please, Mr. Quist, leave it closed. I want to talk privately to you—if you'll let me."

"Of course." He placed a chair for her, again seating himself, and said apologetically, "If you'll just make it as brief as possible. Right now I'm pretty busy, Miss Harmon."

"Mrs. Harmon. I'm Gideon Harmon's wife. You may have heard of him. He owns the Thunderbird Ranch—that is, we do, though"—white, even teeth showed in a ghost of a smile—"I'm not sure just how valuable I am in the outfit's operation."

"I doubt Gideon Harmon has any doubts on that score," Quist said easily. If the remark anent her marital status brought any surprise, it didn't show in his features. "You know, I ran across Gid Harmon two or three times, back in the old days. Lord, I haven't been in these parts since the name of the town was changed to Cenotaph, until today.

16

It used to be Indian Mound—no, I wasn't a close friend of Gid's. Just met him a couple of times and drank with him at the only bar in town then. The town has sure boomed." He paused, waiting for her to continue.

Lilith Harmon had been studying Quist while he talked, wondering if his eyes were brown, or hazel, or really topaz, the way they looked when the light caught them a certain way. In a country where most men were addicted to beards, or at least mustaches, Gregory Quist was clean-shaven. She'd thought, when she first saw him on his feet, that he was but slightly taller than herself, but she realized now that it was the deep chest and wide shoulders that detracted from his height. His features were bony, the nose aquiline, the skin well tanned, except for the lighter strip across the broad forehead where a hatbrim had afforded protection from burning southwestern suns. His expression was quizzical, with a slightly sardonic quality.

Quist's clothing was quite ordinary—woolen shirt, corduroy trousers tucked into knee-length, high-heeled boots; a bandanna was knotted loosely about the shirt collar—but already Lilith Harmon sensed that here was a man out of the ordinary. He was compact, like a steel spring, every muscle in commission, every nerve rock-steady. Already he was gaining her somewhat reluctant approbation, and all the time she was remembering the things that had been spoken of him: hard, tough, relentless. She'd never heard anyone accuse him of being an unjust man, though. Perhaps, just perhaps, she might persuade him to see things her way.

"I scarcely know how to begin," she commenced at last. "I'm desperately in need of help, and—and—"

"It's something about Gid?" he put in helpfully.

"That's it. I think his life is in danger—"

"From what?" Gregory asked abruptly. "Anybody threatening him?"

"I think so. I don't know—that is, I haven't any actual proof. It's this way, Mr. Quist, you're a detective for the T. N. & A. S. Railroad—"

He cut in a bit dryly, "The Texas Northern & Arizona Southern has me down on its payroll as a special investigator, but that doesn't necessarily mean—say, how did you know I was coming here?"

"Early yesterday morning a freight train was wrecked just east of Puma Junction. Such things usually bring investigators—"

"That's not good enough, Mrs. Harmon. Investigators, yes, but for some time now I've been stationed 'way over on the El Paso division. To put it plainly, this isn't my bailiwick. I'm asking again just how you learned I was coming here."

This time she replied frankly, "Sheriff Blackmer

18

mentioned it to one of our hands, who told me, along with several other bits of gossip he brought from town."

"John Blackner always did talk too much." A trace of a scowl crossed the wide forehead beneath the tawny hair. "But it goes back farther than that. The telegrapher . . ." He let the thought dangle in mid-air.

"I suppose it was something like that," Lilith Harmon agreed. "Anyway, a man of your reputation couldn't go many places without being noticed."

"My reputation?" He raised his eyebrows.

"It's pretty well known," the girl smiled. "Even I remember a few things I've heard—read in the papers. Seven years ago you were working for one of the cattle associations. You cleaned out, one after the other, certain rustling rings. Then you joined up with the railroad—"

"Hired out is a good way to put it," he said wryly.

The girl continued, "There were those train robbers up in Wyoming—Union Pacific, then, wasn't it, or was it—"

"It doesn't matter," Quist said amusedly. "What else do you know about me?"

"There was a train robbery in Kansas. You landed those men. Was it in Oklahoma you cleared up that nest of freight thieves? And then you've accomplished various things for the T. N. & A. S.

Something special, no doubt, has brought you here. Oh yes, I just remembered, you had something to do with the apprehension of a gang known as the Hole-in-the-Rock bandits—"

"All but one," Quist smiled. "He got away. The worst of it was, he was the leader. That's always rankled. He just plain dropped from sight."

A mischievous smile crossed Lilith Harmon's lips. This was almost like a contest. "I think," she said slowly, "I could even tell you the name of that man who got away. Let me think . . . he was called Whitey—no! Whitney something—I've got it! Whitney Farrell. Right?"

"Right," he nodded, smiling. There was admiration in his eyes now. "You've sure got a memory for what you read."

The girl sobered suddenly. "But we're far off the subject. I think I've proven to you that you're the man to help me—us—if you will."

"In what way?"

"I want you to protect my husband, see that nothing happens to him. I'm terribly afraid."

"But, Mrs. Harmon, I'm under contract to the railroad. I couldn't take another job, not even if I was willing to. You see, you have no proof. This may all be in your own mind."

"I'm sure it isn't." The girl was twisting her handkerchief between her hands now, her dark eyes pleading for help. "You see, you're right here, anyway, and—and—"

Quist drew a watch from his pocket, then rose to his feet. "Look, Mrs. Harmon, I haven't had my supper yet, and I'll bet you haven't either. If we don't get downstairs the dining room will be closed. I'd like to have you take supper with me if you will, and maybe you can tell me exactly what's bothering you. One way or the other we'll get this business threshed out."

"That's mighty kind of you, Mr. Quist. I'll accept with thanks."

By the time they'd descended to the lobby and rounded the desk of the somewhat still-dazed Toby Nixon, Quist had donned a dark four-in-hand necktie and coat. In the dining room they found a table in a far corner. The crowd of half an hour before had commenced to thin out. Lilith Harmon appeared nervous, unable to concentrate on what she wanted for food when a waitress appeared at the table and said, "Good evenin', Mizz Harmon," and commenced to whisk the previous diner's crumbs from the table top. Quist ordered for both, glanced at his companion for confirmation and received an agreeing nod.

When the waitress had left, Mrs. Harmon continued, "I really don't know what we'll do, Mr. Quist, unless you do decide to help us. I'm really terribly worried."

"Something," Quist told her, "can probably be worked out, though I doubt I'll be able to help much. Just remember, nothing ever happens, good

21

or bad, *until it has actually happened.* There's little use of getting into a stew about what you fear may take place." And when the girl didn't reply, he insisted, "Now is there?"

"I'm not so sure," she said doggedly.

Silence fell between them until the food had been brought to the table. The food was only passable. Neither ate a great deal. Finally Quist opened the subject: "Just what is it you fear may happen to Gid Harmon?"

"That is exactly what I do not know. I do know something has been troubling him for the past two or three months. When I've asked what was wrong, he's always refused to say. He's had several letters—I do not know what they contained—that seem to have upset him considerably. Once, when he said I should be prepared for almost anything to happen, and I asked him why, he just put me off with a few words to the effect that I shouldn't worry, as I was well provided for in his will."

Quist considered. "There are very few things in this world that can't be arranged with money. I understand Gid Harmon is pretty well fixed. I've heard things from time to time. Made his money in mining, didn't he?"

Lilith nodded. "The old Thunderbird Mine. He'd been prospecting when he made his silver strike. Money was needed for development. He took in two pardners—"

22

"Who were they?"

"I really couldn't say. It was before I knew Gideon. Anyway, as he has explained it to me, considerable progress was made, but not all that was expected. A mining company from the East sent men to look over the proposition. The upshot was that the mining company bought out Gideon and his pardners for quite a sizeable sum of money. It all turned out luckily for Gideon and his pardners, as the vein shortly after ran out—petered out, as Gideon said—and the company was forced to abandon operations."

"In other words, Gid unloaded just in time."

"That's about it. But he always felt that name 'Thunderbird' spelled luck for him, so when he went into stock raising he branded a thunderbird design on his cattle. For earmarkings he used an under-half-crop, right and left, claiming it made the cattle's ears resemble thunderbirds. I could never quite see that, however. Once he even tried to get Cenotaph's name changed to Thunderbird, but that never succeeded."

"As a matter of fact, he was rather fanatical on the subject of thunderbirds, I'd say."

Quist's companion looked slightly dubious, then she nodded a little reluctantly. "I guess you could say that he was."

"No harm in that," Quist smiled reassuringly. "Lots of men are obsessed with certain designs, or coins, or something or other they feel has brought them luck. From all I hear that thunderbird luck stayed with Gid in cattle raising, too. Biggest outfit in this neck of the range, isn't it?"

Lilith shook her head. "Not any more. Even before I married him, Gideon decided he was working too hard, and sold off most of his holdings. The present Thunderbird Ranch is a relatively small one, just large enough, as Gideon expressed it, 'to keep his hand in.' The trouble is,"—a frown creased the lovely forehead—"with so much more time on his hands, he took to drinking more than he should."

"And that's caused trouble?"

"It's worried me. No actual trouble—oh, you mean did he become quarrelsome?"

"That's what I was thinking of."

"Not with me," Lilith said promptly. "He's had arguments with various men around Cenotaph. I don't think it was anything serious, though—"

"Men who'd be inclined to kill him?"

Mrs. Harmon forced a smile. "I hardly think it was that serious—just arguments how the best cattle could be bred, politics, and that sort of thing. The usual cow-country politics."

"You're not eating. Maybe I'm talking too much, or making—"

"That's what I came here to do. I'll get enough, don't fear." She forked up a bit of steak and placed it in her mouth.

Quist said slowly, "After Gid sold the

Thunderbird Mine, were his pardners dissatisfied with the division of profits, or did the company that bought the Thunderbird feel it had been cheated in any way?"

"I've never heard of anything of the sort."

Quist frowned. He didn't seem to be getting any place. He asked, "Did Gid ride to town with you?"

"No. Naturally, he didn't even know I planned to see you and ask your help." Her dark eyes widened at a sudden thought. "You won't tell him, will you?"

"Any particular reason why I shouldn't?"

"Good heavens, yes! He wouldn't like it at all. I know! He's so awfully independent, you know. He feels fully capable of handling his own problems. You won't tell him, will you?" she pleaded.

"Not if you put it that way. As a matter of fact, I doubt I'll see him, unless I run across him in Cenotaph. Look, Mrs. Harmon, I think you're making a mountain out of a gopher hole. Something may be on Gid's mind, but if it were serious I think he'd tell you. After all, you've given me nothing I can put a finger on. This may all be in your own mind."

"I just know you're wrong. Even if I haven't been able to give you actual proof of any sort, haven't you any faith in a woman's intuition?"

"As much as I have in a man's—only men call it a hunch. Sometimes it's all right; others, all a fellow gets from a hunch is a bad steer." He drained his cup of coffee and produced a long, thin cigar. "Don't mind, do you?"

She shook her head impatiently, and his match crackled. After a moment she asked, "Am I to conclude you won't help me—us?"

"I'm afraid so. In the first place, I'm under contract to the railroad. I've work here to do. There's a wreck to be investigated—"

"That shouldn't take too long. Afterward—"

"That's one of the things you can't be definite about. I've got to learn what is back of the wreck, whether it was just due to chance, or . . ." He didn't finish the words.

"You—you mean someone may have caused the wreck purposely?"

"That's what I mean."

"But why should anybody wreck a freight train?"

Quist smiled. "Have you forgotten, Mrs. Harmon, that up in my room you recollected my running down some freight thieves?"

Her red lips parted suddenly. She swallowed hard. "You think that is—"

"I don't think anything of the kind—right now. I'll have to see first."

Lilith considered that, then stated frankly, "At the risk of sounding pretty darned blunt I'd like to tell you that we—I—could pay you better money than the railroad people."

26

"For what?" he asked flatly.

"For staying here for a time to—to sort of look out for my husband—see that nothing happens to him. You could become friendly, learn what is on his mind. He might tell another man, even if he wouldn't tell a woman, even though that woman's his wife. You know, it's no secret to me that men know things they never tell women."

"It could be you're right," he conceded, and changed the subject: "Is Gid out to the ranch at present?"

She shook her head. "He left for Tanzburg day before yesterday. He should be back by tomorrow, if you'd consent to see him. As a matter of fact, I thought he might get home this morning."

"He's over there on business?"

"No," Lilith replied. "He's gone to see a doctor there. No, he's not sick. About a month back a horse threw him and he injured his right wrist. Somehow it didn't heal as it should, the local doctor didn't appear to be able to do anything, so Gideon planned to consult a Doctor—er—I think the name is Jorge."

"He didn't take the train." It was more of a statement than a question.

Lilith shook her head. "He went in the saddle. He prefers to ride that way, and mentioned something, before leaving, about intending to make a leisurely trip of it—" She broke off. "Mr. Quist, you will help us, won't you?"

Slowly he shook his head. "My first duty is to the railroad. We have law officers in the county. There are plenty of private detectives you could hire. A minute ago you mentioned something about freight thieves. If this recent wreck should involve me in something of that kind, you can see I'd have no time to devote to Gid's welfare."

"I see." Lilith looked disappointed. She considered a moment, eyes downcast, then suddenly raised her head. "Mr. Quist, suppose Gideon's welfare was in some way connected with freight thieving—"

He asked quickly, "What do you mean by that?"

Before Lilith could reply, the waitress approached the table and said to Quist, "Sheriff Blackmer is outside the door—says he'd like to see you right away. He says it's very important."

Quist rose from his chair, asked to be excused for a few minutes, and left the dining room. In the lobby, not far from the desk, John Blackmer, a thick-bodied man with sweeping tobacco-stained yellow mustaches and the star of office on his flimsy vest, was waiting. Quist approached and the sheriff said, "Bad business ahead, Greg."

"What's on your mind, John?"

Blackmer jerked one thumb toward the dining room. "That's Missis Harmon in there with you, ain't it?"

Quist said shortly, "You probably took a look

28

before you had me called out here. What you asking for?"

"Now don't you get techy with me, Greg. This is serious and you got a duty ahead."

"What duty? What's serious? Let's drop all the mystery and talk up."

"We just got word that Gid Harmon committed suicide."

3. Railroad Business

Scowling, Gregory Quist pushed open the door of his hotel room. A thin, gray-haired man in a suit of wrinkled "town" clothing rose quickly from the bed where he'd been resting. He had tired eyes and wore spectacles. Quist said, "Hello, Jay," and shook hands.

Jay Fletcher, division superintendent on the T. N. & A. S. Railroad, said fervently, "Thank God you got here, Greg."

"While we're on the subject of my getting here, it's a good thing I didn't plan to come in secretly. If there was anybody that didn't know I was due in Cenotaph, it's not your fault."

"You sound testy, Greg. What's up?"

"Why in hell shouldn't I sound testy? That bug man down to the station told the sheriff I was due, so of course the news got spread around."

Fletcher swore. "I'll fire that telegrapher and—"

"You'll do nothing of the sort," Quist cut in bluntly. "He just made a mistake. If you fire every man on this line who makes a mistake, you won't have anybody left to run things. We all make mistakes. Was he warned to keep his mouth shut?"

"Er—no. But that has nothing to do with—"

"All right. Now you make your mistake. Fire him! Who have you to take his place—right now when he's needed bad? Don't talk like a fool, Jay."

"I fire who I like," Fletcher said hotly. "Don't forget I'm running this division—"

"And don't you forget that when I'm here, you'll cooperate with me. If you doubt that, consult headquarters." Quist dropped into a chair and commenced to fit a pair of spurs to his boots. He continued, while he twisted a brown paper cigarette, "Look, Jay, it's useless you and me arguing. Things are enough butched up without that."

"I'm sorry, Greg." The look of anger was again replaced by his mask of weariness. "I've not slept since it happened. We've all gone practically insane rerouting trains over the Albuquerque & Abilene tracks, north of here. God knows what's happening west of Puma Junction."

"Probably having similar troubles over there, too. Jay, you've been out to the wreck?" He struck a match to his cigarette.

"I just returned from there before you came in. Toby Nixon said you were dining with a lady. I couldn't understand, at a time like this—"

"Now, don't go losing you head again." Quist swore. "And what a mess that got me into! That goddam John Blackmer!"

"What's Blackmer got to do with it?"

Quist put it briefly. "The lady was Gid Harmon's wife—"

"I've seen her." Fletcher forced a wan smile. "Maybe I can't blame you, after all—"

"—and while we were eating, Blackmer called me outside to tell me her husband had committed suicide out at the Thunderbird. Blackmer, the bustard, said so long as I was with her, it was my duty to break the news. Cripes A'mighty! I hadn't seen the lady an hour before. And her not even knowing Gid was at the ranch."

"What did you do?"

"What in hell do you think I did? I broke the news."

"And that brought on a lot more trouble, I suppose."

Quist shook his head. "Not much. She took it like a thoroughbred, though I thought for a moment she might keel over. Then she got hold of herself. That hotel clerk got some woman to go with her some place here in town where Lilith—Mrs. Harmon—has some sort of relative—" He broke off suddenly to look at a bottle standing on the table. The words on the label said "Glen Spey." Quist said, "That looks interesting."

"I remembered you favored scotch. It's a bottle from a broken case at the wreck. I've already drawn the cork."

"What are we waiting for?" Quist got two glasses and poured generous servings. They drank. Quist said, "Now tell me about it. Make it short. I've got to get out of here shortly."

"It's a heck of a mess," Fletcher said tiredly. "The whole train is flung antigodlin fashion along the tracks. I suppose the engineer was running fast down that grade getting up speed for the next pull into Puma Junction. A couple of the cars broke loose and plunged down the embankment, but it's taking time to clear the tracks of the rest and get the line back in operation. We had to get the derrick and wrecking crew out from Puma Junction, of course. They're doing all possible—"

"What about the train crew?"

"Engineer killed instantly, I should judge from what I could pick up. The fireman must have jumped. Maybe he'll live, maybe he won't. Somebody said his skull was cracked wide open. Only for the light of the fire—"

"Fire?"

"A Mex sheepherder saw the smoke and flame from some distance off. He'd been a section hand one time, and set out to investigate. He knew what to do and went down the tracks quite a spell to flag the Limited when it came along. Only for that, we might have had two wrecks—"

"I'm still wondering about the fire."

"The caboose caught and burned in nothing flat. Conductor and brakie inside." Fletcher hesitated a moment. "They didn't get out."

Quist's eyes narrowed thoughtfully. "Only the caboose burned?"

"That's all."

"I don't like it," Quist said flatly. "What about looting?"

"Three cars broken open. Lot of stuff bound for the Pacific coast—'Frisco was the destination—wine, cigars, scotch whisky, cases of clothing, some canned goods—a good many thousand dollars, Greg, has been lost. You've got to do something. That's the second wreck within three months, remember." He repeated, "You've simply got to do something. Next time it may be a passenger train. Folks will get afraid to travel on our line."

Quist said shortly, "I'll do something. But t'heck with folks and their fears. I'm thinking about that freight crew." He rose to his feet and slipped off his coat. Then, lifting from the table the short-barreled forty-four six-shooter, in its underarm holster, he quickly fitted the harness about his thick chest.

Fletcher eyed the proceeding with a certain interest mingled with surprise. "That's a new rig-up since we met last, isn't it?"

"I've been toting this about five years now. With this holster, you just pull the gun out, instead of up and out, through the open side. A flat steel spring, sewed inside the leather, holds the gun in place until it's needed. This is a heap more comfortable to wear than a hip gun—and a fraction of a second faster on the draw. Sometimes that fraction is dang' valuable." He put on his coat again.

Fletcher eyed the plain, wide-buckled belt Quist was wearing. "No cartridge belt?"

"Too heavy." Quist dipped into a satchel, opened a box of forty-four cartridges and thrust a handful into a coat pocket. "Any man that can't finish the job he's got to do with what's in the gun and an extra fistful hasn't any business carrying a gun."

"You're a cold-blooded proposition, Greg."

"Not naturally. I merely adapted myself to a job."

"I feel a lot better now that you're here, anyway—"

"Save all that until this business is cleared up. . . . By the way, did you see any wagon tracks in the vicinity of the looted cars?"

Fletcher nodded. "Didn't make any attempt to follow them, of course. The wreck occurred in Murdock County, and the deputy at Puma Junction was to do some investigating. Probably won't learn anything more than was learned last time, when Sheriff Blackmer tried to discover where the stuff was taken. This time Blackmer refused to have anything to do with the business, claimed the wreck didn't take place in his county and that he didn't intend to lay an extra burden of expense on the taxpayers—"

"Goshdarn John Blackmer!" Quist's anger vanished as quickly as it came. "Blackmer's right about it not being his county, of course, but if he won't help out a brother officer—Cripes! Let's forget it. Jay, I want you to wire ahead to Puma

Junction and have a good horse waiting for me when I get to the wreck—no crowbait, mind you. I want something that can travel if it has to."

"I'll take care of it, Greg. I'll walk down to the station with you when you leave. The Limited's engine is waiting to run you up there."

"I won't be ready to leave for a spell yet."

"You won't?" Fletcher's eyebrows raised questioningly.

"I'm riding out with the doctor and Sheriff Blackmer to the Thunderbird. I want to look into this suicide business of Gid Harmon's. I don't like it."

Fletcher scowled. "Look here, Greg, the railroad's business comes first."

"Maybe that's railroad business."

"I don't see how it could be."

"Neither do I," Quist conceded doggedly, "but in my job I have to consider all the angles. I don't try to tell you how to run your job, Jay. You leave my job to my doing. Any complaints you have in mind can be made when I've failed on my end. Good night. With luck I should be back shortly after midnight."

Without waiting for a reply, he slapped the flat-topped sombrero on his head, yanked open the door, strode through the doorway, and slammed the door after him.

Fletcher poured himself another drink of whisky, considered the dark amber fluid against

36

the light, then drank deeply. He shook his head. "I've never yet known any woman to make an impression on Gregory Quist for any length of time. Hell! I still think he should have gone out to the wreck first, Lilith Harmon or no Lilith Harmon." And with that off his mind, he recorked the bottle of whisky and departed in the direction of the railroad station.

4. Suicide?

Quist emerged from the hotel to find a wagon standing at the edge of the sidewalk. There were three saddled horses, and two had riders. One of the two riders was Sheriff Blackmer. Blackmer said, indicating the man on the driver's seat of the wagon, "Greg, shake hands with Dr. Lang, our coroner—and the town sawbones, as well," and jerking a thumb toward the rider on the horse next his own, "This is Stark Garrity who rods the Thunderbird. You'll remember I told you it was Stark who discovered the body."

Quist shook hands with the two men. In the light reflected from the hotel windows, he saw that Dr. Lang was tall, in his fifties, with grizzled eyebrows and stooped shoulders. Garrity was around thirty-two, compactly built, with a well-tanned lantern jaw and dark hair. He was smoking a cigarette. Quist said, "I hope I didn't keep you gentlemen waiting long."

Blackmer said sourly, "Seemed like you was never coming."

"That's a darned lie," Garrity said bluntly. "We just got here, Mr. Quist. Been here sooner, I'll admit, but the horse John got for you at the livery was already lame in the off forefoot. I took the liberty of picking you something better,

38

but that livery don't give a man much choice."
The sheriff didn't make any denials.

Quist said thanks, adjusted the stirrup straps a
trifle, and climbed up. Lang started the wagon,
and the three riders got moving, Garrity slightly in
the lead to show the way.

The stars were bright and the road wasn't
difficult to follow. Now and then a tall
cottonwood made a black silhouette against the
night sky. Once as they slowed around a bend
they heard an owl hoot. Horses and men were
traveling too fast to make conversation easy, and
Quist decided to save such questions as he might
wish to ask until he'd seen the dead man. On top
of that, Garrity seemed considerably depressed,
and Quist didn't want to force him into
conversation until it became necessary. Only the
thudding of hoofs, creak of saddle leather, and
jangle of harness were heard. Behind the wagon a
thin cloud of dust could be seen faintly rising in
the starlight.

In something over an hour and a half they
reached Thunderbird Ranch, the roofs of the
various buildings ghostly under the now rising
moon. The men slowed the animals somewhat as
they came into the ranch yard.

Blackmer said, "There ain't a light on, that I can
see."

Garrity replied, "I already told you nobody was
here."

"You mean to say," Blackmer asked righteously, "that you went away and left Gid all alone, without no light?"

"What was I to do," Garrity answered, "just wait here until Mrs. Harmon came back and leave her to discover him? And what good would a light do anyway—for him?" He sounded irritated with the sheriff.

The sheriff didn't have any reply for that beyond, "It don't hardly sound Christian." Quist and the doctor didn't make any comment.

Horses and wagon stopped in front of the ranch house proper, a long low building built of adobe and rock. As he slipped down from the saddle Garrity said, "I guess you'd better wait until I go inside and light up. I know just where it—where Gid is layin'. You wouldn't want to go stumbling through the dark."

He moved across the wide gallery that fronted the house, thrust a key in the lock and stepped inside. A moment later there was the sound of a match being ignited, then light from a big oil lamp flared into being. The other three, now on the gallery, pushed through the doorway, the sheriff bringing up in the rear, and found themselves in a pleasantly furnished room running the width of the house, with a huge fireplace at the right end. At the opposite end of the room a heavy oaken table stood out a few feet from the wall, and sprawled on the floor, about midway between table and entrance, was the lifeless body of a big man with iron-gray hair.

The corpse lay on its right side, bent at the waist to form a sort of V-shaped figure, the right hand outflung. Not far from the ends of the rigid, outstretched fingers lay a Colt's forty-five six-shooter. Garrity had already told them the bullet had entered somewhere in the middle body, but Harmon's coat covered the wound. Except for a hat, the dead man was fully clothed. The eyes were partly open; the jaw sagged. Quist eyed Gid Harmon's body and judged the man had been in the vicinity of forty or forty-five years.

Dr. Lang broke the silence: "Take a good look, you three. I'll be expecting you to testify at the inquest, and I'd like to have you remember just how this body was placed when found. We'll do some talking in a few minutes, after I've given Gid a quick look-see." He set his bag on the floor and bent over the dead man.

While Lang was making his examination Quist's eyes roved about the room. There were Indian rugs and animal skins on the floor. The chairs looked comfortable and well worn. Mounted deer heads raised pronged antlers toward the beamed ceiling. The big kerosene lamp suspended above the heavy oaken table had a wide shade, and on the table top were a few books, some newspapers and magazines, a man's almost new Stetson hat, and a half-filled bottle of bourbon with the cork withdrawn.

On the wall opposite the entrance, and placed between two doors leading to other rooms of the house, was hung an unusually large Indian rug with wide stripes of black and gray around the edge. Woven in the center of the rug, against a background of white, was the blocky figure of a Navajo thunderbird—a formalized design depicting a bird with outstretched wings, the head turned to the left and the tail feathers placed straight down. The figure was almost square and about a foot and a half wide, being woven in scarlet wool. "A nice piece of rugmaking," Quist mused, "and one more evidence of Harmon's obsession on the subject."

He was aroused from his abstractions by Dr. Lang's voice: "The bullet entered from the front and somewhat to the right of the body. In my judgment it traveled across and through the heart, though I can't determine that without a more thorough examination. His clothing seems to have absorbed considerable blood, but as there is none on the floor, I judge there was a lot of internal bleeding. John, if you want to ask Stark any questions, go to it."

"I don't reckon there's much to ask," the sheriff said dubiously. "We know just about all that happened from what Stark told us when he arrived with the news. In my opinion Gid just took on too much of a load—maybe he didn't do this purposely. Maybe the shot was an accident. You can determine that at your inquest, Doc. Anyway, there's that bottle on the table, and if I know Gid Harmon he'd taken on quite a skinful. Let's get that body loaded so we can—"

"Just a minute," Quist broke in. "There's one or two things I'd like to get straightened out, if you don't mind."

Blackmer said sarcastically, "Thought you had plenty of detecting to do on your railroad, 'thout cutting in on county crime—"

"Are you stating a crime has been committed here?" Quist cut in.

"Certainly not; any fool can see—"

"Maybe we're not all fools." Quist turned to the doctor. "Mrs. Harmon asked me to come out here tonight. I'm willing to help when I can. There's one or two things I'd like to get cleared up. After all, I haven't heard all the story. I was too busy for a spell taking on a job that rightly belonged to our esteemed minion of the law. Why it was up to me to break the news to Mrs. Harmon, I haven't yet figured out, but we'll let that lay as is. Now that I'm in this thing, I don't figure to be pushed aside. Doctor, what time would you say death came?"

"That's easy to figure out," Lang replied. "Stark can tell you closer than I can determine it. What time would you say, Stark?"

Garrity considered. "Well, let me see. . . . Mrs. Harmon must have left for Cenotaph around five o'clock this afternoon—maybe a mite earlier or later. I couldn't say exactly—didn't pay any attention to the time. Gid arrived just a short time after she left and asked where she was, or rather if she was up to the house. I told him she'd gone to town. I put his horse up for him, and he went on up to the house. Maybe a half hour passed before I heard the shot. I was in the bunkhouse going over the tally book. I called up to him, and when I didn't get an answer, went up to see if anything was wrong. I found him layin' just like you saw when we come in. He was already dead—No,"— breaking off at a question from Lang—"I didn't touch the body, Doc. Figured you wouldn't want that. I just locked the door, saddled up, and headed for town."

Quist nodded. "Then it would be safe to say that you think death occurred around six o'clock this evening?"

Garrity considered. "I reckon that would about hit it, Mr. Quist."

"Did you notice anything wrong with Gid when he arrived?"

Blackmer cut in with a short laugh, "Probably normal—drunk as usual."

Garrity shot a steely look at the sheriff. "You and me, John," he prophesied, "are due to have words one of these days. I don't like your attitude.

Gid was the best boss a cowhand ever had." He turned back to Quist. "I hadn't thought of it before, but now that you mention it, Gid did appear sort of upset over something. He didn't appear to have been drinking, though. I'd say he was strictly sober when he arrived here."

"From which direction did he ride in?" Quist asked next.

"I couldn't rightly say. I was in the bunkhouse and didn't know he was here until he rode into the yard. He probably rode in from the southwest. He'd been over to Tanzburg."

"What enemies did he have that you know of?"

"I'd say none that would shoot him," Garrity replied promptly. "There was some that didn't like him—but more that did."

Quist asked, "How come, Garrity, that none of the hands are around today? Where's the Thunderbird crew?"

"Today's payday. Gid always gave the men payday off, right after breakfast. He left their wages here before he went to Tanzburg. Usually they head for Cenotaph, but this morning they all high-tailed it over to have a look-see at the train wreck. By the time they catch up with their drinking at Puma Junction, it'll likely be midnight before they start back for here."

Quist indulged in some mental speculation before putting the next question: "Garrity, could anyone have entered the ranch house without you seeing him, and have been waiting for Gid when he arrived?"

"Probably," Garrity nodded. "I was busy in the bunkhouse most of the day. Of course, it would have to have been between the time Mrs. Harmon left and Gid showed up—"

"Time enough," Dr. Lang put in. "A man hidden out in the brush until he saw his chance to get in the house, after Mrs. Harmon departed—"

"You mean," Blackmer asked, looking startled, "that mebbe Gid didn't shoot himself—that this is murder, 'stead of suicide?"

"I didn't say that at all," Quist answered. "I'm just trying to cover all possibilities. It looks like suicide."

The sheriff relaxed and appeared to breathe easier.

Quist knelt at the dead man's side and picked up the forty-five six-shooter to examine the cylinder. Flipping open the loading-gate of the weapon, he plucked out, one by one, four cartridges—replacing each before removing the next—and two exploded shells, one of the latter sticking a little before it came free.

Garrity said, "Gid always carried his hammer on an empty shell, like most cowfolks. That leaves one exploded ca'tridge."

Quist nodded without looking around. "Yes, I judged as much. That empty that rested under the hammer has been in the cylinder a long time. It was dang' nigh corroded in place."

He felt the cold, stiffened fingers, pushed back the coat sleeve and glanced at the upper arm, then did the same with the other sleeve. Minutely he inspected the clothing down to the dead man's boots, and struck a match so he could better examine the boot soles. The others watched in curious silence. Finally Quist handed the six-shooter to the doctor and got to his feet, saying, "You'll probably want to keep this weapon." He strode over to the table, picked up the Stetson hat, glanced inside the crown, and set it down again, with the remark: "I'd like to look through the house before we leave."

Garrity found and lighted a smaller lamp with which he led the way into a long hall entered from the doorway to the left of the thunderbird rug. Off the hall were three bedrooms. Each was entered in turn, but there was little to be seen except neatly made beds. The far end of the hall led into the kitchen, in which were a spotless range, a table, cupboards, and a couple of chairs. Quist tried the kitchen door and found it bolted. He opened it and glanced out to the moon-drenched night. Several buildings met his eye—bunkhouse, barns, corrals, stable, blacksmith shop. A windmill, with its fans now motionless, reared a skeleton frame against the indigo sky. Beyond was a long ridge of land covered with brush, cedar, and chaparral. Quist closed the door and rebolted it.

Garrity said, "I locked that door before I headed for town."

"It was open all day then?" Quist asked.

"Probably—after Mrs. Harmon unlocked it this morning."

They left the kitchen by another door and entered the dining room, from whence they passed through the doorway to the right of the thunderbird rug and found themselves back in the big main room again.

Blackmer looked at Quist. "Find anything?"

"You saw as much as I did."

"What were you looking for?"

"A muzzle for inquisitive hombres," Quist said shortly.

"I don't understand—" Blackmer broke off, and a flush swept his features. He didn't say anything.

Dr. Lang sighed. "I guess that's about all we can do. John, tomorrow morning early I want you to round me up six men for a coroner's jury. Inquest at three in the afternoon. I want all you men there." He directed his remarks in Quist's direction.

"I won't be there," Quist stated bluntly.

"Why not?"

"I've got other business to attend to."

"I'll need you as a witness."

"If necessary I'll give you a deposition, Doc."

"That won't do. The jury will want to hear your testimony."

Quist said, even-toned, "Look, Doc, if you can point out one bit of testimony that I could give that would differ from what you and John and Stark can give, I'll be glad to show up. Otherwise, I won't be there."

Doc Lang said testily, "I could subpoena you, you know."

"I still won't be there. Sure, you could have John take me into custody—he could try anyway,"—with dry humor—"but he couldn't hold me. I'm employed by the T. N. & A. S., and I've discovered that railroads don't take it kindly when their interests are interfered with. If you think that you have more influence in this county than the railroad, go ahead and make a fool of yourself."

Lang sighed. "Have it your way, Mr. Quist. I'll not attempt to force the issue. I guess we can get along without you. Well, I guess there's nothing more now, except to get Gid's body into that wagon and drive it in to the undertaker's."

"You and John should be able to do that," Quist said, and turned to Garrity. "Stark, I'd like to have a look at Gid's horse."

"Sure, Mr. Quist. Come on, we'll head down to the corral."

Quist accompanied Garrity around the house and down into the ranch yard. They paused a moment at the bunkhouse while Garrity picked up a rope, then continued on to a pole corral in which

49

stood several saddlers huddled at the far side. Garrity removed the top bars of the gateway and stepped inside, shaking out a loop in his rope as he moved. The horses could be seen plainly under the bright moonlight. After a moment Quist followed Garrity inside the enclosure.

Instantly the group of horses—browns, whites, buckskins, grays, and pintos—broke into rippling motion and went flashing around the men in a flurry of hoofs and tossing manes. Undisturbed, Garrity said evenly, "It's that mouse-colored animal—see! Just edging past that palomino." He hesitated a moment, then made his cast expertly when the horse next came near. The loop settled about the horse's neck, tightened, and the animal immediately became docile. Garrity led it over for Quist's inspection, while the remaining animals once more settled down at the far end of the corral.

Quist ran his hands along the horse's flanks, examined its eyes, struck a match and looked at the four hoofs. "Doesn't look as though it had been ridden hard, or anything," he observed quietly. "Of course, it would be kind of difficult to tell at this late hour. Still, there's no sign of fatigue that I can note."

"I took over the horse when Gid stepped down," Garrity said. "I don't think he'd been pushing it any."

"Where's the saddle Gid used?" Quist asked.

"Over in the bunkhouse. If there was one thing Gid didn't like, it was to see a saddle left out overnight. You want to take a look at that, too?"

"Might as well."

They left the corral for the bunkhouse. Garrity lighted a lamp. There were a number of saddles resting here and there about the long room with its double tier of bunks. Garrity indicated a saddle not far from the doorway, standing against the wall. "There she is."

Quist examined the rig from a kneeling position. It was nothing out of the ordinary—just a plain, workmanlike saddle of good manufacture, the leather stained and worn from much use. "I'm surprised," Quist observed, "that Gid didn't have his thunderbirds stamped in this leather. It would have been in line with a lot of things he did."

"Yeah," Garrity nodded. "Gid was sure nutty on the subject of thunderbirds."

"A nice job could have been done, right here below the saddle horn," Quist went on. He sketched with his thumbnail lightly a few lines of the design, the nail cutting slightly into the brown leather. "Then he could have had a row of the birds around his skirts—" He broke off, smiling thinly. "I'm talking nonsense, I reckon."

"Speaking of saddles," Garrity said, as though suddenly struck with an idea, "you go back to the house and take your rig off that livery horse; while you're doing that, I'll catch up one of our horses for you."

"What's the idea?"

"You said something about having work to do. You'll want to get back to town as soon as possible. You can make better time on one of our fresh horses, getting back to town, than you would on that hired horse."

"I call that dang' decent of you," Quist said.

"Don't mention it. It didn't occur to me until just now. I think Mrs. Harmon would want it that way, too. You can leave our bronc at the livery, and I'll pick it up when I bring in the hired horse."

"I'll take advantage of that. Thanks, Stark."

By the time Quist returned to the wagon before the house, Gid Harmon's body lay in the bed of the vehicle and the doctor was on the driver's seat, anxious to get started. Blackmer was mounted, too.

Quist said, "You two go ahead when you feel like it. I'm waiting for a fresh horse."

The doctor and Blackmer hesitated, then got started. By the time Quist got the saddle stripped from the livery horse, Garrity had arrived with the fresh mount, a rangy-looking buckskin with good shoulders and legs.

"Nice-looking bit of horseflesh," Quist commented as he saddled up.

"I think so myself," Garrity responded. "You can have the use of him as long as you're around

Cenotaph, if you want. I know it will be all right. Gid had more saddlers than we actually needed."

"I may take you up on that, Stark. You're putting me in your debt."

"The hell I am. And something else"—as Quist stepped up to the saddle—"I didn't want to mention it while Blackmer was around—he's too gabby—but it's pretty hard for me to believe that Gid Harmon committed suicide."

Quist rolled a cigarette in silence, lighted it, then asked, "Do you know anything I should know?"

"Not a thing. I'm just telling you how I feel about it. Maybe I'm wrong, of course."

"Maybe so." Quist nodded. "Well, I'll see you again, Stark."

"Soon, I hope."

Quist touched spurs to the pony's ribs and moved off.

A short distance along the road he overtook the wagon with the sheriff riding alongside. Momentarily Quist slowed pace and approached the doctor on the driver's seat. "Just wanted to ask a favor, Doc," he said. "I wish you'd probe out that slug and let me know exactly what course it took."

"I expected to do that anyway," Lang replied somewhat stiffly. "Can I get you to reconsider about giving testimony at my inquest?"

"You should know better than to ask," Quist replied briefly.

Blackmer said sarcastically, "Some folks act like their hat had shrunk, or something."

Quist laughed. "When it shrinks to pinhead size, I'll donate it to you, John. S'long, you hombres. I'll see you eventually."

Blackmer's burst of profanity faded in his ears as he raced the buckskin pony toward Cenotaph.

5. The Wreck

It was around one in the morning when Quist reached Cenotaph. He went directly down to the railroad station and found a red-eyed, impatient Fletcher waiting for him within the building. Outside, on the tracks, a locomotive, with steam up and ready to go, waited several yards in advance of the long line of uncoupled, now dark passenger cars. Fletcher stumbled wearily to his feet as Quist entered.

"Darn it, Greg," he snapped, "you said you'd be back around twelve. Here it's one o'clock—"

"I got back as soon as I could," Quist said shortly. "I'm ready to leave now. There's a Thunderbird horse outside. I'm asking you to see that it's taken to the livery and taken care of properly. I sort of pushed it to get here by this time."

Fletcher had him by the arm and outside the station doorway now. "Always putting your duty second to the interests of the Thunderbird," he said irritatedly. "It's darned queer what a pretty face will do to a man—"

"That's about enough of that, Jay," Quist said, level-voiced.

"It's the truth." Fletcher's voice lifted angrily.

Quist gestured toward the line of darkened passenger cars. "There's probably a few people trying to get some sleep. I don't imagine everybody found beds in town. Suppose we hold our voices down. Look, Jay, you wouldn't talk like this if you weren't worn out. I'm pretty danged tuckered myself—had to make a ride to get here, train and saddle—and I'm a little short on temper right now. Anything you got to say can be dropped for the time. We'll talk over your complaints when we're both more clearheaded. Right now there's a job to do."

"You're right, Greg," Fletcher said contritely. "By rights I should be going out there with you, but I've made the trip once. I don't know what more I could do. If I don't get some sleep mighty soon, they'll have to find somebody else for my job. Probably you should push a bunch of knuckles against my jaw for losing my head in such fashion, but I've been short-handed and—"

"Forget it. I'm going now. Just leave things to me. After I'm gone, take care of my horse, then head for that hotel bed. The company doesn't expect you to kill yourself. And before you turn in, a healthy slug of whisky will help quiet your nerves."

They were standing by the locomotive by this time. There was a bit of conversation with the fireman and engineer, then Quist said good-by and climbed into the cab of the engine. The iron monster commenced to pant; smoke plumed back from the stack; cinders rained down on the station roof, and the wheels started to turn.

Quist settled himself on the seat behind the engineer as the throttle was gradually opened and the locomotive drove through the night. None of the three men talked to any extent. From time to time the fireman's shovel made scraping sounds in the vicinity of the tender, the light from the firebox throwing the man's features into crimson, sweat-streaked relief before the door was again closed. Spots of firelight gleamed and danced within the cab, and the heat brought drops of perspiration to Quist's forehead. Now and then a gust of wind whipped through the windows. Moonlight-bathed semidesert country flowed past on either side of the speeding locomotive as it rocked through space.

Quist dozed on the seat in an endeavor to store up a little energy for the task that lay ahead. His eyes couldn't have been closed for more than half an hour when he felt the engine slowing and heard the engineer speak over his shoulder through the rush of wind, "We're nearly there, Mr. Quist."

Quist roused and glanced out of the cab window. The light of a glaring fusee momentarily illuminated the scene as it whipped past. The engine slowed to a long, coasting halt.

"Don't think we'd better carry you any closer," the engineer was saying. "Things are pretty tangled up ahead, I understand. However, it isn't much of a walk from here—just around that bend ahead."

Quist descended from the cab and felt his feet strike earth not far from the ties. He said, "Much obliged for the lift."

"Glad to carry you," the engineer replied. "I understand you won't be going back with us, Mr. Quist."

"There should be a horse waiting for me up ahead," Quist answered. "Good night." He heard the fireman saying something to the engineer relative to having a look at the wreck themselves, but he didn't wait to see if they intended to accompany him. He started out along the roadbed, mentally cursing the engineering genius that had decreed the spacing of railroad ties in such a manner that they weren't compatible with a man's steps. "Hell's bells!" Quist grumbled to himself. "Why couldn't they have placed 'em closer together, so a fellow could skip every other one, or spaced 'em farther apart?"

He followed a curve in the roadbed where the rails rounded the end of a rock-jumbled ridge of terrain and saw what appeared to be a scene of indescribable confusion spread under the moonlight. A man in overalls came running along the track. "You Mr. Quist?" he panted.

"Yes. Are you the wrecking boss?"

"No, I'm just a straw. Mr. Carstairs is up ahead. He told me to be on the lookout for you, but we weren't sure just when you'd get here."

The two strode along side by side. The center of

the activity was placed still farther ahead. Lantern lights bobbed along the track and were paled by the great light of a huge bonfire of flaming timbers that sent sparks and smoke swirling toward the heavens. Men with axes were clearing debris from another point along the rails. There was much shouting mixed with profanity. Beyond the fire, Quist saw the derrick of the wrecking car swing down, grip a ponderous bit of mechanism and deposit it at one side. Men swarmed over the scene, each following some particular job the sooner to get the line once more open and the trains routed through again. Farther on, Quist and his companion passed a group of men gathered around a huge tub of coffee. Another group was filling tin cups from an opened keg of whisky. The men looked dirty, weary, their overalls stained and patched and torn. Smoke smudges blackened features here and there.

The straw boss gestured to a still-smoking heap of charred timbers and twisted metal. "Caboose," he said tersely. "I can't see why those fellows didn't get out."

"Maybe the door jammed, or something, and couldn't be opened."

The other said dubiously, "That could be, I suppose."

They went on. The heat from the huge fire was searing Quist's face, it seemed, and he and the other man left the railroad right-of-way and headed toward a group of three men standing some distance off and watching the fire. One of the men saw Quist and left his group.

"You Quist?" he asked as he approached. "I'm Carstairs." The two shook hands, and the straw boss went about his business.

Quist and the wrecking boss sized each other up as they came to a halt, apart from the other men. Each liked what he saw.

Quist said, "How you getting along?"

"We're making progress. Got the engine and tender rerailed and just sent 'em on to Puma Junction about twenty minutes ago." He lifted one pointing finger. "Those cars are rerailed too. They'll be out of here before too long. We've salvaged quite a bit of freight." The pointing finger indicated several huge mounds of merchandise some distance from the tracks. "I'm keeping guards on those until they can be moved."

"What about this fire? Who ordered that?"

"Fletcher, when he was out here yesterday. Quickest way to clean up the mess. There was just a tangle of splintered matchwood. Couldn't save anything out of it. Once the wood is cleared we can get at the tracks and other stuff. Those other cars, farther on, are the ones that were broken into. We'll get them straightened out before long. I've already sent word to Fletcher that trains can be routed through by sundown tonight."

"Pretty fast work, isn't it?"

"Oh, there'll be stuff along the side of the tracks to clear away, but that can be done later. The main thing is to get the line cleared for operating."

"You're doing a dang' good job, Carstairs."

The light from the fire reflected redly on Carstairs' drawn features. "I've got a darned good crew," he said simply. "Just give 'em plenty of coffee and food and they'll stay with the job until it's finished. If a keg of whisky happens to turn up in the wreckage—and it usually does—that helps too. But very man jack of 'em will drop in his tracks before he'll quit on the job."

Quist considered the fact that only a danged good boss could draw such effort from his crew. He said next, "Has the cause of the wreck been placed yet?"

Carstairs said quietly, "The engine jumped the track coming around this curve."

"You made any sort of examination to determine why?"

Carstairs nodded. "A lot of spikes were drawn— the rails were spread—" He broke off to curse in low, monotonous undertones, then went on, "The engine left the rails and the others piled up behind, in a sort of zigzag fashion, some on the tracks, some off. A couple of cars rolled down a slight embankment up ahead. God, what a mess it was when we got here!"

"I understand the engineer was killed."

"He was pretty badly crushed when we pulled

him out. Probably died instantly." Carstairs hesitated. "The fireman jumped, got a broken leg—"

"As I got it, his skull was fractured or something like that."

"Word came out from Puma Junction just a spell back—about that fireman. I was to pass it on to you when you arrived. The fireman regained consciousness for a bit, but from the little he talked we got some information."

"I'm waiting."

"The fireman got clear of the wreck when he jumped. He lay there quite a spell, knowing he'd broken his leg. Pretty soon he heard voices and he let out a yell for help. After a while he saw a man coming toward him with a club in his hand. The man worked around behind the fireman—well, that's all the fireman remembers."

Quist said grimly, "Clubbed and left for dead, I suppose."

"That's the way it looks to me."

"I hope he lives to identify the bustard."

"The doctors aren't holding out much hope. The railroad sent the company doctor from Tanzburg, you know, so with the sawbones at Puma Junction there's a chance of pulling him through."

Quist asked next, "You figured yet how the caboose caught fire and no other cars did?"

Carstairs shook his head. "There might have been a fire in the stove, of course, but I doubt that.

We're lucky it was just a short train sent to make connections in Puma Junction, so certain cars could be sent on. Otherwise we might have had more dead. As it is, just the engineer, conductor and brakie—"

"You've sent the bodies of the conductor and brakeman to Puma Junction, I suppose."

Carstairs nodded. "We got 'em just as soon as things cooled down enough. Maybe you noticed the timbers were still smoking when you came through. It sure must have burnt fierce. Yes, we got the bodies out—what there was to bring out. They were pretty well destroyed, features and hands charred and so on."

"Were you present when the bodies were removed from the wreckage?"

"I helped carry out one of the bodies myself, though I don't know which one, whether conductor or brakie."

"You didn't see anything that would give you the idea they'd been shot, did you?"

"No, you couldn't tell, of course, without a thorough examination—" Carstairs broke off suddenly as an oath burst from his lips. "You think that's what's happened?"

"I don't know. It's possible. Say the two men are stunned by the impact of the wreck. Before they can protect themselves, they're shot, then the caboose set on fire to burn up the evidence."

"The dirty, murdering snakes! That would

explain why the caboose, 'way at the end of the train, caught fire."

"It would be one explanation."

"An autopsy would determine—"

"I've been thinking of that."

"If you want to send a message from here to Puma Junction, I'll be glad to take care of it for you." He paused, then added, "Oh yes, there's a horse here for you, too. I forgot to tell you before."

"I was wondering about that. Thanks." Quist drew a small notebook from his pocket and with a stub of pencil quickly scribbled a few words. Handing the sheet of paper to Carstairs, he said, "I'll appreciate it if you'll get this off as soon as possible, then I'll let you get back on your job. I've already taken a lot of your time."

Carstairs smiled tiredly. "I'm glad to help. If you want any coffee or food, it's over that way"— gesturing in the direction of the group Quist had passed some time before.

"The coffee sounds good. I'll see you before I leave."

6. Vanishing Wagons

As soon as it was light enough to see, though the sun was still some time from rising above the distant Sangre de Estebans, Quist climbed into the saddle and, starting with the debris of the burned caboose as a center, he drew a huge circle about the scene of the wreckage. Carstairs' crew were still working like beavers. Two more freight cars had been sent to Puma Junction. Another smashed car was flaming and crackling fiercely by this time, with men waiting to clear the tracks as soon as they could get at the unburned litter among the ashes.

Quist was riding the horse—a clean-limbed bay—at a leisurely walk that cast an ever-widening spiral of travel around the point at which the wreck had taken place. As he rode, his eyes were intent on the earth, his keen scrutiny searching past each sagebrush and cactus springing from the sandy soil. He had already located the wagon tracks leaving the railroad in a northerly direction, but for the moment he wasn't interested in these. There were footprints in plenty near the tracks, so many that Quist ignored them, knowing it would be practically impossible to determine which were those of the wrecking crew and which belonged to the thieves, even though the thieves' prints might be made by riding boots, in contrast to the flat-heeled boots of the railroad laborers: each succeeding print had undoubtedly wiped out the one that had gone before.

Finally he spied the sort of tracks he was seeking. Evidently he had missed them previously in his circling progress, or they might not have showed so plainly at other points. At any rate, the footprints—those of a riding boot—now showed plainly in the sand as they picked their way through the various species of semidesert growth. The trail led Quist to a stunted mesquite tree, below the branches of which he saw two five-gallon kerosene cans. Quist got down from the saddle and examined the cans, smelled at the uncorked openings. Both were empty. Had they been railroad property, they would have borne the usual red-lettered T. N. & A. S. R.R. on the sides. There was no lettering on these cans.

Quist's features tightened. He examined again the footprints in the soft earth. Made by cowpuncher riding boots to be sure, but there was little of a distinguishing nature to make them stand out. An average-size foot, heels slightly run over, toes pointed slightly inward.

"Unless," Quist told himself, "I had the actual boot to fit these prints right here, I couldn't uncover much. Someday, darn it, somebody will discover a way of taking an imprint of tracks like these. I should think a mixture of plaster of Paris could be used to fill the tracks—there I go again,

66

always wishing for something I haven't got. The devil with it."

For a moment he eyed the tracks on their return journey back toward the wreck. They didn't take quite the same direction this time, but he saw no need for following them further. He again got into the saddle and turned the pony toward the railroad. Even at this distance he could hear the faint crackling of flames from the burning freight car. The smoke volumed darkly up and then dissolved against the ever-lightening sky. Beyond rose the jagged turrets of Pihuela Range with the long line of reddish-colored buttes running along the eastern slopes. To the north the range was hazy in the distance, but already the rising sun was starting to tip the peaks of the Sangre de Esteban Mountains which lay forty miles to the east, beyond Cenotaph. Thoughts of Cenotaph brought Lilith Harmon to mind, and what had passed between them the previous night. She'd said something of suspicions having to do with freight thieves. Dang the luck! It would probably be two or three days before she'd be ready to talk to him again—probably not until after Gid Harmon had been buried.

As he once more neared the railroad right-of-way, early morning sunlight glistening on the twin rails, Quist turned his pony in the direction of the group gathered about the open fire where a covered tub of coffee bubbled above the glowing

67

coals. At a second fire the odor, almost a fragrance at present, of broiling beef rose in the air. Cans were being opened; a long table made of planks resting on wooden horses held tin plates and cups; Dutch ovens were turning out freshly baked bread. Carstairs noted Quist's approach and left the group about the cooking fires.

He held his voice low when he reached the pony's head and asked, as Quist pulled to a halt and stepped down from the saddle, "Did you pick up anything?"

Quist said tersely, "Ten gallons of coal oil were dumped in that caboose. The empty cans are laying out there on the sand, about seventy-five or a hundred yards from here. I reckon the dirty sons didn't figure we'd look that far." Carstairs started swearing again in that low, monotonous monotone he used when deeply stirred, but Quist cut him off with, "Now that's settled, I've got to pick up those wagon tracks and see where they lead."

"That might prove to be considerable of a job, before the day's done," Carstairs said. "You'd better come get some chow and hot coffee before you start." He commenced swearing again, muttering something about ten gallons of coal oil and a flaming match being enough to destroy evidence—sometimes.

Quist considered the mild features of the man, smoke-smudged, begrimed, and wondered that so much hate could be contained in one man. "You see," Carstairs added after a time, "that brakie was my brother-in-law."

Quist took his arm. "I reckon we can both do with some hot coffee," he said quietly. "That won't exactly fill the bill for what's needed, but it will have to do for the present."

"Blast it, Quist," Carstairs said fiercely, "you've got to run down this gang. If you need help, say the word. I'll quit my job and come on the run if you need me."

"I'll be remembering that," Quist nodded. "It might help to have a man I could trust in Puma Junction. Keep your eyes peeled and your ears open when you get back there." He added as they approached the cooking fires: "But don't quit your job. The T. N. & A. S. needs your kind of quality to keep these trains highballin'."

Half an hour later Quist was again in the saddle, having said "s'long" to Carstairs. Now he was ready to follow those wagon tracks which showed plainly leading to and away from the point at which the wreck had taken place. The rain of the previous few days had softened the earth and made the tracks more visible than they might otherwise have been.

About thirty yards from the slight embankment along which the tracks were laid was a big saucer-shaped hollow with considerable brush growing about the rim and in the bottom. The brush didn't grow high, to be sure, but it made a fit hiding place for the freight thieves to wait until their tampering with the tracks had brought about the wreck. Then, working swiftly, they had left the fireman for dead, set fire to the caboose, broke open certain freight cars. Wagons would have been loaded swiftly with various types of merchandise and driven off to—where? That was what Quist resolved to discover.

The imprints in the hollow were plentiful; wheel tracks too. They led up to the right-of-way and then headed off toward the north, running parallel with the Pihuela Range. Just how many wagons there were, Quist didn't stop to decide. That didn't matter now. Enough to carry away thousands of dollars' worth of goods, as Fletcher had said. Quist guided his pony in their wake, pausing now and then to scrutinize the imprints of moving hoofs and wheels. The wagons hadn't spread out, but had followed, one after the other, making the matter of number more difficult to decide, as the wheel ruts crossed and recrossed at places, adding to the confusion. When he found a hoofmark set clearly apart from the blur of other hoofmarks, Quist gave it some study.

The sun rose higher while he traveled. The way was leading closer to the Pihuelas now, going off on a long gradual northwesterly direction. Quist had the conviction that he had crossed the county line and was now in Murdock County, where, as he expressed it irritatedly to himself, "there'd be no help from John Blackmer, if help was needed."

Once he shifted in the saddle to look back in the direction of the wreck. Black smoke still rose against the vast expanse of sky. Quist turned back in the saddle, removed his coat and folded it across the saddle horn. The sun was growing hotter every minute. Now the tall buttes of reddish rock he'd noticed earlier in the morning were definitely nearer.

Mile after mile Quist pushed the pony at an easy gait. It was no longer necessary to watch the trail closely. So far as wheel- and hoofprints were concerned, he'd seen all there was to see, as regards variety. High above, a trio of buzzards wheeled against the cloudless void. A chaparral cock crossed ten feet in front of Quist's horse in its long swooping, half-running flight, to disappear among the seemingly endless clumps of buffalo grass and sagebrush and cacti that stretched as far as vision reached.

Once Quist paused and dismounted to rest the pony for a few minutes, though the bay animal showed not the slightest sign of fatigue. He eyed the canteen that some thoughtful person had slung to the saddle horn, but decided a drink could be postponed for a time yet. Then he again mounted and pushed on.

By this time the trail was running parallel to and in the very shadow of (had there been a shadow at this early hour) the high red granite buttes which presented an apparently unbroken escarpment for miles into the distance. The great bluffs towered high above horse and man, their precipitous sides presenting an almost smooth, unscalable wall rising abruptly from a nearly level apron of flat rock, shale, and broken bits of granite. Quist eyed it with interest; the formation was somewhat different from any he had seen recently, and though he had passed through this country years before, he had paid but little attention to its geologic aspects. Nor had he ever before ridden so close to the red buttes.

Suddenly the trail he'd been following made a right-angled turn directly toward the buttes.

"Hmmm!" Quist muttered. "There must be a break in this wall after all. There's probably a pass leading through a canyon into a valley, or something of the sort. Or maybe there's just a box canyon where the crooks have a hideout. If John Blackmer had had any gumption when that other wreck happened and the cars were looted, he could have made himself a reputation, maybe. Well, we'll see what we see."

Unconsciously, as he turned his pony toward the buttes, his right hand came up and tentatively touched the forty-four gun in its underarm holster.

Quist was eying the trail more closely once again. Straight toward the steep rock walls went wheel ruts and hoofmarks, until they'd reached the edge of the apron. Here, because of the rock surface, the "sign" disappeared, but Quist continued on, expecting every minute to catch a glimpse of some partially concealed opening in the face of the escarpment. The way grew slightly steeper, while Quist, leaning from the saddle, strained his eyes in the hope of sighting some slight hoofmark to show him he was still on the right road.

Abruptly he saw the pony had halted of its own volition, facing the cliff. It could go no farther, and half turned its head, its reproachful eyes seeming to ask if the rider expected it to fly over, or at least scale, the precipitous wall blocking its path.

"My mistake, horse," Quist grunted, puzzled. "Now what happened to those wagons?" He turned the pony away from the wall, its hoofs slipping slightly on the hard footing, but, as Quist noted, leaving no track.

"This," he told himself in perplexity, "is one of the damdest situations I've ever seen." He considered the problem for a few minutes, his eyes scrutinizing the apron, on which he sat his pony, in either direction. "Looks like," he concluded finally, "they moved up on this stretch of rock, so's anybody that might follow would lose the trail. The question is, did they backtrack at this point, or did they continue on in a northerly direction? There just has to be a passage through

73

these buttes someplace, but where do I find it?"

He manufactured a brown-paper cigarette while he considered the problem, scratched a match and fanned his lungs deeply with the smoke. Finally he decided to continue north, explaining to himself, "I didn't see any openings in the cliffs before, but I may see one ahead."

He spoke to his pony and moved at a walk along the apron. "An unshod hoof might not leave a track on this rock," he mused, "but a wagon tire could scratch someplace. Still, I could look from now until doomsday and not find anything of the sort—"

He broke abruptly off. There, at his left, was a narrow opening in the face of the butte wall. It was just about wide enough to admit the passage of a horse and entered the face of the rock at an angle that wouldn't be discernible from any distance. Quist tensed suddenly. He thought he'd heard the neighing of a horse coming through that opening.

Quist slipped silently down from the pony, dropping the reins over its head. If it had heard the neighing of another horse, his own mount apparently paid no attention. Nevertheless Quist determined to investigate that opening. He dropped his cigarette butt, stepped on it, then, drawing his six-shooter, slipped along the rock apron on noiseless feet.

Drawing near to the edge of the opening, he

peered around the edge before entering the passage. It widened slightly after he was inside, and he made his way along the rocky floor for about seventy-five feet, the high rock walls towering straight above on either side. Ahead lay a bend in the passage, and when Quist had rounded that he found himself facing a huge open space, probably fifty feet across.

What is more, in the center of the open space was a mounted rider, who lifted his head and quickly obeyed Quist's order to "Raise 'em high!"

For a moment the two men eyed each other in silence, then the man on the horse, a dark-complexioned fellow of around thirty, said, "You sure snuk up stealthy-like, mister, but was I you I wouldn't force this business none."

By this time Quist had seen the deputy sheriff's badge pinned to the man's sweat-soaked denim shirt. "Maybe I am acting a bit hasty," Quist conceded quietly, "but I'm not taking any chance this way, either. What's your name?"

"Steve Wilson. I'm the deputy sheriff over to Puma Junction, and if you got any water handy, I'd sure appreciate a few drops. Me and my bronc, we—"

"We'll get to water in a minute," Quist cut in. "What are you doing here instead of Puma Junction?"

The other replied promptly, "Mebbe-so you heard there was a train wreck a few miles outside the junction. There was freight thieves looted some cars. I been out since yesterday, trying to track 'em down, but it just seems like they vanished in thin air. And something else, it wouldn't make me mad if you lowered that gun."

Quist nodded. The man's eyes were honest. He guessed the fellow really was a deputy. "Sorry," Quist said, and put the gun back in its holster. He stepped forward now, offering his hand. "I'm Gregory Quist, investigator for the T. N. & A. S. It looks—"

"I've heard of you." The deputy leaned down to accept Quist's clasp. "Have you uncovered anything?"

"It looks," Quist resumed, "as if we'd both run up against a blank wall."

"You're looking for those same thieves, I reckon. Been followin' those wagon tracks?" Steve Wilson asked.

"Yes, and not getting any place. Lost 'em when they moved up on the apron—"

"That's what I done yesterday. Completely missed the passage into here, then. Didn't spot it until today on my way back."

"Your way back from where?"

"I traveled northerly a good stretch of miles, hoping to find some way through these buttes. No luck. Then I come back here, to take another look around the point where those tracks leave off. This time I spotted the passage and came on in. I was just sort of looking around when you threw that there gun on me—"

"You mean you been in the saddle since yesterday?"

"Except for a bed-down in a sheepherder's shanty last night." He broke off, then continued, "Don't know how I come to miss this place yesterday, except mebbe it was because I didn't stay on the apron when I left. I reckon the opening don't show up so good at a distance. Quarter of a mile along"—he jerked his thumb toward the north—"there's sign showing where several horses left the apron, but they sort of scattered and I didn't figure I'd better trail 'em over into Dawson County. But one thing's certain, them horses must have holed up in here for a spell. Look at the droppings around. I'd say they'd been here several hours. On the other hand I don't find many cigarette butts, so I guess whoever was riding them must have left and took to wagons. But where in tarnation did them wagons get to?" He sounded irritable, as though the problem had plagued him considerably.

Quist smiled. "That one has me guessing too—but I don't seem to have any good guesses." He paused, eyes narrowing. "I wonder if wagon wheels could be padded in some way so they wouldn't leave tracks—"

"Say, Mr. Quist, maybe that's an idea. But how?" Wilson asked.

"You tell me and I'll tell you."

The deputy frowned. "Even if those wagons could get in here, they couldn't get out no way I can see. There's no passage leaving from here. It's just like we were at the bottom of a big, deep well—except that there's no water and I could sure—"

"Come on, I'll give you some water."

Wilson got down from the saddle, leading the horse behind him as he and Quist made their way back through the narrow passage. Once out on the apron again, Quist secured the canteen from his saddle and handed it to Wilson. Wilson removed the top, drank deeply, and sighed with relief. "That's sure satisfactual," he smiled.

"Take what you want. Finish it up."

"But you'll need it," the deputy protested.

"I don't reckon so. You deserve it. You've saved me a lot of travel. No use me looking further for passages through the rock, when you've covered the job. I can get back to Cenotaph now and see if there isn't some other angle to work on. I've wasted enough time in this direction—"

"But Cenotaph is nigh forty miles from here."

"We'll make out all right. I'm certain to run across some water someplace before I hit town."

"Well, thank you kindly, Mr. Quist." Wilson took another small drink, then poured the remainder in the crown of his Stetson and offered it to his pony. The beast drank gratefully.

Quist and the deputy stood talking a few minutes longer. Finally Quist said, "Who keeps mules around here?"

"Mules? Can't say I've seen so many mules since I left Indiany, and that's some smart spell back. There's not many farms in Murdock County. But why you asking about mules?"

"A mule is smaller than a work horse. Didn't you notice the hoofmarks when you were following those wagon tracks—the length of the stride the animals were making and so on?"

"You think those wagons were pulled by mules?"

Quist nodded. "Mules are danged good for hauling freight."

"Maybe you're right," Wilson said slowly. "But those tracks weren't made by regular freight wagons."

"I agree with you."

"I'd sure like to know what became of 'em."

"I agree on that score, too."

"You know," Wilson observed, frowning, "something sort of told me those tracks were kind of different, but it didn't come to me. Mules, eh? I'll be darned."

"Ask some questions around, and if you hear of anybody who has several mules, let me know. I'll be at the Cenotaph House for a while."

"I'll do that, Mr. Quist."

They talked a few minutes longer, then got into saddles and went their separate ways.

Noon came. Quist was getting pretty dry by this time. He got from his coat pocket a chunk of beef and a couple of slices of bread, rolled in newspaper, and chewed while he rode. Far ahead on the horizon he saw the top of a windmill. He'd find water there all right, but there was still a long trip ahead before he reached Cenotaph.

7. Murder?

Quist awakened as Jay Fletcher let himself softly into the room. Morning light penetrated below the drawn shades. Quist sat up, shaking his head of tawny hair and yawning. "What time is it?"

"Awake at last, eh?" Fletcher chuckled. "I thought you never would come to life. It's just a mite after nine o'clock."

Quist stepped from bed and got into his pants. "Lord, I must have been as dead as you looked when I got in last night. Why didn't you call me when you got out of bed?" He drew on his boots.

"Figured you needed the sleep. I had to go down to the station for a while. I warned the hotel clerk not to let anyone bother you because you hadn't had any sleep the previous night."

"Lord, you're considerate when things are going good. Line open for travel again, I suppose."

"The Limited went through there about seven last evening. It's a load off my mind getting things running again."

"You can thank that man Carstairs for that, Jay." Quist poured some water into a washbowl and got out a razor and brush. He went on while he started shaving, "It wouldn't hurt you to put a couple of hundred extra on Carstairs' pay check. He's really earned more than his salary."

"I'll see that he's taken care of, never fear. Greg, what progress did you make?"

"Darn' little. That caboose was set afire with coal oil. I've a hunch the brakie and conductor were shot first. I'll learn later. I followed the track of the thieves and . . ." From that point on, Quist related what had happened, concluding with, "After I left that deputy—Steve Wilson was his name—I figured there was nothing to do but get back here and try working from some other angle. I stopped at a small outfit around one-thirty, watered my horse and rested him, and argued cattle prices and conditions with the old Methuselah who operated the spread, and when the day cooled some more I came on to Cenotaph. You were snoring like one of your locomotives when I came in, so I undressed and got in beside you—and that's all I know until now. Want a written report?"

"You know that's not necessary. Greg, where could those wagons have gone to? They couldn't just vanish!"

"Who says they couldn't?"

"You know better than to talk like that. You sure they didn't leave that apron again and then head out across the country someplace?"

"No." The razor made ringing sounds as it scraped through the lather. "Without facts, I'm never sure of anything."

"Why didn't you look farther?"

"Jay, you haven't been over there. You've no idea how many miles that apron stretches along those buttes. No man can examine every inch. I went part way. Deputy Wilson covered a great deal more. Unless I had a stroke of luck it would be sheer waste of time to do any more riding in that country. Besides,"—he grinned—"I thought I'd better get back and get some sleep if you wanted me to continue on the job."

"That goes without saying."

"Don't be such a blamed slave driver then. You know, Jay, when you were just an engineer charting surveys, you used to be human. Now that you've got to be division supe, you're thinking this whole dang' world revolves around the T. N. & A. S. And what will it get you? Sure, you'll probably get to be president of the road someday and you'll have a lot of money, but by that time you'll have indigestion and your hair will be falling out and you'll be gnashing store teeth everytime anybody reports a hotbox. And you won't ever have had any fun. I don't know what gets into some fellows when they get a little authority."

Fletcher smiled. "All right, rub it in, Greg. But I've got a job to do, the same as you. I'm concerned about what goes on over my division. I'm not trying to rush you, but in a nutshell what have you discovered so far? I have my reports to make out too, you know."

"All right, here it is in a nutshell. I've already told you how the thieves caused the wreck. They waited in a hollow with wagons, looted the freight cars, and headed toward those buttes I mentioned. Where the wagons went to, I don't know yet. I did find a well-concealed opening in those buttes where a number of horses had waited, probably until their riders had delivered the wagons someplace." He wiped the last of the lather from his face and continued. "I've a hunch if the thieves aren't caught there'll be another wreck at about that same spot one of these days; it's mighty convenient to those buttes."

"Great God, no! But how are we going to stop it?"

"My suggestion is that you put some guards out there patrolling the right-of-way, until such time as the trouble is halted. Cut in on a wire and have the guards report frequently. If too long a time passes without a report, get somebody out from Puma Junction to learn why."

"Guards cost money," Fletcher protested, shaking his head.

"Well, wrecks don't build any profits for stockholders, either."

"I guess you're right, Greg. I'll see what can be done."

Quist ran a comb through his tousled hair and searched out a black sateen shirt from his satchel. He knotted a red bandanna about his throat, adjusted the shoulder holster to his body, then slipped into his coat. "I suppose you've already had breakfast, Jay?"

"Couple of hours ago. I'm planning to catch that nine forty-three to Loboville, back to headquarters. I just wanted to say good-by and much obliged for getting here, before I left."

"Always glad to accommodate the authorities," Quist smiled. "Say, did you attend that inquest on Harmon yesterday afternoon?"

"You know I wouldn't have time for that. I heard something about a verdict of suicide being turned in."

"I wonder if Mrs. Harmon testified."

"I understand she did. Just appeared briefly and then left. Toby Nixon said she bore up wonderfully. Queer what a pretty face will do to some men."

"You're not getting cynical, are you, Jay?"

"I'm talking common sense. I've wondered if you were entirely immune to her fatal beauty, or if there really was something in what you said about the freight thieving being tied up with Harmon's death. Are you still holding the same opinion?"

"I've not come to a definite decision yet," Quist said shortly.

"Oh yes," Fletcher remembered, "the deputy sheriff was here to see you, earlier. I told him you were asleep."

"What did he want?"

"I guess it wasn't important. He said he just wanted to ask your opinion of that suicide verdict. He said he'd see you later. Name's Pete Dewitt. Didn't look to me as though he had much ambition. Rather indolent manner."

"I'll run across him eventually."

"That's likely. . . . Look here, Greg, just how much time do you plan to devote to this suicide business of Harmon's?"

"No time at all to a suicide. All the time that's necessary to a murder."

"Great Scott, Greg! Do you think it's murder?"

"I don't think there's any doubt of it."

"On what are you basing your opinion?"

Quist said noncommittally, "Just a couple of ideas that entered my head."

"Meaning you don't want to talk about it yet?"

"Meaning I'm not sure enough of my ground to talk about it yet. I'd like to make a few facts dovetail before I do any talking."

Fletcher said seriously, "Maybe you should have stayed here yesterday and testified at that inquest."

Quist laughed scornfully. "A fat chance I had of doing that, with you practically grabbing the seat of my pants and running me down the tracks where that wreck took place. It's darn' funny how you always think of the right thing to do, once your division is operating smoothly. Otherwise, nothing exists except the T. N. & A. S."

"But, Greg—murder! I didn't realize before—"

"Forget it, Jay. In the first place there was nothing I could have testified to that would have changed the verdict much, in face of the stand John Blackmer and Doc Lang were taking. In the second place, while you probably won't believe me, I was just as anxious to get out to that wreck as you were to have me there. Don't forget, Jay, I have a pretty good reputation for looking out for the railroad's interests. If I wasn't convinced that somehow Gid Harmon's murder was mixed up with the people doing the freight thieving, I wouldn't waste any time on it. There's law officers in Dawson County to take care of such things, and if they're inefficient, it's none of my affair—unless it affects the railroad."

"Lilith Harmon wouldn't have had anything to do with that matter of convincing you, would she?" Fletcher asked dryly.

A slow flush crept into Quist's features. He picked up the division superintendent's satchel and thrust it into the man's hand. "Jay, if you're intending to catch that nine forty-three to headquarters at Loboville, you'd better mosey on down to the station. I've got to catch some breakfast. I'll keep you posted on anything special that turns up."

Taking Fletcher's arm with one hand, while the other seized the flat-topped sombrero, Quist steered him toward the hotel-room doorway.

8. Danged Loyal

The two said good-by in the hotel lobby, and Quist started toward the dining room, only to find his way barred by a sleepy-eyed individual, with a deputy sheriff's badge on his open vest, who rose from a chair as Quist started to pass.

"The dining room's closed, Mr. Quist. How about me staking you to a stack of wheats? I'd like to talk to you if you can give me a few minutes. I'm Dewitt—Pete Dewitt. John Blackmer's deputy."

"Any particular reason you should pay for my breakfast?" Quist asked as they shook hands.

A ghost of a twinkle appeared in Dewitt's sleepy eyes. "Well, I rather gathered from what Fletcher said, when I tried to see you earlier, that railroad men were entitled to some sort of special treatment." Dewitt spoke in a drawly manner. He was thin, dark-complexioned, loose-jointed.

Quist smiled. "You don't want to let that stiff attitude of Fletcher's bother you. He's all right when you get under his skin. He's just so interested in making the T. N. & A. S. the best road in the country that he just doesn't have time for any other interests. And furthermore,"—Quist studied the sleepy eyes—"I don't think you're the kind of man that would let himself be impressed by Fletcher's attitude. So I'm still wondering why you want to buy my breakfast."

"Well, now, it's this way, Mr. Quist. I've noticed when you buy a man a meal, he sort of feels under obligations to listen to anything you've got to say."

"You're frank, anyway."

"No, I'm Pete. And you've probably heard that one before. I'm gettin' kind of sick of using it myself."

Quist said quietly, "That much is clear anyway. So you're willing to buy me a meal so I'll listen to you?"

Dewitt shook his head. "No, I'm planning that you do the talking. I'll listen."

"What's the subject?"

"Gid Harmon."

"You mean the suicide?"

"It wasn't suicide."

"How do you know, Dewitt?" The topaz eyes were sharp.

"I knew Gid Harmon," the deputy drawled.

Quist nodded shortly. "All right, where do we get this stack of wheats you mentioned?"

"We'd better go over to Carrie Trent's Stopgap Restaurant. She don't like to be called Carrie, though. Her name's Car'line."

"I'm ready when you are."

They stepped out into the midmorning sun of Main Street. A few pedestrians moved along the plank sidewalks. Ponies and wagons stood at an almost unbroken line of tie rails on either side of the rough, unpaved thoroughfare. Most of the buildings were of frame structure with high false fronts. Quist had a brief glimpse of a brick-constructed bank building, a general store, and a real estate office. It was the first time he'd seen the town in daylight—that is, for a number of years. It had grown considerably since his last visit.

Pete Dewitt steered him in a diagonal direction across the street from the hotel, and they entered a restaurant, on the window of which were painted the words THE STOP-GAP, in white letters. It was clean and neat within. Two men sat at a long counter running along the left side of the entrance. The remainder of the room was given over to several oilcloth-covered tables with straight-backed chairs. At the rear of the long counter a swinging door gave access to the kitchen.

A girl emerged from the kitchen bearing platters of food which she placed before the two men at the counter, as Quist and Dewitt seated themselves at a table in the far corner. The girl was slim and more than attractive in a green-checked gingham dress and white apron. Her hair—well, there was no doubt about it: it was brick red!—was gathered in a great shining knot at the back of her neck. Quist judged her to be twenty-three or -four. When she approached the table a few minutes later, he saw she had hazel eyes with long lashes, and a dusting of freckles across her nose.

"Morning, Pete."

"Morning, Car'line. Have you decided yet when you'll marry me?"

"No," the girl replied crisply.

"Meaning you haven't decided, or you won't marry me?"

"Both." The girl's lips twitched at the corners.

"We-ell . . ." Dewitt looked puzzled. "Maybe we'd better get to the less important business. Car'line, this is Mr. Gregory Quist—Miss Car'line Trent." Quist liked the cordial hand the girl proffered him as he rose from his chair. It was firm, friendly; there wasn't anything wrong with her ready smile, either. She told Quist to sit down and waited to take their order.

Dewitt said, "I promised Mr. Quist a stack of wheat cakes. I might even throw in some coffee. But anything beyond that, he pays for himself."

"Darn you, Pete," the girl frowned. "You might know we wouldn't have wheats at this late hour. The batter is all gone, long since. Cookie will be fit to be tied if I ask him to mix another batch."

"That's what I like about this place," Dewitt explained blandly to Quist. "You never have any trouble getting what you want."

"All right, I'll mix some fresh batter myself," Caroline surrendered.

"I knew you would," Pete chuckled. "And that will keep us here longer and we're going to have a lot to talk about, maybe. And——"

"Look here," Quist protested, "I don't have to have wheat cakes. Anything else will do."

"Like wheat cakes, don't you?" Caroline Trent smiled.

"It's my favorite breakfast—with a slice of ham on the side and lots of sirup and coffee."

"Wheat cakes you get, with all the trimmings," the girl said briefly and turned toward the kitchen.

"What a girl!" the deputy drawled admiringly. "Y'know, she started this place three years ago— just selling beans. What she can do with beans— yessir, just baked beans, bean soup, coffee and pie. Now who'd ever think the cow country would go for beans when the hands come to town."

"Maybe the girl had something to do with it," Quist said dryly.

"That could be. But what Car'line can do with a bean is something like heaven. And then the business grew and——"

Quist broke in, "I'd be much obliged if you'd explain what all this has to do with Gid Harmon."

The deputy's eyes lost their enthusiasm and assumed that sleepy expression again. "You know, I never can keep my mind on business when I come in here," he said slowly. "I'll just tell you that Car'line serves the best food in town and we'll say no more about it."

"Exactly what is it you want to know from me?"

Dewitt said, "What makes you think Gid Harmon was murdered?"

"Have I made any statement to that effect?"

"I don't know. John Blackmer seems to think you hinted at something of the sort."

"And Blackmer sent you to pump me to see what you could learn?"

They were holding their voices low, so the tones wouldn't reach the men at the counter.

A slow flush mantled the deputy's cheeks. He half rose from his chair, then sat down again. "I understand," he said slowly at last, "that you knew John, years ago."

"I was acquainted with him."

"That being the case," Dewitt pursued, "can you imagine Sheriff Blackmer showing that much initiative? So far as he's concerned, it was suicide. That's the easiest way to wash up the case. But you know how he talks. You must have said something. Anyway, he told it around, like he always tells things, figuring it was a joke on you. Now, though, a lot of people are commencing to wonder, and Cenotaph is full of arguments today as to whether it was suicide or murder. Now, if you think I'm siding with Blackmer—"

"I don't, as a matter of fact—now," Quist conceded. "I wasn't sure in the first place. I wanted to see how you'd accept such an accusation. I found out."

Dewitt nodded. "But didn't you say something about the murderer coming in the back way of the Thunderbird ranch house and—"

"I did some speculating along those lines. I offered nothing definite, Dewitt."

"Uh-huh, I see. Well, you have got Doc Lang wondering now if he should recall the jury, there's so much talk around town, and this time he'd want your testimony. The sheriff says the idea's crazy."

"That's no more than is to be expected from Blackmer."

"You figuring John had anything to do with Gid Harmon's death?" Dewitt asked.

"What do you think along that same angle?" Quist countered.

Dewitt replied promptly, "Not John Blackmer. Oh, I know, he's inefficient, he talks too much, but there's nothing dishonest about John. He's just willing always to take the easiest way. That's how it generally goes when a politician remains in office too long, and John's no exception—now wait, maybe this sounds disloyal as hell, but I don't mean it that way. But I did figure to do a little investigating on the quiet, if I could."

"What makes you think," Quist asked bluntly, "that Harmon didn't commit suicide?"

"I knew Gid Harmon," Dewitt said for the second time that day. "He liked life too well. Generally, there's only two reasons for a man's committing suicide: financial troubles or bad health. Gid was well fixed, and he was as healthy as they come—that is, for a man of forty-three. He could hold his own riding with any of us. I've never heard of him being sick. Worst I ever heard of him getting was a sprained wrist a spell back."

"How about his enemies?"

"Didn't have any that I know of. Gid and John Blackmer didn't get along too well."

"Why?"

"For one thing, they were on opposite sides of the political fence. For another, Gid was always trying to get into office a sheriff from his own party. But that's not a killing matter."

"Sometimes it has been in the past."

"Not in this particular instance. John's no killer."

"There's always a first time."

"Why, darn your hide," Dewitt said, even-voiced, "are you trying to build a case against John Blackmer?"

"Darn yours—no." Quist's voice was just as quiet as Dewitt's. He smiled. "You're pretty loyal, aren't you?"

Dewitt said simply, "John's my boss. If I thought he was crooked, I'd resign my job."

"All right," Quist nodded cheerfully, "we'll forget Blackmer for the moment. I've got *you* pegged now."

"What do you mean?"

"I wanted to learn exactly where you stood. You think Harmon was murdered. You want to uncover

95

his killer. There's rumors around town he was murdered, despite the verdict of the coroner's jury. You're afraid people will remember past political arguments that Blackmer and Harmon had and suspect Blackmer. You don't want that."

"I can't forget that John was pretty decent to me a few years back when I was broke," Dewitt said slowly. "It was him that got me this job. But you had me mad for a minute."

"I intended that. When a man gets mad, he doesn't think clearly. Occasionally he lets slip things he wouldn't otherwise. You came through all right."

Dewitt gave him a twisted smile. "Thanks. It's nice to know I passed your inspection."

"With flying colors," Quist laughed. "Tarnation! I'm letting you buy my breakfast that I see coming right now. I'd never let an enemy do that."

Caroline Trent distributed dishes about the table and placed a cup of coffee in front of Dewitt. Dewitt said thanks and added, "I thought maybe you wouldn't open up today."

"I'll be closed tomorrow, during the funeral," the girl said.

"How's Mrs. Harmon?"

"Holding up mighty well. Lilith has a lot of courage, you know."

"That's how I figured. I suppose she'll be staying in town until after the funeral?"

Caroline Trent nodded. "I'm going back to the

ranch with her for a day or so, when she returns."

If Quist had been paying any attention to the remarks, he gave no sign. He had just slipped a sirup-soaked forkful of wheat cake into his mouth. He tasted a moment, then said gravely, "Miss Trent, will you please place my name on that list with Pete's—preferably ahead of his?"

"What list?" the girl looked puzzled.

"I heard him ask you to marry him. He can't be the only man in town that feels that way. There must be a list of applicants." He tried another forkful. "I know why, now."

The girl laughed. Dewitt said sorrowfully, "I was afraid I was making a mistake by bringing you here."

The three made small talk for a time, then the girl departed in the direction of the kitchen. Quist continued eating. Dewitt drank coffee and smoked a cigarette. Quist said, after a time, "I take it Lilith Harmon's staying with Miss Trent."

"Sure. I thought you knew. Didn't you?"

"I was the one told Mrs. Harmon about Gid's death. Blackmer said she had gone to stay with a relative. I didn't know who it was."

"I figured the sheriff had probably told you. And Car'line is a relative, in a way."

"How? You mean she's related to Mrs. Harmon?"

"You'd call it that, I reckon. You see, Gid Harmon was Car'line's uncle."

"That's news. Where are Miss Trent's folks?"

"Both dead. Gid's first wife—she died several years ago, ten or twelve, anyway—was Car'line's mother's sister."

"Oh, that's how it was. It's a wonder to me Miss Trent didn't stay on the ranch with her uncle."

"She used to—" Dewitt paused suddenly. He looked miserable.

Quist forked a chunk of ham between his lips, chewed meditatively for a minute. "All right," he said quietly, "you might as well finish it, Pete. Miss Trent's mother died, she went to live with Gid Harmon and his wife, then the first Mrs. Harmon died. What's next? Did Miss Trent leave when Lilith Harmon came to the ranch?"

Dewitt shook his head. "She'd left before the second Mrs. Harmon ever appeared on the scene."

"Why'd she leave?"

"That I don't know. Exactly what happened, Car'line never said, and neither did Gid. Anyway, Car'line packed up and came back to Cenotaph and opened her restaurant. Gid was pretty sore about that for a spell. He offered her money to live on, but Car'line is mighty independent. Then, about a year after Car'line left, Gid married Lilith—er— I've forgotten what her name used to be."

"How did he meet her?"

"That's something you'll have to ask Mrs. Harmon. It was up in Denver, I think, but I don't know the details."

Quist went on eating for a time. Caroline Trent appeared briefly with another plate of wheat cakes and more coffee. When she had returned to the kitchen, Quist said, "Harmon, you said, was pretty well fixed financially. Do you know if he left a will?"

"Probably so. The Judge could say for sure."

"Who?"

"Judge Eli Harnsworth. He's Cenotaph's J. P. He handles legal matters for folks around town."

"How well do you know him?"

"Ever since I was a button around these parts."

"You can do me a favor if you'll learn from him just how the money is to be distributed—how much to Lilith Harmon and how much to Caroline Trent, if anything."

Dewitt's face whitened with anger. "Dang you, Quist," he said in a low, tense voice, "are you trying to throw suspicion on those two girls?" He half rose from his chair.

Quist said coldly, "Sit down and don't act like a fool. God, how darned loyal you are!" He smiled thinly. "I'm getting to like you more all the time, Pete Dewitt. Now if you can tell me why I should try to throw suspicion on two women I'll be glad to listen. Otherwise, settle down and act sensible."

By this time the two men at the counter had departed, and Quist and Dewitt had the big room to themselves. Caroline Trent was out in the kitchen with her cook. Some of the color flowed back into Dewitt's features. He finally found his voice. "All right, maybe I'm not seeing things straight. But why should that will concern you?"

"Harmon is supposed to have been well fixed. His wife is entitled to the bulk of his property, but it seems natural he'd leave his niece something too. Suppose the will shows he had very little to leave, or that somebody else is left a great deal. We might uncover new angles to investigate. See what I mean? Anything you can learn for me from Judge Harnsworth might tell us something, Pete."

"I'll do what I can. Sorry I went off half-cocked that way. But you see, I've heard things about you in the past."

"What sort of things?"

"That you didn't much give a darn who you hurt so long as you could run down a criminal—that you were hard as nails."

"Do you think," Quist asked mildly, "that anyone should be protected, if such protection gave a criminal an opportunity to escape?" Without giving Dewitt a chance to answer, he laughed shortly. "Sometimes I wonder if I'm as black as I'm painted. A man with enemies hears queer things about himself sometimes. Let's forget that, too. Come on, show me your town. The food was everything you said it was, and it must be nearly first-drink time. I'd like to pay you something on account for that breakfast."

9. Definite Evidence

Quist and the deputy left the restaurant and started out along Main Street on a tour of the town. There were various places of commercial enterprise, at least two general stores, four or five saloons, two pool halls, a photograph gallery; the jail and sheriff's office, a rock-and-adobe building, stood at the corner of Main and Cochise streets; there was a hay-and-feed store, and a two-story frame structure known as the county house.

"I understood the sheriff to say," Quist commented as they walked along, "that Gid Harmon was a pretty heavy drinker."

Dewitt nodded. "He didn't used to be, but the past year or so he's been hitting it up right heavy."

"A man doesn't generally take to drink, all of a sudden, unless something's troubling him a lot," Quist mused. He changed the subject abruptly, "Where would I be likely to find some mules?"

"Mules?" Dewitt looked surprised. Then he laughed shortly. "The town's full of 'em."

"I don't mean the two-legged variety."

"There's no mules in this neck of the range to speak of. 'Most everybody uses horses naturally. Why you asking?"

"I'll go into that later. Let's drift down to the station. I'm half expecting a message."

They turned off Main at the corner of Lincoln

Street and headed down toward the railroad tracks in the direction of the red-painted T. N. & A. S. depot on its raised-dirt platform. Entering, Quist found a message awaiting him. He took the paper and read:

Forty-five slugs found in skulls of brakeman and conductor. What can I do to help?

The message was signed, "Carstairs." Quist turned to Dewitt, asking, "What do you know about Steve Wilson?"

"You mean the deputy at Puma Junction? Steve's all right. A mite slow at times, but he's a plugger."

"Thanks. That's about the way I had him figured."

Quist got a sheet of paper and, after addressing it to Carstairs, scribbled on it:

Keep your eyes peeled for mules. Steve Wilson can explain. Talk to him.

QUIST.

Handing the message to the telegraph operator, Quist said, "I don't want this advertised around, if you know what I mean."

The operator flushed and admitted that he knew what Quist meant. Quist rejoined the deputy and they started back toward Main Street. "That other wreck, about three months back, had some looted cars if you'll remember, and you and Blackmer followed some wheel ruts—"

"Only to the Murdock County line," Dewitt said a trifle bitterly. "John allowed our jurisdiction didn't extend farther."

"That's the sort of thing I hold against Blackmer," Quist said. "The railroad had an investigator on the matter, too, but he was unfamiliar with western country and didn't even make a start toward learning anything. That's why I was brought over here this time. I followed some wagon tracks yesterday, but the wagons disappeared over near that stretch of red buttes. Strange formation, those buttes; they seem to be a sort of granite, rather than the usual sandstone—"

Dewitt cut in, "What do you mean—the wagons disappeared?" Quist gave him the story, while Dewitt's eyes widened. When Quist had concluded, the deputy exclaimed, "You mean to say they just plain vanished? But how could they?"

"Steve Wilson and I couldn't figure it out. Maybe you can dream up an answer. The wagons were drawn by mules. Now if I can find a bunch of mules someplace I'll have some questions to ask their owner."

"Those freight thieves are danged smart. But the wagons—"

"Maybe they're smart. I'm not yet ready to

admit it. I do know they're murderers. On that point I've definite information. Take a look at this." He handed Dewitt the message he'd received from Carstairs. The deputy read it through, handed it back to Quist and swore a long wrathful oath.

Quist waited until he had calmed down a trifle, then observed, "For an easygoing-appearing man, Pete, you can sure work up a lot of temper at times. Sure, sure, I know, those thieves are a dirty crew of—well, just what you called them."

"Good lord! How can you take it so quietly?"

"Because I more than half expected that message from Carstairs. It was at my request that the matter of the brakie and conductor was investigated. Besides in my business it's necessary to keep a tight rein on my feelings. An angry man doesn't think clearly."

"I reckon you're right," Dewitt conceded moodily.

"I haven't forgotten I promised you a drink. Where do you do your drinking generally?"

"Sometimes the hotel bar, if I want to learn who's arrived in town. Mostly, if I want to see folks I know, I drink at Johnny Webb's Sundown Saloon."

"The Sundown sounds all right to me."

They entered the saloon at the southeast corner of Main and Waco streets. There were several men standing at the bar to whom Dewitt nodded as he and Quist sought a vacant spot at the far end of the long mahogany counter, apart from the others. Within a few moments Johnny Webb came to take their orders. The proprietor was a thin-faced, quiet man. Quist and the deputy got bottles of beer.

Quist sipped his drink slowly. Now that his eyes had become accustomed to the relatively dark interior after the bright sunlight of the street, he let his vision range slowly along the men at the bar. There were a few individuals in puncher togs, with a sprinkling of townsmen among them. Only two of those present captured Quist's attention.

One was a tall, good-featured man with wide shoulders and slim hips, clothed in puncher's togs. He was probably in the vicinity of thirty-five years, though his dark hair showed a slight sprinkling of gray. A six-shooter was slung at one hip of his faded Levis, and there was about him, at present at least, a careless laughing manner, as he joshed Johnny Webb about the quality of the liquor served in the Sundown Saloon.

The other man brought to Quist's mind a memory of a toy he had once owned when a child. The toy, made of cardboard, had been shaped like an egg and was weighted at the smaller end, so that no matter how hard one pushed it about, it always sprang erect again. The toy had been decorated in bright colors to represent the nursery-rhyme character, Humpty Dumpty.

This man had the form, but none of the bright

color. He was unbelievably fat, and his ears appeared to rest on his shoulders. His thick eyebrows were arched above a wide-nostriled nose. Beneath the soiled-looking sombrero was clustered in tiny locks a head of oily black hair that ended in sideburns on either fleshy chop. The lips were wide, pendulous, and a double chin swelled into the knotted bandanna about the man's neck—if he had any neck. That was a point Quist couldn't decide.

Dewitt said, at Quist's shoulder, "You seem to be interested in the Egg."

"The what?"

"The Egg. That's what he's called around Cenotaph—but not to his face. His name's Voit—Hugo Voit."

"Egg suits him better."

Dewitt dropped his voice still lower: "If he hears you, you might have trouble on your hands—no, don't underrate him! He's a mighty deceivin' hombre. Powerful. And fast!"

"Now who are you ribbing?" Quist smiled good-naturedly.

"I'm telling you," Dewitt said earnestly. "I've seen him take a horseshoe in his two hands and bend it out straight. All that fat is just padding for a lot of steel muscle. I've heard it said, by hombres who saw him do it, that he's fast enough to pick a live rattler from the ground before it can strike him."

"So you're trying to tell me he's fast with his gun?"

"That's something I've seen. Last Fourth of July we had some shooting contests in town. The Egg beat everybody who competed—both in accuracy and speed tests. He's mean. I've seen him shoot a dog, just to watch it jump and squirm. I protested that, and for a minute it looked like Voit would kill me, too. But Belvard cut in and stopped Voit with a couple of words. Belvard can handle him, apparently. I've never seen any reward dodgers for Voit, so I judge anybody he's killed has been killed in fair fight. With Voit's speed, he can afford to give an opponent an even break."

"You mentioned somebody named Belvard."

"That's him with the Egg—Hoddy Belvard. He runs the HB-Connected, which was formerly part of the Thunderbird. Gid Harmon sold him the land and cows about four years back, when Belvard first came here."

"Are you telling me the Egg punches for Belvard?"

"What he's on the payroll for, I don't know. I never heard of him punching cows."

"Did you ever inquire?"

"Nope. I mind my own business, unless folks break laws—which Voit hasn't done, *so far as I know.* I saw him knock a man down one time."

"Did you interfere?"

"Nope," Dewitt drawled. "A man could get hurt

107

that way. Besides, I figured the fellow had it coming when he cast aspersions on the Egg's parentage, with a remark that Voit must have been sired by a kid's spinning-top and dammed by a garden beet. Voit just hit him once, but the fellow's lower jaw was plumb fractured. Since then folks are mighty careful how they speak of the Egg."

"That description of Voit's parentage explains the shape but not the size of the man."

Dewitt said, "There's a hell of a lot about the Egg that's unexplained, in my estimation. . . . No, the rest of Belvard's crew are just ordinary run-of-the-mill cowhands. I've never heard they didn't do a good job raising beef stock."

At that moment Belvard came laughing down the bar, followed by Voit, who minced along on small feet with all the lightness of step of a professional dancer. Belvard said, "Pete, how about you and your friend having a drink with me? You might as well get in on a good joke."

"I reckon it can be arranged," Pete said genially. "This is Mr. Quist—Hoddy Belvard and Hugo Voit."

Quist shook hands with Belvard. Voit was engaged in rolling a brown-paper cigarette and nodded to Quist. Quist marveled at the Egg's deft manipulation of tobacco and paper, considering the fat man's wide hands and stubby fingers. In contrast, Voit's feet were almost tiny, more nearly the size of a woman's feet than a man's.

Johnny Webb took the order. Belvard tossed a silver dollar on the bar. The men drank. Belvard set down his glass and started laughing again. Voit, too, laughed. No, it wasn't a genuine laugh. It was more like a giggle than anything else. His voice had a sort of high-pitched quality that was exceedingly unpleasant to Quist's ears.

"You said something about letting us in on a joke," Dewitt remarked.

"Oh yes." Belvard grinned. He turned to Quist. "As I get it, you've been sort of interested in Gid Harmon's death, said it was murder, or something of the sort."

"I don't recollect," Quist said quietly, "making any public statement to that effect."

Hugo Voit giggled. "Oh, now, Mr. Quist, don't back down. The sheriff led us to believe you did, and most folks around town have taken up the idea."

"I'm not backing down," Quist said, even-toned. "I didn't say it was murder. I did do some speculating that may have led John Blackmer to think—"

"Let it drop, Hugo," Belvard chuckled. "The point is, Quist, that all day yesterday Blackmer went around maintaining it was suicide. Now that the town is commencing to take the opposite view, Blackmer has swung to the murder theory. Isn't that just like a politician—give the public what it wants to hear?" He went off into another peal of laughter.

"Maybe," Dewitt said resentfully, "Blackmer is commencing to use his head."

Belvard sobered instantly. "Don't tell me you're thinking it's murder, Pete." A series of short giggles escaped the Egg's thick lips.

"I'm not saying," Dewitt stated flatly.

Belvard swung around to Quist. "It's about time you came into the open with your opinion, isn't it?"

Quist said good-humoredly, "Any particular reason why I should?"

Belvard chuckled. "Come on, now, there's no use you acting secretive. Everybody knows you're a detective of some sort. A detective should have an opinion, one way or the other."

"Even a railroad detective," the Egg tittered derisively.

By this time the conversation had drawn the attention of the other men in the barroom. Quist felt there was some purpose behind this heckling attitude on the part of Belvard and Voit. Perhaps they wanted to learn how much he knew or suspected.

Quist laughed softly, but there was no laughter in his topaz eyes. "Yes, even a railroad detective should have an opinion, Egg," he stated, and each word carried an insult all its own. "I'll express my opinion for your benefit. It is this: you just think you're a bad egg, but if you don't keep a civil tongue in your fat head you'll get your shell

110

cracked and everybody will see the yellow run out."

A gasp ran through the barroom. No one had ever talked in such fashion to Hugo Voit. Both Belvard and Dewitt started to speak, then fell silent. The smirk left Voit's face, his heavy-lidded eyes blinked in surprise. In an instant he regained control of himself.

"You're going just a little too far, Mr. Quist," he purred, and his eyes, glancing quickly below Quist's coat, spied no six-shooter. "And now you're going to get down on your knees and apologize for those remarks, or I'm going to shoot off your right ear. Or"—a ghost of a giggle escaped the loose lips—"shall it be your left? Are you prepared to apologize, Mr. Quist?"

His right hand went leisurely to the gun at his hip—and then the movement stopped abruptly.

Quist's left hand had flipped back the left lapel of his coat, and the underarm forty-four had seemed to fairly leap into his right before Voit's gun muzzle had cleared its holster. A thin smile played about Quist's lips.

"Whose ears were you going to shoot off?" he asked softly.

A murmur of surprise lifted through the saloon. Carefully, Voit lifted the hand from his gun butt and moved back a pace. Grudging admiration appeared in his eyes. "Ah, so you do carry a gun, Mr. Quist. And you're, oh, so swift in the drawing. Tricks. Like a magician. And I say to myself, 'Hugo, you idiot, for once your jokes have got you into trouble, and how are you going to square yourself with this Mr. Quist who is so quick to misunderstand?' And I think this time, perhaps—"

"This has gone far enough," Belvard found his voice. "Look here, Quist, Hugo was only fooling—"

"So was I," Quist chuckled, and replaced his six-shooter in its holster. "Looked sort of serious for a moment, didn't it?" Behind him he heard Pete Dewitt draw a long breath of relief.

Voit said in a tittering voice, "I think the drinks are on me. What will you have, Mr. Quist— Hoddy—Pete?"

"I've still something left from the last round, Voit," Quist refused, as did the other two. "Just remember, I don't like to be ribbed."

"Another time I will know better," Voit stated. "Perhaps I did push you too far, but it's a weakness of mine to learn what a man is made of." He wagged his huge head ruefully. "To my sorrow I have learned. Another time I shall act differently." The hidden threat in the words didn't escape Quist.

Johnny Webb, looking very pale, announced that drinks were on the house. By the time bottles and glasses had been place on the long counter, conversation was somewhere near back to normal.

"I'm still interested," Belvard ventured at last, "in knowing what you think of Harmon's death, Quist."

"Murder," Quist said flatly.

"I think you're wrong."

"Why?"

"Who would murder Gid Harmon?"

"You tell me and I'll tell you."

"But he had so many friends," Voit put in. "Everybody liked Gid Harmon, Mr. Quist. Are you suspecting anybody in particular?"

"Everybody who knew him—practically," Quist replied.

Belvard laughed. "I'm glad I have an alibi, then."

"Airtight, I suppose?"

"Couldn't be better." Belvard turned to Johnny Webb. "Johnny, everybody knows Gid Harmon died around six o'clock, day before yesterday. Do you remember that I was in here about that time?"

"You were in here all afternoon that day," Webb replied promptly. "You went out for supper and then came back just a little while before news came in that Gid had killed himself—"

Belvard turned to Quist. "That satisfy you?"

Quist laughed. "Cripes! I'm not the man to be satisfied. Pete Dewitt and John Blackmer are enforcing the law in this county. I came here for the railroad people to investigate a wreck—as everybody seems to know."

"And what have you learned, Mr. Quist?" asked the Egg.

"That," Quist said, "is railroad business and none of yours."

"Excuse me for asking." The Egg giggled. "It is probable, also, then, you are not interested regarding my alibi for the death of Mr. Harmon?"

"Not in the least," Quist said promptly. "I couldn't believe it anyway."

"You are very humorous, Mr. Quist. Someday we shall become better acquainted. Then I shall know just how to take you—no?"

"No," Quist smiled icily. Again he had caught that hidden threat in the words. He turned to Dewitt. "Let's get going." And as the two left the barroom he nodded and said, "See you again, gentlemen. You too, Voit."

10. Proof

When they had reached the sidewalk Dewitt took a deep breath and said ruefully, "Darn your blasted hide! Giving me a scare like that. What got into you?"

"They were looking for trouble when they came up to us. I had noticed the pair of them talking and glancing along our way, shortly before Belvard came up with that talk about letting us in on a joke."

"But what was the idea?"

"I don't know. Maybe they wanted to learn how much I knew. If they're mixed into the skulduggery around here, they may have wanted to see if I could be easily bluffed. I saw it was up to me to get the jump on 'em before they rode me too much."

"So you took the bull by the horns."

"Let's say I dehorned the bull," Quist smiled.

"You did that. Geez! I never knew you had a gun."

"These shoulder guns are convenient at times. The triangular end of this bandanna I've got around my neck covers the harness strap that runs across my chest. With my coat on, I appear unarmed."

"Cripes I never dreamed you had a gun. There was a bad second or two when Voit started his

115

draw. I didn't like the way he was going at it—slow and leisurely, like a cat plays with a mouse. I couldn't really believe he'd use it against an unarmed man, so hated to draw my gun. And there was something in your manner that told me you wanted to handle the show by yourself."

"Maybe I should have shot him," Quist said quietly. "He started to draw first. I had all the excuse in the world. I've a hunch I may someday regret holding my fire."

"You'll admit now he's a bad proposition—plenty tough?"

"I figured him tough when I first saw him: anybody that looks like he does would have to be bad to stay alive this long. But, imagine it, a fat man who giggles. It's amazin'."

"I'm talking seriously, Greg."

"So am I."

Dewitt said, "Oh darn" in a hopeless tone.

They sauntered over to the shady side of the street and crossed at the intersection of Lincoln and Main. The deputy went on, "What did you think of that alibi that Belvard offered?"

"It's too pat to be any good. Belvard was too anxious to let us know he had an alibi."

Dewitt said slowly, "Still, if Johnny Webb swears he was there that afternoon, I'd believe Johnny any time. He's straight."

"I'm not doubting Webb's word as to when Belvard was in the Sundown. As to the Egg—if he has an alibi, it's probably as good, or as bad, as Belvard's."

"You really feel then," Dewitt persisted, "that Belvard's alibi won't hold water?"

"It's water- and airtight both," Quist stated, "provided Gideon Harmon died the afternoon of the day it is claimed he committed suicide."

"And you don't believe he did?" Dewitt asked curiously.

"Not for a minute."

The deputy pondered that. Finally he drawled, "You sound pretty dang' certain. I'd like some proof."

Quist didn't reply for a few moments as they progressed along the plank sidewalk. After a minute or so he nodded. "Perhaps I can give you proof. Where can we locate Dr. Lang right now?"

"Unless he's been called out on a case, he's probably at his home. That's almost directly opposite here, over on Second Street. He has his office there, too."

"Let's go see him. No, wait,"—consulting his watch—"it's dinnertime now. You ate breakfast a lot earlier than I did, Pete. Tell you what, you go get your dinner. I'll meet you on the hotel porch when you get through."

"That's the best way," the deputy nodded. "I should be down to the jail right now, anyway. Got a couple of prisoners to feed. No, they're nothing special. One's a cowhand and the other's a town barber. They both got to celebrating a mite too freely last Saturday night, and the J. P. thought he'd give 'em a few days to contemplate their sins. I'll see you later, then."

He strode off down the street, and Quist turned back to the hotel. Not feeling hungry, he settled himself on the long veranda that ran along the Lincoln Street side of the hotel building, leaned back in a wooden chair and erected his feet on the railing. A few feet behind, and to one side, were the swinging doors of the hotel-bar entrance, from which emerged from time to time patrons of the dining room who had stepped in for an after-dinner libation. Quist lighted a cigarette and let his gaze rove idly on the pedestrians moving along the sidewalks. At his rear the swinging doors banged and then came to a rest.

"I was just wondering where you were," came a voice at his shoulder. "Looked for you in the dining room, but they said you hadn't been in." It was Sheriff Blackmer, at that moment in the act of swabbing the back of his hand across his wide tobacco-stained mustaches.

"I'd say you looked in the bar, too," Quist observed.

"Yes, just dropped in for a minute to get a touch of stomach bitters. Seems like my dinner don't agree with me lately, and I have to have something to settle my food."

Quist said gravely, "Probably everything you eat goes to your stomach."

"That might be it," Blackmer said dubiously. He sat down in the chair next to Quist's. "Have a cigar?"

"Thanks, no, John. What's on your mind?"

"I've been thinking things over," Blackmer commenced awkwardly, lighting a thick brown weed to cover his embarrassment, "and mebbe I was a mite hasty in my judgment regarding Gid Harmon's death."

"I heard you'd said something about its being murder."

"Well, I wouldn't go that far,"—cautiously—"but the more I think on it, the more it seems unlikely Gid would kill himself. He had everything to live for—money, a beautiful wife, not a care in the world. Now you can't tell me a fellow like that would commit suicide."

"But you're not sure it was murder. What do you think it was—a sort of natural death from lead poisoning?"

"Lead poisoning. Huh! Pretty good. It was that, all right. But I'd like—"

"John, you didn't have any love for Harmon. Why this sudden interest?"

"Sudden interest? Cripes A'mighty! If a murder's been committed I've got a duty to do, ain't I? Sure, I didn't have any love for Harmon— but I didn't have any hate, neither. I got to thinking this morning as to how I'd miss him. Him and me, we used to have some bang-up arguments as to which was the best, the Democrats or the Republicans."

"And which is?"

"Well, you know what side I'm on, but just between the two of us, I don't think there's much difference."

"Speaking of arguments," Quist said, "do you know of anybody who ever had any real serious arguments with Harmon?"

Blackmer shook his head. "Not serious, that I know of. The only time I ever saw Gid look like he was real mad was one time he was arguing with Hoddy Belvard. When he walked away, he shook his fist in Hoddy's face."

"Yes? What was the argument about?"

"Can't tell you that. They were standing on the corner of Main and Cochise, kitty-corner from my office. I listened real hard, but Gid wa'n't yelling like he usually does, and I couldn't hear a word."

"When was this?"

Blackmer scratched his chin and puffed hard on his cigar. " 'Bout a year back, I'd reckon."

"I understand it was about a year ago that Harmon took to drinking pretty hard."

"I'd say that was about right."

"To me it's all wrong."

"Huh?"

"Never mind. What was it you wanted to see me about?"

"Oh yes. Well, it's like this, Greg. I've been

talking matters over with Doc Lang, and he thinks maybe we should hold another inquest with you testifying. Now if you'll just tell me what murder theories you have, I'll run down the clues, and maybe we'll learn that Gid was murdered, after all."

"John, I haven't a thing I'd give you. I'm going to talk to you like a Dutch uncle for a minute. You're not going to like it, but it's time somebody told you. In the first place, you haven't sense enough to keep things to yourself. You blab everything you hear. You've been in office so long, you think you don't have to work at your job any more. You're leaving the whole business to Pete Dewitt—"

"Here! You can't talk to me like this, Greg. I won't—"

"Yes, you will stand for it. It's Dewitt that's keeping you in office, if you'd only realize it. He won't hear a word against you—and there's plenty being said, too. You always did talk too much for your own good, John, but there was a time when you were a good man in office. Nowadays you aren't even that."

"Have you gone crazy, Greg?" Blackmer was panting like a fish out of water, his face purple. "Pete Dewitt! What does he know that I didn't teach him? I trained that boy and—"

"He knows enough to keep his mouth shut when it's necessary. You blow and brag, and that's about all. If there's two ways to do a thing, you always look for the easiest. You're an insult to the badge you wear."

"By God, I won't stand for such talk!"

"You won't have to stand for any more. I've said what I intended. You can take it or leave it, but what I've said was for your own good."

For a moment the sheriff looked as though about to explode. Then he lifted himself from the chair, glared at Quist, left the gallery, and walked stiffly down the street. Quist looked thoughtfully after the pompous figure until it was lost to view. "Either that talk will do him some good," Quist mused, "or I've just made another enemy."

Pete Dewitt put in an appearance in about a half hour. "What happened between you and John?" he asked curiously, as Quist descended the veranda steps to meet him. Quist related the conversation he'd had with the sheriff. Pete nodded. "You've got John's dander up. As I was leaving I heard him muttering about showing up that lousy, two-bit, gall-sored so-and-so of a railroad dick."

Quist laughed. "I like John almost well enough to hope he succeeds."

They found Owen Lang seated on the porch of his white frame house which served as both dwelling and office. "I was just thinking about looking for you, Mr. Quist," he said. "Here—sit down. There's a chair for you, Pete."

They seated themselves. "I take it," Quist said,

"you wanted to see me in connection with Harmon's death."

Lang nodded. "There's a lot of talk around town. I'm afraid I'm going to have to recall that coroner's jury and ask for your testimony."

"You know what started the talk," Quist reminded. "Sheriff Blackmer picked up something I said and magnified it. As usual he talked too much and rumors started flying."

"Then you think," Lang asked, "that it was really suicide?"

"Not at all," Quist replied promptly. "Pete and I were talking it over a while back. I said then I didn't believe it was suicide. Pete said he wanted proof. That's why we're here."

"I can't tell you any more than you already know."

"I just want a checkup on certain theories of my own," Quist said. "Now, taking Stark Garrity's word for it that he heard a shot around six o'clock, the time of death was established at that hour, wasn't it?"

"Right," Dr. Lang nodded.

"All right," Quist pursued. "Now, let's pretend that Garrity wasn't there when death occurred and that you had to determine the time of death from the condition of the body. Think back, Doc, and remember I examined Harmon's body, too. I personally felt that the body was in quite an advanced state of *rigor mortis*, considering that Harmon was supposed to have died but a few hours before we saw the body. I was surprised you didn't comment on it at the time."

"I know what you mean," Lang replied soberly. "I've thought about it a great deal since. But in face of Garrity's testimony, I figured I might be mistaken—"

"*Rigor mortis,*" Pete broke in, "means that stiff condition a dead man gets in, doesn't it?"

"You're right," Lang replied. "*Rigor mortis—* the rigidity of death. Generally it commences about two hours after life has left the body, and in eight to twelve hours following death *rigor mortis* is complete. Had it not been that Garrity said he heard the shot around six o'clock, I should have been more inclined to give heed to the knowledge gained in my training. However, you can't make fast rules. *Rigor* has a tendency to set in, in the very aged, much quicker than in, say, a man of twenty. Sometimes, strange to say, *rigor* may be hastened by the temperature of a very warm day, or delayed by freezing weather."

"It was plenty warm the day Harmon died," Pete remembered.

Lang agreed. "That's one thing that made me doubt my better judgment."

"All right," Quist continued, "I think we can assume that Harmon died considerably before six o'clock that day. Let's consider the form of the body when we saw it. It was bent to a sort of V shape—remember?"

Lang remembered. Pete said, "I had to stay in Cenotaph that night, but I recollect John telling me what the body looked like. But does that V shape mean anything in particular?"

Quist replied, "It could mean that Harmon's body stiffened in that shape while slung, head and feet down, across a saddle."

"You mean"—Lang's eyes widened—"that Harmon died someplace else, then was brought home and left in his house?"

"That's how I see it," Quist nodded.

Pete said, "I'll be danged!" Then, "But when the body was carried into the house, wouldn't it straighten out again?"

"Not necessarily," Lang said. "We come back to the matter of heat—the warm day—again. The muscles may have been very rigid, and unless an effort was made to straighten them out—"

"And there'd be no particular reason for that, probably," Quist said. "Anyway, the position of the body gave me that idea, and I still think it a good one. Here's another thing to think about: What became of Harmon's hat? He was otherwise fully clothed."

"His hat was right there on the table," Lang said. "You saw it. I remember you picked it up and looked inside."

"Oh, I don't doubt it was his hat all right—but not the hat he wore that day, Doc. The hat I saw was practically new, hadn't been worn scarcely at all."

"Maybe he put it on for the first time that day," Lang said.

"All right." Quist smiled. "Where was Harmon supposed to have come from that day?"

"Mrs. Harmon guessed that he'd been to Tanzburg. That's where he said he was going when he left. I didn't inquire into that too much, as I could see just appearing at the inquest was an ordeal for her."

"Tanzburg is a right long ride from the Thunderbird," Quist stated. "Particularly under a hot sun. A man could do a lot of sweating on a ride like that."

"Harmon probably did," Lang said.

"If so," Quist smiled thinly, "it sure didn't show any on the sweatband of that hat I examined. That sweatband was hardly stained."

"By God, I never thought of that!" Lang exclaimed.

"It's not your job to think of such things," Quist responded.

"You know, Greg," Pete spoke admiringly, "you've got a head on your shoulders."

Quist smiled deprecatingly. "That sort of thing is just routine in my kind of work. The point is that the hat Harmon wore that day was lost someplace—maybe it fell off while he was being transported on the back of a horse. At any rate, when he was brought to the Thunderbird, fully clothed, somebody figured his hat should be near,

126

inasmuch as he was supposed to have just got home. And whoever it was, was acquainted with the house, and knew where another hat could be found."

"But where's the hat he wore that day?" Lang asked.

"I wish I knew," Quist responded. "If we could locate that hat, it might lead us to the place where he was killed."

"I'm convinced," Pete said. "I asked for proof and you've given me more than enough. Now——"

"I'll give you a couple of more things I picked up," Quist interrupted. "When I examined Harmon's gun that night, you'll remember that we found one old shell—the one on which he carried his hammer—one exploded shell, and four cartridges. Three of those cartridges had been in the gun for some time, and matched, in the finish of the metal, the exploded cartridge. By finish of the metal, I mean they matched in the degree of dullness the finish of the metal had acquired while being carried in the cylinder. The fourth cartridge had been placed in the cylinder at a much later date; the metal was much shinier."

"And that means what?" Pete asked.

"I'm not sure, but to me it means that two shots were fired from Harmon's gun that day, but that one of the exploded shells was replaced by an undischarged forty-five cartridge by someone."

"But why?" Lang frowned.

"You found only one bullet in his body, didn't you?" Quist asked dryly. "It wouldn't have done to have left two exploded shells in the gun—not when the first one killed. And it must have been the first one that killed. I can't imagine a suicide missing himself. Incidentally, Doctor, did you trace the course of that bullet?"

Lang nodded. "It entered just to the right of the navel, below the right ribs, and took an upward direction to reach the heart—"

"Think what an awkward position a suicide would have to hold his gun in to shoot himself that way," Quist pointed out. "Besides, suicides generally aim for the head."

"Dang it, you've convinced me," Pete growled, "but I don't yet see why that other ca'tridge was fired."

"Neither do I—yet," Quist admitted. "And now there's one more point. I looked at Harmon's horse's hoofs that night. For some reason they were quite clean, like they'd been washed. Of course, it had been in the corral with other horses, but still they didn't look like the hoofs of an animal that had made the long trip from Tanzburg."

"What reason would there have been for washing the hoofs?" Lang asked blankly.

"I'm not sure. But mud on those hoofs might indicate the horse had crossed a river someplace. I know of no river between Tanzburg and the Thunderbird Ranch."

"The Rio Esteban is the nearest stream in these parts, and that runs east of the Thunderbird," Pete pointed out.

"So maybe Harmon didn't go to Tanzburg," Quist said. "After all, it was Mrs. Harmon who said that he said he was going there, to see a—Dr. Jorge, I think the name was. Know anything about him, Dr. Lang?"

Lang smiled. "Ezra Jorge," he said, "has the reputation of being the best, the very best, doctor of veterinary medicine in Tanzburg."

"Just a plain old horse doctor, eh?" Quist said. "I can't see why Harmon should consult him about a sprained wrist."

"There's a reason for that," Lang said. "We medical men hate to admit it, but Jorge has had a certain success in curing human ailments—setting broken legs and so on, lame backs, that sort of thing. He'd be no good, it's likely, with organic ailments, but—"

"You think it's likely he may have started to see Jorge?" Quist asked.

"It's possible. That sprained wrist of Harmon's has bothered him quite a spell. If he'd followed my instructions when he first injured it, all would have been well, but he had an idea that because it was only a sprain he could use it as much as ever. Consequently, it required longer to heal. After all, Harmon was past forty. Injuries at that age don't mend as quickly as they would with a younger man. It wasn't really serious, of course, but he did a great deal of grumbling when he came in to consult me a couple of weeks back. At that time he said he was thinking of riding over to Tanzburg to see if Jorge couldn't fix him up better than I was doing."

"What did you tell him?" Quist asked.

"Told him I was doing all possible, but that if he insisted"—the doctor's eyes twinkled—"I could recommend Jorge as being mighty good for spavined mules—Harmon was just as stubborn as a mule when he was drinking, and he was pretty tight that day. He got mad and tore out of my office."

"Speaking of Harmon's wrist," Quist said, "when I examined his body that night I noticed some scratches on his wrist. Did you?"

Lang replied that he had. "I put it down that he'd got those abrasions off some brush, or cactus, or something of the sort. I don't think they meant anything."

"All this spells just one thing to me," Pete said.

"What's that?" Quist asked.

"Stark Garrity's a liar. Greg, you've proved that Harmon died earlier than six o'clock that day. Garrity maintains that Harmon rode into the ranch shortly after Mrs. Harmon left for town—I wonder what she came to town for?" he finished suddenly.

"I can throw some light on that," Quist replied.

"She came to see me to ask me if I wouldn't protect her husband from some danger she feared. . . ." He briefly related what had happened.

The other two heard him through in silence. "I think we'd better see to it that Garrity is brought in for a spell of questioning," Pete Dewitt said. "I always liked that hombre, but—"

"Let that ride for a time, Pete," Quist advised.

"But surely, Mr. Quist," Dr. Lang protested, "you can see that we should hold another inquest, supplementing the one we've held, so you can offer as testimony the various things you've told Pete and me."

"I can't prevent it," Quist replied. "I'll even testify, if you insist, but what will you get? A change in the verdict from suicide to murder 'by person or persons unknown.' And then where are you? All you can do is recommend that Sheriff Blackmer take steps to apprehend the murderer—and we'll be no farther along than we are now."

"What do you think we should do?" Pete asked.

"Keep to ourselves what we've talked over today. So long as the killer don't know we're aware of those facts, we have a certain advantage. But once we make them public, we just make things more difficult for ourselves."

Dr. Lang sighed. "I guess you're right. I'm willing to hold off another inquest if Pete feels it's the thing to do."

"I can see sense in what Greg proposes," Pete replied.

"It's agreed then that nothing is to be done until I say the word?" Quist asked.

The other two replied in the affirmative. Dr. Lang asked, "I suppose you plan to attend Harmon's funeral tomorrow afternoon, Mr. Quist?"

"I haven't decided," Quist evaded. "I may have to run down some other business."

"I keep forgetting," Lang said, "that you're supposed to be working in the interests of the railroad while here—or shouldn't I ask?"

Quist smiled, as he rose and prepared to leave. "I guess it's no secret."

Only after Quist and the deputy were heading down the street did it occur to Lang that he hadn't had a direct answer to his question.

11. Motive?

It was early, the following morning, when Quist rose from his breakfast in the hotel dining room and strolled out on the veranda of the hostelry to smoke a cigar and adjust his thoughts to the day that lay before him. He hadn't been seated there long when Pete Dewitt mounted the steps to the porch.

"You had breakfast?" Pete asked.

"Finished not ten minutes ago."

"Sort of looked for you over to Car'line's Stopgap, but you didn't show up."

Quist smiled. "I figured the place would be so popular it would be crowded, so I ate here where I could get my food without waiting."

"Maybe you were smart, at that," Pete conceded, "though between Car'line and her food—well, the wait might have been worth while. Car'line's figuring to close up, right after breakfast, until the funeral's done with this afternoon. She's got to help Mrs. Harmon, I suppose."

"Help her with what?"

Pete shrugged. "I dunno—whatever it is one woman helps another with at a time like this, I expect." He dropped into a chair at Quist's side and changed the subject. "After I left you, yesterday afternoon, I went over and saw Judge Harnsworth."

"You mean about Harmon's will?"

"Yeah. The Judge was pretty canny and refused to talk about it at first. Said it wouldn't be ethical to talk of such matters to an outsider, and that after due legal process the contents of the will would be made public. He'd just been over to see Mrs. Harmon, at Car'line's rooming house, where she's staying."

"So you couldn't learn anything?"

"Well, I got some idea. Y'see, I took the Judge into confidence and told him you had a special reason for wanting to know, so he finally consented to give me some general information without stating definite figures. As I got it, Harmon's original will left the bulk of the estate to Mrs. Harmon, around one thousand dollars, probably, to Car'line, and some odds and ends to the crew of the Thunderbird. The Judge kept one copy of the will and gave Harmon another."

"What do you mean—the original will?"

"I'll explain. That will was made out about a year and a half ago; then about seven months back—maybe it was less, the Judge couldn't remember, offhand—Harmon told the Judge he'd decided to have another will drawn."

"Did you learn why?"

"The Judge isn't exactly sure, but Harmon mentioned something about leaving more money to Car'line, stating he hadn't been fair to the girl in the first will. The Judge didn't press for details, as Harmon didn't appear to want to talk about it at that time. Harmon said he wanted to think things over first, and that he'd write out what he wanted, then bring his draft in to the Judge to be put in legal form and witnessed."

"And Harmon never did it?"

"The Judge never saw it, if he did. On the other hand, he thinks Harmon may have written out a new will, but never brought it in to be fixed up legal. Of course, if such a will was found, it wouldn't be legal without witnesses and so on."

"Did Harnsworth say that?" Quist asked sharply.

"No," Dewitt replied, looking up in surprise. "That's just my idea."

"You might be wrong," Quist said slowly. "If Harmon did write out another will, all in his own handwriting, it might be declared legal as a holograph will, providing it was properly signed, dated, and written on perfectly blank paper—" Quist broke off suddenly. "You said the Judge had been to see Mrs. Harmon. Did he mention the wills?"

"Yeah, though he said he hadn't intended doing so when he called to express his sympathy, and so on. But as Mrs. Harmon appeared to be right sensible about the whole business, he did bring it up, asking her if she knew of another will. So far as she knew, she told Harnsworth, Harmon had never drawn up a second will. She promised to look through Harmon's things for it when she returned to Thunderbird Ranch."

Quist said slowly, "Do you think Lilith Harmon was in love with her husband?"

The deputy said slowly, "I couldn't say as to that. I'll admit, I've wondered. But Gid was a lot older than she was. I remember when he brought her back from Denver, it came as a sort of surprise, him getting married so sudden and her being younger. It would be my guess she thought a lot of him without actually being in love. I know they used to seem to have good times together— before he took to drinking so heavy."

Quist said, "Pete, did you ever know of Harmon and Hoddy Belvard having any trouble?"

"Can't say that I did."

"John Blackmer mentioned, yesterday, about witnessing an argument he saw them having one time."

"What about?"

"John didn't know. He wasn't close enough to hear. But he says he saw Harmon shake his fist in Belvard's face."

"Was Harmon drunk?"

"John didn't say so."

"I guess that's once John didn't run true to form: he never mentioned the matter to me."

"Maybe it didn't seem important enough to him." Quist drew deeply on his cigar, knocked off the long ashes with his finger and said, "I understand Belvard bought the HB-Connected from Harmon."

Pete nodded. "Yes. Harmon had plenty of money at that time, and, as he used to say, he couldn't see much sense in working just to pile up more, so he sliced off most of the Thunderbird holdings and sold to Belvard."

"Belvard pay cash?"

"I don't know."

"Where did Belvard come from?"

"That's something else I can't tell you. I remember him saying once that he'd lived up in Wyoming, or Montana—one of those northern states, leastwise—but I don't remember much about it." He changed the subject: "I was thinking, Greg, if Harmon was killed away from the Thunderbird, then brought there across a saddle, there might be traces of blood on the saddle. What do you think?"

"I thought of that the night I was out there." Quist smiled thinly. "I asked Garrity to show me the saddle."

"And did he?"

Quist nodded. "There wasn't any blood on it."

Dewitt looked disappointed, then said suddenly, "Are you sure you saw Harmon's saddle that he was supposed to have arrived on?"

"No," Quist said quietly. "So I scratched my thumbnail on the saddle Garrity showed me, so I'd know it if I saw it again. I want to check that saddle with somebody else's opinion and make sure it was Harmon's. Course, he might not have been brought back on his own horse, either." He broke off. "I wish we could learn just what financial arrangements were made when Belvard bought his ranch. Was there a ranch house on the property he got?"

"That I can tell you. There wasn't. Belvard had to throw up some adobe buildings."

"I wonder if he had the cash for those?"

"I don't know that, either, but maybe I can find out something. There's a lot of such business done through the bank. Henry Vogel—he owns the bank—is a pretty good friend of mine. I might ask him what he knows about Belvard's finances. I could explain that it's to be held confidential, and why. What do you think?"

"I think it's a dang' good idea, Pete. Glad you thought of it—that is, if Vogel will keep his mouth shut."

"He will. Vogel is straight as a die. He was a pretty good friend of Gid Harmon's, too. I think he'll welcome a chance to help, when I tell him that we suspect Gid was murdered and that it wasn't suicide." He looked at his watch. "The bank won't be open for a spell yet."

"There's something else, Pete, you can do for me. I don't want you to think I'm using you for a messenger boy, but I've a hunch my moves are being pretty well watched."

"Forget it! What can I do?"

"Do you know anybody in Tanzburg who's reliable and can keep his mouth shut?"

138

"Sure," the deputy responded promptly. "Sheriff Max Egan. Tanzburg is the seat of Murdock County, you know. Egan's a good man."

"Send a message to Egan and ask him to do a bit of inquiring for you: I'd like to learn if Harmon visited Dr. Ezra Jorge a day or two before he died."

"That's a job I can get at pronto," Dewitt said, getting to his feet. "I'll head right down to the station."

"Tell that telegrapher you're doing it for me," Quist suggested. "And thanks a lot, Pete."

"Don't mention it."

Pete had scarcely passed out of sight down Lincoln Street when Quist spied Sheriff Blackmer approaching from the west on Main. Blackmer came directly to the hotel porch and mounted the steps. "I was hoping I might find you here, Greg," he said.

Quist cocked one eye in the sheriff's direction. "You going to give me a chance to choose the weapons?" he asked gravely. "Or is this a peace powwow?" His topaz eyes twinkled.

"It's a peace powwow, so far as I'm concerned." Blackmer came around behind Quist and dropped into an adjoining chair. "Greg, you sort of laid into me yesterday."

"I reckon I did," Quist acknowledged. "I've been thinking since maybe I should have kept my mouth shut."

"You made me right mad, that's a fact," Blackmer nodded. His face flushed, and he added, surprisingly enough, "I thought it all over, Greg, and I came to a decision: every word you said was correct as the dickens."

"What!" Quist straightened in his chair. "What's that, John?"

Blackmer smiled ruefully. "You called it correct, Greg. I've been an old fool. I've loaded more work than's fair on Pete's shoulders and I've taken the credit. He's the one that really should be sheriff of Dawson County—not me. There he was last night, working late to make out the reports that I should have turned in long ago. Him, covering up for my shortcomings. I've been a disgrace to the badge I wear—"

"You don't need to make it so strong, John."

"I know what I'm talking about. Today I've turned over a new leaf. There'll be no living on a reputation I made years ago. From now on henceforth I aim to earn my salary. And I just wanted to say there's no hard feelings and I'd like to shake your hand."

"Why, sure, but you don't want to be too hard on yourself." The two shook hands.

Blackmer breathed a long sigh of relief. He laughed sheepishly. "Well, that job of eating crow is off my chest, anyway. And now I'm going to do my dangedest to run down Gid Harmon's murderer—no, don't get me wrong. I'm not asking for any information you may have, unless you want to give it, but I'm ready to give you anything I turn up."

"That's mighty decent of you, John."

"Not at all. You've got the head for such business, far better than mine. And besides I've felt you knew what you were doing ever since I heard how you handled the Egg yesterday. But I'm afeared you've made a bad enemy."

"I'm not worried about Voit."

"You'd best be on your guard, nonetheless. . . . Say, you going to the funeral this afternoon?"

"I suppose practically everybody in town will be there," Quist said evasively.

"Probably, but"—Blackmer lowered his voice and glanced cautiously around—"I may not be."

"What are you aiming to do?"

"I'm going to sort of hang back when the procession forms at the undertaker's. If there's anybody from any of the ranches hereabouts who's in town and doesn't attend the burial services, I'm just aiming to tag along and see what he does. I might pick up a clue that way. What do you think?"

"You could try it," Quist said gravely.

They talked a few minutes more, then Blackmer rose from his chair. "Well, I reckon I'd better sort of mosey around town a mite. I've been sitting on my breeches too much the past few years."

Quist eyed the man as he rounded the corner of

Lincoln Street. "John," Quist mused, "you never will make a good detective, I reckon, but I'll say one thing for you—you'll be trying now, at least."

There were more people along the sidewalks by this time. Horses and rigs commenced to gather at the hitchracks. Some twenty minutes slipped by, and then Pete Dewitt again mounted the porch steps. He didn't sit down, but stood rolling a cigarette by Quist's side. "Yeah," he was saying, "I sent the telegram to Sheriff Egan. I learned something else too."

"What now?"

"It's too early yet for the bank to open, but I ran into Henry Vogel—you know, I told you he owns the bank—on the street. I told Henry what we'd like to know. At first he didn't want to talk."

"I take it you got something."

"Yes, but not the exact amounts involved. It's this way: When Belvard bought his outfit from Harmon he didn't pay cash outright. Harmon had Vogel handle the deal as his agent. Belvard paid a certain amount down, and was to make a payment, through the bank, every three months, at a certain per cent. When the entire amount was paid in, Harmon contracted to give a deed, but not before."

"Then the deed to the HB-Connected holdings is still in Harmon's name?"

"Yes. And here's something else. Belvard hasn't kept up the payments, claimed he hadn't the money and was trying to arrange a deal to get the payments made smaller. Harmon was opposed to that. But for some time now Belvard hasn't paid a cent on the ranch."

"How about the ranch buildings?"

"The bank loaned Belvard the money to build those. He's behind in payments there, too, but not so far behind."

Quist pondered the question, his topaz eyes narrowed. "It looks," he said finally, "as though Belvard was short of money. But what could he gain through Harmon's death?"

"You don't reckon Belvard might come up with a forged receipt for payment in full, do you?"

"I'm not sure the bank would accept anything like that without a fight, so long as the bank is acting as agent in the deal."

"Well, then I can't see where Belvard could improve his situation any through Harmon's death. He'd just owe Mrs. Harmon the money—" Pete broke off, as though a fresh idea had occurred to him. "Belvard might figure," the deputy said slowly, "that he could prevail on Mrs. Harmon to reduce the payments. Sometimes a widow is right gullible, if you can get to her before she's recovered from the shock of her husband's death."

"With some women, maybe," Quist conceded. "But Lilith Harmon looks pretty levelheaded to me. I don't figure you're on the right track there, Pete."

"Or anywhere," Dewitt growled. "This whole business has me running around in circles. Why anyone should want to kill Harmon in the first place, is more than I can—"

"I'll ask you something I've already asked Mrs. Harmon—though she didn't know anything about it and couldn't give me an answer. I understand Harmon made his money in a mining deal—"

"The Thunderbird Mine, up in the Sangre de Estebans."

"Harmon had pardners in that deal, and later the mine was sold to a mining corporation. Did you ever hear any squawks from the pardners?"

"On the contrary, they were well satisfied. One of 'em is living in California now. The other is in the East someplace."

"Was the corporation that bought the Thunderbird Mine satisfied—that is, did it blame Harmon in any way when the mine failed to be successful?"

"Not as I ever heard of. That was just bad judgment on the part of the corporation's mining experts, or maybe it was just bad luck. You see, the silver just plain petered out. But that wasn't Gid Harmon's fault. He sold in good faith."

"No use following that idea further, then," Quist said. "It just heads into a blind alley. I was looking for some sort of revenge motive, thinking Harmon might have pulled a swindle someplace in his transactions."

Dewitt shook his head. "Whatever you say, Harmon was honest." He drew on his cigarette and blew smoke into the air. "Say, I saw the Thunderbird crew ride in a little while back. In case you wanted to look 'em over, we could probably find 'em in the Sundown."

"Considering the fact the funeral isn't until this afternoon they're in rather early, aren't they?" Quist asked.

"I thought of that too."

"Stark Garrity with 'em?"

"I didn't see him."

"Let's drift over to the Sundown."

They left the hotel, walked along Main to Waco Street and then crossed over. There were a couple of the town's citizens at the bar, drinking eye openers, and farther along stood four men in what was probably considered their Sunday-best raiment, despite their high-heeled boots and worn Stetsons. They were clean-shaven and looked rather glum as they hovered over their drinks. They spoke to Dewitt and glanced curiously at Quist.

Dewitt said, "Boys, I'd like to have you meet my friend, Greg Quist—Greg, this is Gid Harmon's crew: Gus Judkins, Herb Moody, Ike Palmer, and Skillet Osborn."

The four shook hands solemnly. Quist judged Osborn, from his name, to be the ranch cook. The other three were typical leather-faced sons of the range.

"This is a pretty sad day, Mr. Quist," Judkins commented. "It's tough to bury a good boss like Gid Harmon was."

"I know how you feel, I guess," Quist nodded.

"You never know," Moody said, shaking his head. "Here one day, gone the next."

"It seems just like yesterday," Palmer put in, "that Gid was bawling me out for not oiling the windmill—and I deserved it, too."

"And the times he's praised my biscuits," Skillet Osborn mourned. "He always did like my cooking—him and the missus both. When I'd take a pie up to the house, they were right pleased."

The other three nodded solemn agreement, though at any other time the cook's remarks would have brought down on his head a hail of abuse.

"Drink up," Quist said. "I'd like to buy a round in honor of Gid's departure."

Johnny Webb set out bottles and glasses. Dewitt said, "Didn't Stark come in with you?"

Herb Moody nodded. "Yeah, he rode in. Right now he's over to Car'line Trent's, where Mrs. Harmon is staying, to pay his respects for her bereavement. Stark is sure taking it hard. He thought a heap of Gid Harmon. You could see him brush at his eyes every time he caught sight of any of Gid's gear hangin' in the bunkhouse."

"I reckon it's my turn to buy a round," Ike Palmer offered.

"Maybe we'd better not," Judkins said. "We still got a long day before us. We got to go easy on the liquor. Stark wouldn't like it if—"

"You fellows came in early enough," Dewitt said carelessly.

"That's Stark's doings," Osborn said. "Generally I'm up first, naturally, but something roused me and I saw a fire burning in the yard—"

"Fire?" Quist asked.

Osborn nodded. "I pulled on my pants and went out to see it, and there was Stark, aburnin' up Gid's saddles. He said he couldn't bear to see them in the bunkhouse any longer."

"Saddles?" Quist asked. "How many did he have?"

"Probably a half a dozen," Palmer said.

"But he just burned two," Osborn said. "I told him Mrs. Harmon might not like it, and Stark said he hadn't thought of that, and he wouldn't burn the others."

"I can't say I blame Stark, at that," Moody put in. "The sight of those saddles was always bringing him memories. Like Gid's favorite saddle—Stark shoved that under his bunk and kept it covered with a blanket and asked none of us to drag it out—but even that was too much for him, I reckon."

"And so he burned it," Osborn said glumly. "Well, I was wide-awake by that time, so I got breakfast earlier than usual, and Stark said we

147

might as well get to Cenotaph, as there was no use sitting around the bunkhouse with long faces, waiting to start."

"Probably he was right," Quist remarked, exchanging a quick look with Dewitt.

"Say," Judkins said suddenly, "I got you placed now, Mr. Quist. You're the railroad detective. You were out to the ranch the night Gid—er—died. We've heard a couple of stories around town—"

At that moment, Stark Garrity came pushing through the swinging doors at the entrance. He wore a black suit, cow boots, a white shirt and black tie, and his usual sombrero. He didn't have a gun on. He looked rather drawn. "Hello, Mr. Quist—Pete. Boys, remember what I told you; go easy on that liquor." He said to Quist, "God, how I wish this was over." He looked as though he meant it, too.

"I don't care much for funerals myself," Quist said.

"Not when it's somebody you think a heap of," Garrity said. He added in a lower tone, "I ran into John Blackmer on the street a few minutes ago. John tells me you had a little run-in with Hugo Voit yesterday."

"It didn't amount to much. I can't understand why this town lets the Egg run roughshod over everybody."

"He's a pretty mean customer. You'd best keep your eyes peeled for trouble." He looked steadily

148

at Quist, then continued, "Speaking of trouble, I hope you didn't have any with that buckskin I loaned you the other night."

"Any reason I should have had?"

"That horse has a right tender mouth, and if he isn't handled just right he's inclined to go to bucking."

"The buckskin was a perfect gentleman with me. I've been intending to return it before this, but I've been busy."

"Don't let that bother you. Keep the horse as long as you like. I'll pick it up when you're through with it."

He paused as Hoddy Belvard and Hugo Voit entered the saloon and found a place at the bar, nodded briefly to them, then resumed his conversation with Quist: "I got a job I hate worse than poison this afternoon. It's bad enough to be attending Gid's funeral, but I've got to drive a rig to carry Mrs. Harmon and Car'line Trent."

They talked a few minutes more, then Quist caught Dewitt's eye and the two prepared to leave the saloon. As they passed Belvard and Voit, the HB-Connected men gave them short nods, with Voit adding, "You seem to be keeping your health, Mr. Quist," and that nasty giggle ran through his tones.

"That's due to my diet." Quist laughed insolently. "I never have anything to do with eggs—I just can't stand 'em."

The smirk left Voit's face. "Someday, Mr. Quist, you may not be able to avoid the egg you do not care for. What then?"

"In that case," Quist said carelessly, "I'll do my own cooking. I never yet saw the egg I couldn't scramble."

A slow flush spread through Voit's fleshy features. He started to reply, then a short laugh from Stark Garrity caught his attention, and he swung around on his small feet to face Garrity. Garrity stared at him a moment, then looked away.

By this time Quist and Dewitt were once more on the street. Dewitt said, "What are you trying to do, needle the Egg into starting a fight?"

"Exactly. He's looking for trouble. The sooner I can force him into the open, the better."

"Phew!" Dewitt breathed. "You've got more nerve than I have."

"It's not nerve," Quist denied. "I'm just putting up a bluff and getting away with it. I haven't any more nerve than the next man, Pete."

Dewitt thought that over. When next he spoke it was on another subject. "Anyway, we know where a couple of saddles went—up in flames."

Quist nodded. "Garrity sensed what I was up to when I scratched that saddle with my thumbnail the other night. And I've a hunch that other saddle had blood on it, all right. Yet, at times, Garrity seems on the square to me. I can't figure him out."

"What's your next move going to be, Greg?"

"For one thing, I'm not attending the funeral. With everybody away, this should be a good time to visit the Thunderbird Ranch. Meanwhile, if anybody misses me or asks where I am, you just act like I'm still around Cenotaph, so far as you know—even if you have to take an oath I attended the burial services."

12. Knockout

With Harmon's funeral planned for that day it wasn't surprising to find more people on the streets of Cenotaph than was usual during the week. Consequently no one paid any attention to the rider on the bay horse who led behind him a saddleless buckskin pony and, after leaving the town livery stable, took the most direct route out of Cenotaph, which led along Waco Street, crossed Second and Third streets, and then struck open country.

As he rode, Quist avoided the road to the Thunderbird which ran north, although his course paralleled that trail, and picked his way through the growth of cottonwood trees and brush that denoted the approach to the Rio Esteban. After a time the cottonwoods gave way before yellow-leaved aspens shivering in the slight breeze, and within a short time the man caught the glint of sunlight on flowing waters where the stream curved slightly to the southwest.

Quist speculated as he rode: "Let me see . . . it's four days back since Harmon was killed. There should be some sign someplace to show where he crossed the river or where his horse crossed to get him to the Thunderbird. That horse's hoofs had been cleaned. I still think they must have had mud on 'em. By following this river, I might find the place where his horse climbed out."

He proceeded at a leisurely fashion, eyes fastened continually on the earth in his search for hoofprints. The buckskin pony came behind without trouble, probably sensing that it was nearing its home corral. It was pleasant riding through the groves of aspen with their yellow filtered sunlight bathing man and beasts as they moved along, the soft music of the river's flow ever present in their ears. At any other time Quist could have enjoyed such a ride, but now he was too intent on his search for hoofprints to indulge in any enjoyment of Nature's beauties. By this time he judged he must be nearly opposite the point where the Thunderbird Ranch was located, farther to the west.

Abruptly he drew rein, then stepped down from the saddle to give the earth a closer scrutiny. There, running at right angles to the direction Quist had been taking, were hoofprints. A great many leaves from the trees had fluttered down since the hoofs had first been imprinted in the earth, but many of them still remained uncovered and were plainly to be seen.

Crouched closely to the earth, Quist moved back and forth, studying the trail. Finally he straightened up, considering. "Two horses," he built the picture slowly in his mind, "coming due west from the river, one following the other. That means they probably crossed the river from the other side." He bent his steps in the direction of the stream murmuring lazily not twenty-five yards away, and on its sloping banks saw the hoofmarks where two ponies had clambered out.

Returning to the horses, he led the buckskin down to the water and let it drink. Then he returned, tethered the buckskin to a low-hanging branch of a cottonwood, and got into the saddle of the bay horse. He crossed the river on the bay, pausing only long enough to allow the pony to dip its muzzle into the cool running waters, then horse and man emerged on the opposite bank. It took but a few minutes to again pick up the hoofmarks of the ponies that had traveled this point previously. The trail headed due north, with Quist's eyes ever alert for the hat he felt sure had been dropped from Harmon's head somewhere along the trail. "Providing," Quist amended the thought, "that Harmon's body was on one of the horses whose prints I'm following—and I feel, now, right certain he was. Even if I don't find the hat, I may discover something else to show where Harmon was that day he met his death."

The search was to uncover even more than Quist had expected.

It was about four in the afternoon when Quist returned to the buckskin waiting patiently where he'd left it tethered to the limb of the cottonwood tree. Without dismounting from the bay, he secured the buckskin's lead rope and turned the bay in the direction of the Thunderbird Ranch, which now lay not more than a mile or so to the west.

The trees commenced to thin out as Quist rode, leading the second horse at his rear, and a little later he broke into open country. Within another five minutes he had struck the road that ran from Cenotaph, and now he saw, ahead, the buildings of Thunderbird Ranch. He followed the road and was shortly entering the ranch yard.

He could hear the clanking of the windmill as he approached the house, and saw horses moving in the corral beyond, but otherwise there seemed no sign of movement about the place. The bunkhouse door was shut tightly, though Quist doubted that it was locked. He started past the house, to leave the buckskin at the corral, then hesitated and glanced toward the sinking sun, already picking out high lights above the purple shadows on the far distant peaks of the Pihuela Range.

"That crew," Quist mused, "will be arriving from the funeral at any moment now. For all I know, Lilith may be with them. I reckon if I want to do any searching around, I'd best do it right now, and put that buckskin in the corral later. I wouldn't want to be caught snooping through the house."

He pulled the pony to a halt at the corner of the wide gallery that fronted the house, wrapped the lead rope around the horn of the bay's saddle, and stepped down to earth. Reaching the gallery, he strode across to the front door, and wasn't greatly surprised when the knob turned easily under his hand: this time, Quist told himself, there wasn't any dead man to be secured behind a locked door until the coroner could arrive.

He stepped into the house, leaving the door open, and surveyed the big living room of the house. Things appeared pretty much as they had on his last visit, though there'd been some attempt to clean up the debris on the top of the oaken table—probably Stark Garrity's work, Quist imagined. The chairs stood about as usual, and on the wall, directly opposite the entrance, hung the large Navajo rug with its scarlet thunderbird design.

Quist hesitated, musing, "Now if I only knew where Harmon was accustomed to keep his papers, maybe I could locate—"

He broke off short, a tiny golden gleam on the back of one of the easy chairs catching his eyes. Someone had sat in that chair, in the not too distant past, and that person's head, resting against a cushion, had left a couple of fine reddish hairs, a few inches long, on the rough surface of the cushion's material. Ordinarily the hairs would have passed unnoticed, but the afternoon sunlight, streaming through the side window, had highlighted them for Quist's wandering gaze.

Quist picked the hairs from the chair back.

"Now I'd like to know just when those were left here," he muttered. Curling them around one finger, he folded them into a cigarette paper and deposited the tiny package in his wallet.

He glanced around the room again, then started for the doorway opening to the left of the thunderbird rug and found himself in the hall that gave access to the three bedrooms.

And on the floor of the first bedroom he entered, he saw evidence that someone had been there ahead of him. On the floor, in the middle of the room, lay a wooden box, metal-covered, about a foot square and six inches deep. The lock had been smashed and the cover was thrown back to expose, in the box's interior, a number of folded papers.

Quist knelt by the box to examine the papers. There was the land grant to the Thunderbird holdings, several insurance papers, a brand-register certificate, a bankbook, some shares in a Colorado gold mine, various letters, and other odds and ends which Quist skipped through in a hurry. A scholarly piece of writing on one folded paper told him it was a will. Opening the paper, Quist saw the name of Eli Harnsworth, and knew it wasn't the will he sought. A theater program caught his eye; he glanced along the lines of printing and saw one name that caught his interest. . . .

Abruptly Quist got to his feet, folding the

program and sticking it into a hip pocket. He heard riders approaching and stepped back into the hall. It was probably the Thunderbird crew returning from the funeral. It wouldn't do for Garrity to learn he had been inside the house.

Quist started quickly toward the kitchen, prepared to slip out the back door and then come around the house to meet the approaching riders.

As he started across the kitchen floor in the direction of the back door, which he noted was standing open, Quist noticed a partly filled bottle of whisky on the table. Then, with a sudden shock, something else caught his gaze:

At the other side of the kitchen a doorway led into the dining room on the way back to the big main room of the ranch house. The door stood about three-quarters open, and stretched full-length across the threshold, feet in the dining room, head in the kitchen, with both arms flung wide, lay the body of a man, face down.

Despite his urgent rush to get out of the house— the hoofbeats of the approaching ponies were coming much closer by this time—Quist wanted to know who the man was; the outlines of the back of the head and shoulders were very familiar. Stooping swiftly by the side of the motionless form, Quist turned the body half over—and found himself looking into the expressionless, glazed eyes of Sheriff John Blackmer. The sheriff was quite dead.

And at that very instant something round and steely hard descended with crushing force on Quist's head, and he felt himself falling, falling across the lifeless body of the dead sheriff, as a black curtain of oblivion closed in, engulfed his fading senses.

13. Framed

He was drenched, deluged, with water that had the odor of scotch whisky. A second wave crashed over his head, and now he was conscious of a splitting headache, and he opened his eyes and groaned with pain. The room swam before his gaze. A number of men, towering above him, rocked back and forth, came near, receded, then slanted once more, terrifyingly, above his head. He heard somebody say, "The murderin' son is coming out of it, now."

And somebody else: "Who'd ever thought *he* couldn't handle his liquor?"

And a third voice—it sounded like Skillet Osborn's tones: "You never can tell. Some fellers are periodicals and when they start drinkin', they just go crazy."

There were further comments. The smell of scotch whisky pervaded an atmosphere that gradually cleared. Quist's head still ached intolerably, but he realized now that he was stretched on his back on the floor of the living room of the ranch house, while standing around him was the crew of the Thunderbird, all gazing down with extremely angry faces. In his hand Ike Palmer held a bucket of water, all ready to throw more of the fluid in Quist's face.

Quist looked up at them, forcing a wry smile. "That's no way to waste good whisky."

"It ain't funny, Quist," Gus Judkins scowled.

And then Quist became aware of something else. He was bound hand and foot. What in the hell was this all about? He suddenly remembered Sheriff Blackmer and asked, "Did you find the sheriff?"

"What are you doing, trying to run a whizzer on us," Stark Garrity half snarled. "Did we find the sheriff for geez' sakes! What a question!"

"You know danged well we found him—" Herb Moody commenced.

"Say, what the devil is this all about?" Quist demanded. "What's the idea of tying me up this way?"

"You can't bluff your way out," Palmer snapped. "Next thing we know you'll be trying to tell us you didn't kill Blackmer."

"Tarnation!" Quist protested. "Any fool would know better than that."

"We're not fools, Quist," Garrity said shortly. "You killed John, and you might as well 'fess up. I've heard of you railroad dicks being pretty tough customers sometimes, and now I've got to believe it. For that matter, I've heard *you* can be right hard on occasion."

"And this must have been one of the occasions," Judkins exclaimed angrily.

"And I want to know what in blazes you and the sheriff were doing here in the first place," Garrity growled.

"And us laying poor Gid away in the ground!" Palmer commenced.

"And Gid himself scarcely cold," Osborn put in hotly.

"What were you doing here?" Garrity asked again.

Quist didn't reply at once. There was something funny going on. None of the men had drinks, yet that odor of scotch pervaded his nostrils. And how much should he tell? Finally he spoke to Garrity, "Look, regardless what you believe, and I'm reaching the point where I don't much give a darn about your opinions, is there any reason why I should be kept down here on the floor? I'm getting pretty sick of looking up at you hombres."

"You're getting sick of looking up at us!" Moody said hotly. "If I had my way you never would get off'n that floor until they carried you out—feet first."

"Devil with your way," Quist said shortly. "Garrity, do I get up or don't I? If you're so blamed afraid of me, you don't have to untie my hands and feet. Just let me sit up."

"All right, boys," Garrity said reluctantly, "put him in a chair."

The room swam a trifle when they lifted Quist, then sat him down. After a moment things cleared again.

Quist glanced at the glaring features confronting him. "All right, Garrity," he said at last. "Now if you'll just tell me what you think happened, I'm ready to listen."

"So drunk you don't remember, eh?" Garrity snapped. "Well, anyway, that much is believable—"

"I asked you a question," Quist cut in evenly. "I'm entitled to a reply, anyway."

"I don't know as you are," Garrity said in ugly tones, "but I'll give you the benefit of that doubt. All right, if you've forgotten, here's what happened: You and the sheriff came out here—though I'm danged if I know why—and got to drinking. From that point on, I figure you had some sort of argument—"

"About what?" Quist asked mildly.

"How in blazes do I know what you argued about?" Garrity scowled. "There was some difference between you and John. The night you arrived here, I heard you had some sort of argument with John at the hotel—"

"I told him what I thought of him that night for putting off on me the job of breaking the news of Gid's death to Mrs. Harmon," Quist explained. "There was no argument—"

"That's your story," Garrity sneered. "It's well known that you had different beliefs as to Gid's death—oh, the devil with all this explaining. We'll just say there was bad blood between you and you shot him while drunk—and how drunk you must have been!" Garrity paused.

"I didn't shoot him, but go on," Quist urged.

"This gets more and more interesting. I didn't even have a drink with him—"

"And that's a darned lie," from Moody, "with the both of you smelling like a distillery."

"Just to give you a fair break," Garrity continued, "I'll give you the rest of the story. We rode into the ranch yard, and then I saw our buckskin and that other horse standing at the corner of the gallery. Next I noticed the front door was open. I thought that was danged funny, so we all pulled up at the house and came in. And there in the kitchen we found you sprawled across John's dead body. You bustard! You didn't even give him a chance to draw."

"Shot him and then passed out, right on top of him," Osborn said angrily. "I suppose you figure you can convince a jury that you didn't know what you were doing and receive a suspended sentence or something simple like that."

"Suspended at the end of a rope," Moody snarled, "and even that's too good for you."

"Look," Quist said patiently, "you'll find my gun in its shoulder holster. Just take a look at it and you'll see it's not been fired."

"Not fired?"

"Shoulder holster!"

"My Gawd! Trying to put across that kind of a bluff!"

"Your gun was fired all right," Garrity said coldly, "and it's not in your shoulder holster, because we found it on the floor, right near your hand."

"I'd like to see that gun, regardless of where you found it. I didn't fire it; that I know."

"Show him the gun, somebody," Garrity said, as though humoring a child.

Osborn brought a gun and shoved it under Quist's nose. "Take a good look, killer," he said angrily.

"That's not my gun," Quist said instantly, as he gazed down on a Colt's forty-five six-shooter. "I carry a forty-four with a shorter barrel."

"Oh, Christ, what's the use of talking to him?" Palmer growled. "We're just wasting time. We'd better notify Doc Lang and Pete Dewitt—cripes! Pete will be sheriff now, won't he?"

"For the time being probably, anyway," Garrity nodded. "Ike, you ride in and notify 'em. Tell 'em to get out here as soon as possible—"

"That suits me," Quist cut in. "Maybe they'll show some sense. You hombres have already made up your minds before you've heard my side of this. Garrity, you said something about giving me a square break. How about letting me tell you exactly what happened?"

"We-ell," Garrity said grudgingly. "Make it fast. We don't want to waste any more time."

"This won't waste your time." Quist marshaled his thoughts. "It must have been about four-thirty, or a little later, that I arrived here with the buckskin pony and saw the front door standing open. I thought that was danged peculiar—"

"Wait a minute," Garrity cut in. "Why did it take you until four-thirty to get here? You left town this morning, shortly after I saw you in the Sundown Saloon—"

"And how do you know that?" Quist asked quietly.

Garrity flushed. "Don't get the idea I was checking up on you," he said. "I went to the livery a little before two to get a rig to drive Mrs. Harmon out to the cemetery and the liveryman mentioned that you'd ridden a bay and led our buckskin behind—but why did you pick today to come here in the first place?"

"Because," and Quist made his tones as frank as possible, "I saw no reason for attending the funeral. I don't like funerals. And I thought it about time I returned that horse you loaned me."

"And it took you from this morning until four-thirty this afternoon to get here, I suppose?" Garrity asked sarcastically.

"Aw, why don't we ram a forty-five barrel down the bustard's throat and shut him up?" Moody snarled.

"What I was doing from the time I left Cenotaph until I got here about four-thirty," Quist said in even tones, "is my business and the railroad's. If the railroad authorities give me permission to release such information, you can have it, but not otherwise. Anyway, when I saw the door of the house open I entered. I didn't see or hear anybody—by the way, how did you fellows reach the kitchen when you came in?"

"We went through the dining room," Garrity said promptly.

"I went through the hall that leads past the bedrooms. Have you been through there?"

"Why should we?" Garrity wanted to know.

"In the first bedroom you'll find that somebody broke into a box of—well, I suppose it's a box of Gid Harmon's private papers, though I can't say for sure—anyway, the box had been opened—"

"Check into that, Ike," Garrity said.

Palmer left the room and returned bearing the opened box of papers. "Somebody busted it open, all right," he scowled, placing the box on the table.

"I went on to the kitchen," Quist continued, "and saw Blackmer's body laying there. As I bent down to see who it was, something hit me on the head and knocked me out. I imagine it was a gun barrel." He smiled ruefully. "I was just a darned fool for not suspecting somebody might have been hidden behind that door, but I was so surprised to find the sheriff that I wasn't thinking straight for a minute."

"And that's your story?" Garrity asked sarcastically.

"That's my story. Those are the things I actually know." Quist mused that most of it was truth anyway. "Now I'll tell you what I think happened. Whoever hit me on the head stole my gun and left his—the gun that shot Sheriff Blackmer."

"And then faded into thin air, I suppose?" Judkins said.

"No, he just faded out the back door and ran to his horse in the brush back of the bunkhouse, while you fellows were coming in the front way. He could have made a getaway while you were all busy wasting time over me, instead of looking around outside as you should have been doing. And up to a certain point the murderer's scheme is working: because you found his gun, you're ready to see me framed for the murder."

Despite their beliefs, Quist could see the men were half convinced there might be some truth in his story. Then Osborn said, "Blazes, it's a nice yarn, but it doesn't explain you stinking drunk with whisky."

"Did you find any whisky bottles around?" Quist asked.

"Yes, there's one in the kitchen. I'll get it," Osborn said.

"Don't bother, Skillet," Garrity said quickly. "This story of Quist's won't hold water—"

"No bother, Stark." Osborn was already on the way to the kitchen. He returned in a few moments with a bottle from which nine tenths of the contents were gone. He set the bottle on the table. "There you are," he announced triumphantly.

Quist eyed the bottle, read the label which advertised, "Glen Spey Scotch Whisky." Quist said, "I remember seeing that bottle when I entered the kitchen, only then it had a lot more whisky in it."

"Meaning," Moody bristled, "that we drank it?"

"Meaning," Quist explained, "that the murderer poured whisky on my clothing to make you think I was drunk—maybe on Blackmer, too. Any traces of dampness were covered up when you threw water on me. When I was hit on the head, my hat probably softened the blow some, but I'm betting there's a lump there. And no man can drink whisky without it showing on his breath. I'm asking that you hombres smell my breath and examine my head for a blow."

They hesitated until Garrity said, "All right, it can't do any harm." They took turns smelling his breath. There was a lump at the back of his head. No one said anything when they were finished, but Quist read the verdict in their eyes. Garrity finally spoke for the rest, "All right, you came through the test. There's a bruise on your noggin. I can smell whisky on you, but not on your breath."

"Go out there and examine Blackmer," Quist suggested.

"A corpse doesn't have any breath—" Garrity commenced.

"Check on his clothing," Quist said.

Garrity nodded, and Palmer and Moody left the room. They returned shortly. "Whisky on his shirt collar," Palmer announced. "We didn't turn him over to check on the front of his shirt, but the shirt collar's still damp, and the smell is real strong."

Quist said, "Well, what about it, Garrity?"

"I don't know what to think," Garrity frowned. "Ike, go ahead now—get Doc Lang and Pete Dewitt out here. We'll let them decide. Meanwhile, Quist, we'll keep you tied up for safety's sake."

The sun was down by this time, and it was growing dark in the room. Palmer departed to mount his pony. Garrity lighted the hanging lamp above the oaken table. Palmer's pony drummed away from the house.

Quist said, "Do me a favor, Garrity. Send somebody out to the brush and see if there's any sign out there where a man might have left on a horse."

"Aw, we'd better wait and let Pete decide about that," Garrity protested.

"You'll probably find the sheriff's horse out there someplace, too," Quist persisted. "It's getting dark fast, but there might be some sign around, even if you had to look by lantern light."

"Maybe it's worth trying, Stark," Herb Moody put in. "I'll be glad to take a look-see."

"I'll go too," from Judkins. "If we are wrong about Quist, we owe him that much."

Garrity looked about to refuse, but finally shrugged his shoulders and gave permission. The men departed, Skillet Osborn going with them to see about rustling up some supper. Quist was left alone with Garrity in the big room. Neither spoke for a time.

Garrity finally said awkwardly, "I'd like to untie you, Quist, but I don't dare. Is there anything else I can do to make your wait more comfortable?"

"Thanks. You can roll me a cigarette and hold it to my lips. Also, I see some scotch still left in that bottle. Now that you know I wasn't drunk, I'd take a drink. My head is still thumping some."

Garrity lighted a cigarette and held it while Quist drew on the smoke. He held the bottle to his lips. Then silence fell between them again. After a time Quist said, "Good thing Mrs. Harmon didn't come out with you today."

"She'll be out tomorrow," Stark said. He sounded weary. "I'll be glad to have her take hold here again and decide what's to be done. She's mighty capable."

"I understand Caroline Trent's going to spend the first few days with her."

"That's what I hear. Thought they'd both be coming out today, but Car'line—" He stopped suddenly.

"Yes, what were you saying?"

Garrity looked uncomfortable. "Car'line left right after the funeral. I don't know where she went, but somebody said they saw her riding out of town—"

"Yes?" Quist said softly. "What time was the funeral?"

"It was scheduled for three o'clock, but everything was ready a mite after two, so we got started. It didn't take long."

Quist said, out of a clear sky, "Stark, why was Gid Harmon murdered? You know."

"Why, er—" Garrity went red, then white. "What in the devil you talking about, Quist? Have you gone crazy? How should I know? What's got into you?"

"All right," Quist said quietly, "let me know when you're ready to talk. I'll see that you get a break if you want it—and if you deserve it."

"Darn you, Quist!" Garrity shouted wildly. "You don't think I know anything about that, do you? By God, I'll—" He paused suddenly and calmed down. Footsteps were heard at the back door, then came nearer by way of the hallway off the bedrooms. Moody and Judkins came into the room. They looked strangely at Garrity, then Quist.

Garrity said gruffly, "Well, did you find anything?"

"Yeah," Moody replied. "For one thing we found the sheriff's horse—yeah, it was John's horse, all right, tethered out there in the brush. I'd know that wall-eyed beer barrel any place. And we found sign at another spot, where a horse had

172

waited and then headed off toward Cenotaph."

"And there were some footprints too, though in that grass over that way they didn't show up too plain," Judkins put in. "They were smaller than average—"

"The Egg," Quist interposed, "has mighty small feet."

"Yeah," Garrity said moodily, "and for all we know Mrs. Harmon might have been over that way a few days ago. You can't count much on prints like that." He added, "Especially by lantern light."

"I reckon not," Herb Moody agreed. "The prints don't stay in the earth like they might have a few days ago, after that rain we had."

Silence fell again. After a time Osborn brought food up to the house and placed it on the oaken table. Quist's hands were untied, and he was helped to another chair where he could partake of the food, though the men watched him warily. They noticed the first thing Quist did when his hands were unbound was to reach to his shoulder holster as though still half unable to believe his gun was gone.

Supper proceeded in silence. When they were finished, cigarettes were lighted. Finally Moody said somewhat sheepishly, "If we have been wrong about you, Mr. Quist, I'm apologizing right now." The others added similar words.

Garrity said shortly, "Naturally, that goes without saying."

The conversation turned to the dead man, still stretched between the kitchen and dining room. "This is one night I wouldn't care to eat out in that dining room," Osborn said.

Garrity said shortly, "Forget it."

"Aw, what's the odds?" Moody shrugged. "A dead man is a dead man. He can't hurt you."

"Darnit, I said to forget it!" Garrity snapped irritably.

His eyes met Quist's. Quist gave him a thin smile. Abruptly Garrity rose from the table. "I'm going down to the bunkhouse—got something to do," he mumbled and left the room.

Moody, Osborn, and Judkins exchanged glances. Judkins said, "Stark is edgy as the devil the last couple of days."

"Gid Harmon's death hit him right hard," Moody said. "And now all this on top of it is a mite too much for him, I reckon."

Osborn said, "I wish we'd brought a bottle out from town."

"There's some left in that bottle on the table," Quist pointed out.

Osborn shook his head. "There's four of us and only about one drink."

"Anyway, who wants to drink scotch?" Moody said. "Give me bourbon every time." The other two added similar remarks.

"Somebody around here must like scotch," Quist persisted.

"Yeah, Stark drinks it—but Stark never was what you'd call a real drinker," Moody said. "There might be some of that Old Crow of Gid's in the kitchen."

The men looked at each other. Osborn said, "I reckon Gid wouldn't begrudge us a bottle under the circumstances. I'll go see." He went to the kitchen and returned bearing a bottle, from which the cork had been drawn, and four glasses. Drinks were poured. After a time Stark Garrity returned. He eyed the bottle, started to say something, then picked up the bottle of scotch and finished that off. Talk continued in rather desultory fashion.

It must have been nearly half past ten when Ike Palmer returned, bringing with him Dr. Lang, driving a light wagon, and Pete Dewitt. The doctor looked worried; Pete appeared grimmer than usual. He nodded to the others and turned to Quist. "You sure got a knack for attracting trouble," he grunted. He glanced down at Quist's ankles. "Oh, for God's sake, you still got him tied up? Take them ropes off."

"You're taking the responsibility?" Garrity asked.

"Certain I am," Pete snapped. "I'm acting sheriff for this county now—until I get thrown out, leastwise. Ike told me the story. Anybody with half a brain could see it was an attempted frame-up. Greg told me he was coming here to return that buckskin pony, this morning. You act like there was something mysterious about his

175

actions. You just ought to be mighty glad he stumbled in when he did. Suppose that killer had decided to wait and bump you off, Garrity."

"Why should he bump me off?" Garrity looked puzzled.

"Why should he bump off John?" Dewitt countered.

"But what was the sheriff doing here? Why wasn't he at the funeral?" Garrity wanted to know.

"If I knew that," Dewitt said shortly, "maybe I could tell you who killed him and why."

"An inquest may bring out certain facts we're overlooking," the doctor put in. "We'll hold it tomorrow afternoon." He said to Quist, "This time you'll have to testify."

"This time I'll be glad to," Quist nodded.

The doctor said, "Hummph!" and added, "Let's have a look at that body."

Quist's ankles were unbound. He rose and stretched. His head wasn't aching so badly now. There was a lamp lighted in the kitchen. The men trooped out to gather about the dead sheriff. The doctor examined him closely, then turned the lifeless figure on its back. The front of the shirt was stained darkly. There was blood on the floor beneath the body. Dr. Lang said, "Plugged plumb center."

Quist said, "How long ago, Doc?"

"When did you get here?"

"Four-thirty or thereabouts."

The doctor pondered. "At a rough guess, and as near as I can figure it, Blackmer died not much previous to the time you arrived. I'd say sometime between four and four-thirty. Nobody can strike it exact, but that's good enough."

Now that he had an opportunity to look over the kitchen, Quist stepped back from the group about the body and scrutinized the floor. Just within the bedroom hall he saw a few drops of blood on the floor. There were further scattered drops leading to the point where Blackmer had been found dead. Quist drew this to the attention of the others.

Garrity said, "All right, does it mean anything?"

"It means that Blackmer had just entered the hall when he was shot. He probably surprised the murderer while the dirty cuss was rifling Harmon's box. Then the murderer dragged Blackmer, by the feet, to the spot where he lies now."

"You figured out," Dewitt frowned, "what was the idea in that?"

"I think I have. The murderer probably saw me coming and dragged the body over here, figuring I'd stoop down to have a look when I saw it. At the same time this door gave him a convenient place to hide behind—"

"Dang," Garrity protested, "why couldn't he have shot you just as well?"

"You and your crew were just riding into the yard," Quist reminded Garrity. "You'd maybe have heard the shot and immediately scattered to catch who'd done the shooting. As it was, you took your time and entered by the front door. Then you were held up when you saw me and the sheriff sprawled on the floor. Meanwhile, while you were engaged in bringing me to, the murderer made his escape through the brush out back."

"Sounds reasonable," Dewitt nodded. "Greg, run over your story for me, will you? I want to make sure Ike Palmer didn't miss anything."

Quist related once more what had taken place, then Dewitt questioned the other men. No new facts were forthcoming. Within a short time Blackmer's body was placed in the wagon bed. The doctor took the forty-five six-shooter, from which but one shot had been fired recently, and the box containing Harmon's papers and prepared to return to Cenotaph, with the dead sheriff's horse tied to the end of the wagon. Quist got into the saddle of the bay that still waited outside, though one of the men had watered and fed the beast, and Dewitt climbed up on his own pony. In a dry voice Quist thanked the Thunderbird crew for its hospitality and received again certain apologies. As the wagon rolled off and Quist and Dewitt got their ponies moving, Quist heard Garrity giving orders to get "that bloodstain scrubbed off the kitchen floor."

14. The Missing Hat

Beyond a few speculations on the doctor's part, to which Quist and Dewitt gave small attention, there was little conversation on the return trip to Cenotaph. Dewitt and Quist would have liked to go on ahead, but didn't want to leave the doctor alone on his grisly journey, in the more slowly moving wagon. Consequently it was well after one in the morning when the vehicle pulled to a halt before the door of the town undertaking establishment. The undertaker was waiting for them, as he had been advised of Blackmer's death before Lang and Dewitt departed from the Thunderbird. The body was quickly carried inside and the undertaker's curiosity satisfied with a brief story of what had happened.

Lang yawned when they were again on the street. Dewitt said, "You go on along home, Doc. Greg and I will get this wagon to the livery. We've got to take the horses down there anyway."

"Thanks," Lang said. "I'll make a more thorough examination of that body tomorrow morning when I'm more wide-awake. Inquest at three, Pete. I'll depend on you to have a jury for me. Good night."

The wagon and horses were driven along a darkened Main Street. Only a few lights showed here and there, and Quist noticed but one pedestrian as they passed. Fifteen minutes later he and Dewitt were seated in the sheriff's office. Before saying anything Dewitt lighted the lamp over the sheriff's desk, drew down the shades, and locked the door. "Now," he stated, "if you're ready to talk, I'm almighty eager to listen. You've had quite a day, Greg."

"What a day!" Quist said fervently. "Only for you being willing to stand responsible for me, I might be in jail now, charged with murder."

"They'd never make a frame-up of that sort stick—not on Gregory Quist. You're too well known."

"That has nothing to do with it. After all, I have no legal standing in state law. There's lots of people don't like railroad detectives. With all due respect to John Blackmer, suppose you were the type John was a week back? You'd been glad to have a case that could have been cleared up so easily. Yes, with a little less luck I could have gone to trial for the murder of Sheriff Blackmer. I might never have been convicted, but my operations hereabouts would have been considerably curtailed."

"It's too darn' bad you had to lose that gun of yours."

"I've a hunch I'll find it again. Meanwhile I've got its mate at my hotel room. Bought a pair of those forty-fours at the same time—there's no difference, same hang and balance—cripes! I'm wasting time and you want information." Quist threw open his coat, unbuttoned his shirt, and, reaching around to the back, drew out a gray sombrero that had been crushed flat against his body. This he threw on the desk before Dewitt, saying, "And the sweatband of that hat shows it's been worn. For more than one reason, I'm glad Garrity and his crew didn't think to search me."

Dewitt seized the hat, straightened it out. "Blazes, yes," he said, "I've seen Gid Harmon wear this hat—fact is, he wore it most of the time. Where'd you find it?"

"Not where I expected to. This morning when I started out, I was looking for hoofprints and thought I might find the hat along the trail."

"And you didn't?"

Quist shook his head. "I found sign where two horses had crossed the Rid Esteban in the direction of the Thunderbird. Crossing the river to the eastern bank, I followed the trail north, and it finally led me to an old cabin of peeled logs, set down in the lower foothills of the Sangre de Estebans—"

"I know where it is," Dewitt interrupted. "That's Harmon's old shack he lived in years ago when he was prospecting. After he made his Thunderbird strike, sold out and went to ranching, he erected the present ranch house. But what did you find at the cabin?"

"A rusty stove, a table, a bunk with blankets."

181

"You figure somebody's been living there?"

"I couldn't say. There was no door and no glass in the windows. Anyway, three people had been there—there were three distinct sets of footprints, one much smaller than the other two. Two horses had been tethered in the brush back of the cabin; one horse had been tethered in the brush facing the front of the cabin, so I gathered that all three hadn't arrived at the same time."

"That's a reasonable deduction."

"Below the paneless rear window were footprints, as though someone had departed that way—it was those led me to the horses' prints in the brush back of the house—but when those footprints returned they came around to the front, as would be normal. Figure that one out. There was dust on the floor within the cabin, and that dust showed prints. From the marks it looked like some sort of scuffle had taken place. I found Harmon's hat under the bunk. I suppose it had fallen off and rolled there unnoticed."

Quist paused to roll a cigarette. "I also found this"—reaching into a pants pocket and producing a somewhat battered lead slug—"imbedded in the floor of the cabin. I dug it out, and only that the wood is starting to rot, it would have been quite a job getting it."

Dewitt studied the leaden bullet. "Forty-five, I'd say."

"Without doubt."

"You said you thought more than one shot had been fired from Harmon's gun. You think this came from that second ca'tridge?"

"That's my guess."

"You think Harmon was killed in fair fight and that his shot missed—no, wait, what about the other shot? Was he shot with his own gun? If so, why did—"

"I've not got that doped out yet, Pete. It needs some thinking over before I can make a guess as to what happened. Let's get back to the hoofprints I'd been trailing. The ones that led me to the cabin had been traveling south—the return trip to the Thunderbird with, I think, Harmon's body on Harmon's horse. But I was interested in the tracks that carried the riders to the cabin. These I followed along the west side of the river. Just to make it a mite clearer I'll go back and tell you what I found."

Quist drew deeply on his cigarette, fanned the air with gray smoke that swirled around the lamp chimney. He went on, "One rider had come from a southwesterly direction and—so it looked—had hid out in the brush for some time with his horse. Maybe he'd stayed there all night. I couldn't say for sure, but there were plenty of cigarette stubs around, and the grass was pressed down where he had stretched out. The footprints were none too clear at that point, so I couldn't tell much else."

"Lord, I'd like to have eyes that could read sign like that," Dewitt said enviously.

"It's a matter of practice," Quist said tersely and continued, "A second rider had traveled in a northerly direction from, I think, the Thunderbird Ranch, and then had been trailed by the rider who'd been hidden in the brush. This second rider, farther on, had been joined by a third rider, coming from the direction of the HB-Connected Ranch. They had gone to the cabin and been followed there by the man who had stayed in the brush all night—"

"HB-Connected—Belvard!" Dewitt exclaimed. "He must have made an appointment for Harmon to meet him at that cabin, then when Harmon passed, the man hidden in the brush followed and he and Belvard killed Harmon at the cabin. They picked the cabin so nobody would be likely to see, if anyone chanced to be riding past. That man hidden in the brush was Stark Garrity and—"

"You make it sound danged simple," Quist said dryly.

Caught up short, Dewitt looked a bit crestfallen. "Well, it could have happened that way," Dewitt said.

"Sure it could. Maybe it did. I don't know, Pete. I'm just telling you what I found. I've got to think this thing out. By the way, was Harmon the noisy type when he was drinking?"

"I guess you could say he was—no, not quarrelsome. He just talked pretty loud."

"How about when he was sober?"

Dewitt considered. "Well, Harmon always was inclined to let folks know he was around, after he got money. Maybe he got sort of arrogant in his ways, like lots of moneyed men do, but he never hurt anybody's feelings intentionally. He was a right kind sort of man, and was mostly easygoing with folks who had less than he did."

Quist ground out his cigarette butt under his heel. "So much for the trailing today," he said. "Now I'll tell you what happened when I went to the Thunderbird. You know, I wanted to see if I could find trace of another will. Well, when I reached the ranch house it looked as though it was deserted, so I went right in. When I found that box of papers open on the floor, it should have warned me, but aside from realizing somebody had been there first, I was too anxious to look through those papers to give the matter proper thought. Then when I went to the kitchen and saw Blackmer laying there and the back door standing open, I figured the murderer had left. When I knelt at Blackmer's side, the murderer stepped from behind the door and let me have it. I probably wasn't out more than twenty minutes, though it could have been more. But you know all that. I want to get back to that box of papers a moment."

"You didn't find another will, did you?"

"No, there was just the one there, drawn by Judge Harnsworth, but I did find something else—an old theater program." He drew the folded paper from a hip pocket. "See if there's any name there that looks familiar to you."

Dewitt accepted the paper and glanced at it. "Coronado Opera House, eh? I know that place. Went there one time when I was in Denver, a year or so back. It's not really what you'd call a high-class opera house, though." He looked at Quist. "I don't mean there's anything wrong with it, but they don't have regular play performances like an opera house. There's girls to sing and dance on the stage, and fellows that tell jokes—but mostly it's girls singing and dancing. The customers sit out in front at tables and have drinks, and sometimes the actresses, or the singers, or whatever you call 'em, come down and drink with the customers. It's sort of a high-class honky-tonk, if you know what I mean, without any gambling."

"I know the place," Quist said shortly. "I've been there—once. But I wanted you to look over the names."

Dewitt's gaze traveled down the program. He paused suddenly, "Is this what you mean?"—reading from the program—" 'Act III, The Rocky Mountain Rose—Miss Lilith Farrell, in Songs Your Mother Used to Sing.' "

"That's the one," Quist nodded.

"You mean that name, Lilith?"

"It's not a common name, Pete. And for some reason—probably sentimental—Gid Harmon kept that program."

"And you think Mrs. Harmon was an actress?" Pete looked aghast at the thought. "I'd never have believed it."

"There's nothing wrong with it, is there?"

"No, but it just comes as sort of a surprise." Pete consulted the date on the program, then said, "Yep, that's just about the time Harmon went to Denver and surprised us all when he came back by bringing a wife."

"You any idea what took him to Denver?"

"Not the slightest. And I suppose it's too late to learn that now, unless Mrs. Harmon would know."

"We won't ask her—for a time yet, anyway. No use bothering her until we have to."

"But does this mean anything in particular—I mean as relates to Harmon's murder?"

Quist shrugged. "You tell me and I'll tell you." He changed the subject. "I understand Caroline Trent went riding right after the funeral today—I should say yesterday, now."

Pete nodded. "Yes, I saw her riding out of the livery when I was taking my horse back."

"Where'd she go?"

"You got me. She keeps a horse and often goes riding."

"What time was the funeral finished?"

"I don't know exactly. It was scheduled for three, but we got quite an early start. It must have been over by three—of course, the slower ones

187

maybe didn't get back to the center of town until after three, but some left as soon as the coffin was lowered into the ground." He paused, then, "Car'line drove out with Garrity and Mrs. Harmon, but I saw her getting into another rig that pulled away early."

"Caroline Trent could have reached the Thunderbird—"

"Good God, Greg!" Pete started from his chair. "Do you realize what you're saying?"

"What am I saying?" Quist was eying Dewitt quietly.

"You as much as intimated she was the one that—went out to the Thunderbird—Blackmer—now, look here, Greg—"

"Sit down, Pete. I didn't accuse her of killing Blackmer, if that's what you mean. I'm just covering all the angles."

"But why Caroline?"

"You're too touchy, Pete. Let's forget it. Was Belvard and the Egg at the funeral?"

Pete replied, a trifle sullenly, "Belvard was. Hugo Voit didn't show up."

"Maybe," Quist proposed, "John Blackmer followed Voit out to the Thunderbird."

Pete brightened. "Say, that sounds like an idea."

Quist rose to his feet. "All right, you follow it through and give me some definite facts, if possible. I'm going to quit thinking about it for the night. I'm ready for bed, and I've got to go to the station, first, and send a telegram."

Pete too rose from his chair. "Look here, Greg, you haven't any gun."

"I'll get my other forty-four as soon as I reach the hotel."

"No saying, you might need one before you got there." Pete drew a loaded forty-five from his desk. "I'd feel better if you carried this until you get your other forty-four."

Quist nodded, accepted the gun, and said thanks. After a few moments they said good night and Quist headed for the railroad station and thence to his bed at the hotel. Pete's fears proved to have been groundless, as nothing untoward took place. For a time, however, thoughts of the dark-eyed Lilith disturbed Quist's dreams.

15. Due to Crack

The following morning Quist left the hotel dining room and stepped out to Main Street, where he spied Dewitt just nearing the hotel. Quist took the forty-five six-shooter he'd borrowed the night before from the waistband of his trousers and handed it to Pete. He said thanks again and flipped back the lapel of his coat to show his other forty-four in its holster. Quist said, "Do you know anything new,"—putting a certain mock respect in the tones—"Mr. Sheriff?"

"Devil with that," Pete scowled. "I'm just doing the same as I've always done. Come election time, I may not be sheriff."

"You looked riled. What's up?"

"I'm trying to round up a coroner's jury for the inquest this afternoon. It's dang' funny how busy folks get when you ask 'em to perform a civic duty. It's even funnier how they'll all be there, anyway. But it's a job to get intelligent hombres—"

"Look, Pete," Quist broke in, "let me give you some advice. Don't look for intelligent jurors. Just grab anybody you can scrape up. Yes, I know that sounds crazy, but in this case I don't want intelligent men on the coroner's jury."

"I'll be danged if I get you!" Pete frowned.

"Pete, you know as well as I do what the verdict

is going to be when that inquest is finished—'Murdered by person unknown.'—"

Pete nodded. "Yeah, and then the coroner will recommend that the sheriff take steps to apprehend the murderer—and we'll be no farther ahead than we are now. But why are you against intelligent men serving?"

"Because intelligent men ask questions, and when I'm testifying this afternoon I don't want to be questioned as to why I went to the Thunderbird yesterday. You and I know certain things, but I'm not yet ready to have that knowledge made public. Now do you understand?"

Pete brightened. "You know what you're talking about. I'll not be so particular in the type hombre I ask. Maybe things will go easier. . . . Have you thought of anything new regarding what you learned yesterday?"

"Nothing new, but I haven't mentioned it to you before."

"What's that?"

"Pete, the freight thieves that looted that wrecked train made off with a good many cases of Glen Spey scotch whisky. I know that particular whisky was carried on the freight, because Jay Fletcher brought me a bottle from a broken case that was left behind. There was a bottle of Glen Spey at the Thunderbird yesterday. Somebody said that Garrity favored scotch. On the other hand, the murderer may have brought it with him, either to drink or leave there for Garrity—if Garrity is tied in with the freight thieves. Or maybe the murderer had nothing whatever to do with it."

Dewitt looked interested. "More and more, you keep putting a noose around Garrity's neck."

"I'm not sure. I'm confident he knows something, but he's not the type you can force. I talked to him alone for a couple of minutes yesterday, and he's getting pretty edgy. I'd guess he was due to crack right soon."

"Anything else you know?"

"I want some information on something, but I'm not asking you, because it concerns Caroline Trent and you always hit the ceiling every time she's mentioned."

"Well, cripes!" Dewitt snapped. "I can't see why you keep pulling her into the case. She's got nothing to do with it, except that she's related to Harmon—or was."

"You see?" Quist smiled thinly. "You're flying off the handle already."

"But what do you want to know about Car'line?"

Quist said seriously, "I want to ask her for something—the recipe for those wheat cakes she makes."

"Oh, you go to the devil!" Dewitt looked much relieved.

Quist chuckled. "All right. Now that you've pumped me dry, have you anything new to offer?"

"Not a danged thing. I've thought over everything you told me, but I can't seem to solve the puzzle. I still think Belvard and Garrity—and probably Voit—had something to do with Harmon's death—and likely Blackmer's too. But—I can't prove it. Oh yes, something else. I talked with Doc Lang a few minutes ago. He decided there'd be no necessity to call Lilith Harmon in on the inquest, as she wouldn't know anything, anyway."

"Has she left for the Thunderbird yet?"

"Doc Lang was over to see her this morning and showed her the box with the papers in it to ask if she noticed anything missing. She didn't. She said she had no idea what Harmon kept in that box. After the inquest the box and papers will be turned over to Judge Harnsworth for safekeeping. Mrs. Harmon and Car'line are leaving for the Thunderbird today—if they haven't left by this time. Mrs. Harmon hired a Mexican girl to stay with her. Car'ine found somebody to run the Stopgap while she's away, but she'll be back Sunday night. Oh yes, Harnsworth plans to call Mrs. Harmon and others concerned in to hear a reading of the will Monday."

"Can you have Harnsworth stall that off for a time?"

"Probably, if necessary. It will have to go through probate, in the regular way, of course."

"All right. Just have Harnsworth postpone that

reading for a time, until we get things straightened out a mite. He can claim that the regular processes of the law have to be observed or some such fooforaw as lawyers spout when they want to confuse the public."

"I'll take care of it, Greg."

"I don't think Mrs. Harmon will think anything of it if the will isn't read at once. I wonder if Caroline Trent would."

"Hell no!"

"How do you know?"

"Well—er—I don't—now dang it, Greg!—I—"

"Take it easy, Pete. I'm just calculating all the angles again. One angle may interest you."

"What's that?" Dewitt asked quickly.

"I was talking to the hotel clerk this morning—you know, Toby Nixon."

"Yes, I know Toby Nixon. Who doesn't? The biggest gossip in Cenotaph. What about him?"

"Toby tells me," Quist said quietly, "that Belvard and Caroline Trent used to ride to town frequently, back in the days when Miss Trent was living at the Thunderbird. You know anything about that?"

"Tarnation!" Dewitt swore and then paused. After a moment he said in a quieter tone, "Now look here, Greg, you can't make anything out of that."

"Have I said I intended to?"

"Cripes! I knew he used to ride with her now

and then. But that was over three years ago, when she was living at the Thunderbird. What's that got to do with now?"

"Did I say it had anything to do with now?" Quist asked mildly.

Dewitt's eyes narrowed. "What you got on your mind, Greg?"

"I've been thinking about that argument Harmon had with Belvard some time ago—the one that Blackmer told me he witnessed. Now you told me yourself that Harmon was rather noisy in his speech. If it'd been about money matters, or cow business, or anything like that, there'd been no reason for Harmon to hold his voice down. But where a woman's concerned, a man isn't likely to tell his troubles to the world. Right?"

Dewitt said after a moment, reluctantly, "Right. But maybe it had nothing to do with Car'line at all. Maybe—maybe—look here, Belvard might have said something to Mrs. Harmon that didn't set right with Gid. How do you know that wasn't it?"

"I don't," Quist said carelessly.

Dewitt snapped angrily, "But you're convinced that it concerned Car'line Trent."

"I didn't say that either. In my business you're never convinced of anything until you have actual facts, Pete. Now cool down and don't jump down my throat every time I start speculating about something."

They talked a few minutes longer and then separated.

Quist strolled down to the Sundown Saloon, entered and ordered a bottle of beer from Johnny Webb. There weren't many people in the bar. Webb was curious about Blackmer's death, but Quist put the man off with a statement to the effect that he wasn't legally allowed to give out any details until after he'd testified at the coroner's inquest that afternoon.

After a time the other customers drifted out. Quist dallied over his beer. He commented idly to Webb, "I suppose these deaths spoil business for you to some extent, Johnny."

"Not for me," Webb said. "Folks hang around and buy extra drinks while they talk about it."

"Yeah, I suppose," Quist conceded. He smothered a yawn with one hand. "I didn't mean that exactly. What I meant was you'd lost a good customer for scotch."

"Who's that?"

"Gid Harmon."

"Harmon?" Webb laughed scornfully. "Cripes, Gid wouldn't touch scotch. He was strictly a bourbon man—always said he wanted something that would take the throat out of him when it flowed down, and that scotch didn't have any bite. What gave you that idea?"

Quist didn't mention that bottle of scotch at the Thunderbird. He shrugged, "I don't know. I thought somebody said he was a scotch drinker. I must be wrong."

"Where scotch is concerned, you'd be wrong 'most any place in the Southwest," Webb said seriously. "We're hard-liquor drinkers in this country." He jerked a thumb in the direction of a squat bottle on the back bar. "I keep that bottle of Dewar on hand just in case anybody does call for scotch whisky. Stark Garrity takes scotch now and then, but Stark's no drinker compared to most folks. I understand there's quite a call for scotch in the high-toned places in San Francisco, but you don't see much in this country."

"I suppose not." Quist appeared to have lost interest in the subject. He yawned again, finished his beer, and departed.

The coroner's inquest over the body of John Blackmer that afternoon produced nothing startling in the way of facts. Quist testified that he had gone to the Thunderbird to return a borrowed horse—which in a way was the truth—and that, upon seeing the door open, he had entered the house and discovered the dead body of the sheriff, then had been knocked unconscious by a blow on the head, probably with a gun barrel in the hand of a hidden assailant.

There was some discussion, in view of the opened box of papers, as to whether the assailant had gone there for purposes of robbery, and some speculation as to whether the man had been discovered in the act by Sheriff Blackmer, but no one was particularly interested in the papers, which Dr. Lang described as "old receipts, insurance papers, and so on." So far as was known, the opened box had contained no money. As to why Blackmer had gone to the Thunderbird on the day Harmon was being buried, that seemed unworthy of investigation by the jury.

The verdict was, as Quist had prophesied, ". . . killed by some person unknown," and the coroner directed Acting Sheriff Dewitt to take the proper steps at once that would eventuate in the apprehension of the murderer. And with that weighty problem lifted from its collective mind, the jury of six retired to the nearest saloon—which proved to be the Sundown, just across Waco Street—to more thoroughly discuss the known facts of the case in a more congenial atmosphere. Only then, and under the stimulus of three fingers of bourbon, did the jurors commence to think of questions they might have put to the different witnesses.

When the inquest was finished, Quist watched Stark Garrity and the rest of the Thunderbird crew get into saddles and ride out of town, then he approached Dr. Lang, who was just leaving the two-story frame structure known as the county house.

"You said," Quist opened the subject, "that the murderer's bullet had entered Blackmer's stomach—"

"And ranged upward," Lang completed, "passing close to the heart."

"But didn't penetrate the heart? In that case, would you say that Blackmer died instantly?"

"Not necessarily. I judged from the nature of the wound that he might have lingered on twenty minutes or so after being struck."

"Could he have made any sort of outcry, or even a moan?"

"Possible, though it would have been feeble, provided he were conscious. After all, John Blackmer was no spring chicken. The shock from the impact of a forty-five slug has knocked unconscious many a younger man. Why do you ask?"

"I was in that house several minutes before I discovered Blackmer's body. I've wondered why the murderer didn't attack me before he did, and it occurred to me that Blackmer may have been partially conscious, and it may have been necessary for the killer to hold a hand over his mouth, or strangle him or something of the sort, so I wouldn't be warned of anyone else being there."

Dr. Lang considered. "I was preoccupied mostly with the bullet wound. Nothing of that sort occurred to me, of course. If you like I'll make a very thorough examination of the body and—"

"Never mind, thanks, Doc. It doesn't matter one way or the other. I simply wanted to know for my own curiosity. You're already overworked in Cenotaph as it is."

"Has the idea come to you that perhaps whoever killed Blackmer lacked the courage, or the necessary aptitude with firearms, to confront you?"

"Yes, I've thought of that, too."

"After all, we just took it for granted it was a gun barrel that struck you on the head, Mr. Quist. It might have been something else of a hard, weighty nature. For instance, I noticed several old brand irons standing at the corner of the fireplace in the ranch house. Perhaps one of those was—"

"The bullet that killed Blackmer," Quist smiled thinly, "didn't come out of a branding iron, and I've a strong hunch the same weapon was used on my head."

"Probably you're correct," Lang nodded. They talked a few minutes longer, then Quist and the doctor went their separate ways.

The following day was Saturday, bringing an unusually large crowd to town not only for week-end buying but to attend the funeral of John Blackmer which was held in the afternoon. Quist joined the procession that wended its slow way out to the Boot Hill, north of Cenotaph, more to see who attended than for any other reason.

It was a large turnout. Now that he was gone, John Blackmer had increased in popularity, achieving in death a stature he had never attained in life, though his long tenure in office affirmed the esteem in which he'd been held by a certain majority group. The truth was that never before in Cenotaph had there been sufficient real crime to demand the services of a more efficient law officer. That Blackmer had, toward the last, realized his own shortcomings was to the man's credit and, in a fashion, made him worthy of the tribute attested by the unusually large attendance at his burial service.

That night, in the sheriff's office, Quist mentioned something of this to Pete Dewitt. Pete nodded slowly. "You're pretty much right about John, Greg," he admitted. "Even while I tell you I owed him a lot for things he did for me, I've got to admit that he was something of a blowhard, he didn't take care of his office the way he should have—but what the devil! Things have been peaceful, mostly, in Dawson County. When election time came, John usually handed out the most cigars and free drinks. That gave him votes."

"He was always a pretty generous cuss," Quist nodded.

"Yeah," Dewitt said glumly, "he gave his life."

Quist saw that Dewitt was harder hit by the sheriff's death than he liked to admit, so changed the subject slightly. "I expected to see Belvard and Hugo Voit at the funeral."

"I didn't see 'em either," Pete said. "They haven't been in town all day. Now if either of them had had a hand in John's murder, it might have made them look more innocent had they come to the funeral and staged some sort of act to show folks how much they regretted John's passing. Fact, is, I expected 'em to do just that."

"Maybe," Quist said slowly, "they were smart and had already figured you'd think that way. You talk like you're sure one of 'em did the killing."

"Oh, I'm sure Belvard didn't do the actual killing, but I think he had something to do with it. Remember, Belvard was attending Harmon's funeral that afternoon. I don't think he could have got out to the Thunderbird in time enough to—"

"Some people left Boot Hill early that day—remember?"

Dewitt shot Quist a sharp look, but held back the words that rose to his lips. He said instead, "Don't you think Belvard is back of this business?"

"Right now I've no *definite* opinion. This much I will say, I'd hoped Belvard and the Egg would be in town tonight. I'd figured to ask 'em both some direct questions, with the intention of making them mad, in the hope they'd get riled enough to make a slip of the tongue of some sort."

"They're usually in town on Saturday night. Let's take a stroll around. Maybe by this time they'll show up. There's some HB-Connected hands in town, too."

"I saw the Thunderbird crew in the Sundown

awhile back—but not Stark Garrity. He left right after Blackmer was buried. . . . Are you going to get a deputy here to help you out, Pete?"

Dewitt nodded. "I swore in Luke Rutson just before supper. He'll make a good man, I think, until election comes and we can learn where we're at. Rutson? Oh, he raises chickens here in town, but he was a deputy for some time up in Three-Sleep County. He knows the ropes and has the town council's approval."

They left the sheriff's office and meandered around town, entering the various saloons and keeping a sharp lookout on the streets, but nothing of Voit and Belvard was to be seen. An inquiry addressed to an HB-Connected puncher in the Longhorn Bar elicited only the reply that "Hoddy and Voit are out to the ranch, so far as I know." Quist and Dewitt considered the man was telling the truth and knew but little of the whereabouts of his employer or the Egg.

The following day was Sunday, and Cenotaph proved to show little activity of any sort. After breakfast Quist took a walk around the town, stopping at the station to see if any messages had arrived for him. None had. His steps next took him to the sheriff's office, where he met Luke Rutson, a tall, skinny, blond man with long mustaches, who had nothing much to say. Dewitt was laboring over some past reports that should have been made out by Blackmer a week before, and as it looked as though he'd be busy all day, Quist decided to leave him to his labors.

He returned to the hotel, took a seat on the wide gallery, and figuratively sat in a fever of impatience chewing his fingernails. He smoked three cigars and eventually went into the dining room for dinner, more to pass the time than because he was hungry. When afternoon came he was again sitting on the porch, surveying a Main Street which seemed deserted. Finally he could stand it no longer, and, rising, bent his steps toward the livery stable.

A few minutes later he was in the saddle, loping easily along the road that ran to the Thunderbird Ranch.

"Maybe I'll be welcome, maybe I won't," he mused, "but if things break right, I may get a little information from Lilith Harmon."

16. Thunderbird Warning

When he arrived, at about four o'clock that afternoon, Quist found both Lilith Harmon and Caroline Trent on the wide gallery that fronted the Thunderbird ranch house. Mrs. Harmon was seated in a wide armchair, with some sewing in her lap. She wore a dark maroon-colored dress of some soft clinging material that succeeded admirably in bringing out the lines of her figure. There were touches of lace at her throat and wrists, and her heavy black hair was done in braids that coiled thickly about her well-shaped head. Her dark eyes were warm and friendly as they rested on the approaching Quist.

Caroline looked tired in a divided riding skirt, masculine woolen shirt, Stetson, and riding boots; wisps of the red hair with its golden glints appeared beneath the brim of the hat. She was seated next to Mrs. Harmon, fanning herself with a handkerchief. At the corner of the gallery Herb Moody was just taking away Caroline's horse when Quist rode up and dismounted.

"I wasn't sure if you were ready for company yet," Quist said uncertainly, "but Cenotaph offered nothing in the way of entertainment, and I thought I might ride out and say hello to Stark Garrity, anyway."

"I think it's awfully nice you've come," Lilith

Harmon said in her husky contralto. "It's been rather lonely here, too. Herb,"—to Moody—"take Mr. Quist's horse down to the corral with you— no, wait a minute. I'm going to give Mr. Quist a drink, and I know men generally don't like to drink alone." She raised her voice and called to someone within the house.

A rather pretty Mexican girl appeared in the doorway, and Lilith spoke quickly in fluent Spanish. The girl smiled and withdrew. Herb Moody and Quist found seats on the gallery.

Caroline was saying something about going in and changing her clothing. Quist smiled and asked if she had placed him on her list as yet. That brought an answering smile to Caroline's lips.

"What list is that?" Lilith Harmon asked.

"As I get it from Pete Dewitt," Quist explained gravely, "there's a long list of applicants for Miss Trent's hand. It has something to do with her wheat cakes, I imagine."

"Caroline has much more than her wheat cakes to offer," Lilith laughed.

Herb Moody said, after a time, "Stark isn't here right now, Mr. Quist. He saddled up right after breakfast. There's some HB-Connected cows working over this way, and he stated he was aiming to drive 'em back. We offered to take the job, but he told us we might as well take it easy, and that he didn't mind. Stark seems to like to get off by himself ever since—" He stopped abruptly and grew red, having nearly mentioned the passing of Gideon Harmon.

If Lilith Harmon knew what had been in the man's mind, she gave no sign, but quickly covered up the rather awkward silence with, "So long as Caroline insisted on going off so early, she might just as well have gone with Stark."

"Stark wasn't going my way," Caroline said. "I wanted to get up into the foothills. You should have seen those golden aspens against the purple of the Sangre de Estebans. It was glorious—and I'm nearly dead. It's so long since I've had a ride like that."

"I was sort of looking forward to riding with you tonight," Quist said. "Pete Dewitt said you were returning to Cenotaph tonight."

"I had planned that way," Caroline nodded, "but I've decided to return early tomorrow morning instead."

The Mexican girl returned to the gallery at this moment, bearing a tray on which were whisky and water for Moody and Quist, and two glasses of something known as "raspberry shrub" for the women. The drinks were consumed, and Herb Moody started to take the horses down to the corral.

"And Herb," Lilith said, "ask Skillet if he can't do something along the lines of an extra pie, because Mr. Quist will be staying for supper."

Moody said, "Yes, ma'am," and took the horses away.

Quist protested he wasn't equal to eating an extra pie and that he hadn't intended to stay for supper at all.

"Nonsense," Lilith Harmon smiled. "Of course you'll stay to supper, and overnight as well. There's plenty of room in the bunkhouse, and, anyway, there's no telling when Stark will return, if you want to see him. Besides, you can return with Caroline early tomorrow morning—"

The two women and the man talked on the gallery awhile longer, then as the sun settled and it grew chilly, they removed to the big main room. Caroline remained but a moment, then excused herself on the plea that she had "to go wash off some dust and tidy up."

Almost the instant the girl had left the room, a change came over Lilith Harmon. She no longer smiled and acted the part of the gracious hostess. She asked quietly, "I suppose you've learned nothing as yet."

Quist shook his head. "I seem to encounter a blank wall."

"But this business of the sheriff—John Blackmer—here at this house last Thursday— what could that have had to do with—with things?" Quist noticed her lower lip tremble, and she caught it between her teeth impatiently.

"That's something else I haven't figured out."

"You've had better luck, I hope, with your own business—the wreck on the railroad?"

"Not much," Quist answered. "We know a great deal of merchandise was carted away by freight thieves, but where it was taken to is a mystery. The wheel ruts just plain vanished against those red buttes of the Pihuela Range—"

"Vanished?" Lilith's brows drew together in a frown of uncomprehension. "But how could they?"

Quist gave her the story, and saw the lovely dark eyes widen in astonishment. "But—but it couldn't be," she exclaimed.

"I agree with you. Nevertheless that's what happened."

"But—but even if horses could fly, I can't imagine wagons taking wings—"

"Well, you see, Mrs. Harmon—"

Quist was interrupted by the reappearance of Caroline Trent. The girl had changed to a green dress that brought out her coloring to advantage, and her reddish hair was once more neatly combed in place. Much of the weariness had left her eyes. She sat down for a few minutes, then offered to go to the kitchen and see how the Mexican girl was getting along with supper.

When Caroline had left, Lilith said, "I've discovered something I want you to see." She left the room and quickly returned with a rather soiled, folded sheet of paper which she handed to Quist.

Quist took the paper and opened it. It was an

ordinary sheet of cheap letter paper, ruled with blue lines. On it were printed in lead pencil a few crudely formed words:

You have three more days to make up your mind.

The paper bore no address. What caught Quist's attention was the signature, which consisted of a roughly sketched figure of a thunderbird in red ink. There was no name signed to the paper.

Quist studied the paper a few moments, then raised his gaze to meet Lilith's eyes, in which showed something of fright. He said, "Where'd this come from?"

"I found it in the pocket of one of Gideon's coats yesterday."

"You haven't any idea what it means?"

"Not the slightest, Mr. Quist. I hoped you'd be able to offer—well, some idea."

Quist shook his head. "It's just one more mystery to add to the others. You haven't any idea when Gid Harmon received this?"

"I didn't even know it existed until I found it in his pocket when I was going through his clothing, before putting the things away. He may have had it months, or—well, the message might lead us to believe he received it only a few days before— before he died. Would you say there was anything there to make a man commit suicide, or—I might as well say it, as I don't, I can't, believe that he killed himself—"

"I can't quite figure it out," Quist said slowly. "May I keep this?"

"Of course, I expected you to." Something like a shudder ran through her lovely form. "I don't want to see it again."

Caroline came into the room a minute or so later to announce that supper was on the table. Quist sat down with the two women. When they were nearly through, Stark Garrity came into the room, apologizing for his dusty condition. He said something about having had a long ride and finding but few of Belvard's cows, which he had turned back toward their home range. He said he'd see Quist later and withdrew in the direction of the bunkhouse.

With supper over, Quist and the two women returned to the main room of the house. Lilith brought out a box of Harmon's cigars, and the three discussed various subjects, none of which was serious, for a time. Conversation dwindled. A moth fluttered about the lamp suspended above the oaken table. Quist commented admiringly on the big thunderbird rug hanging on the wall.

"I can't tell you where, or when, Gideon got that," Lilith said. "He had it long before I knew him."

"Uncle Gid went to an Indian reservation and had it woven to his order," Caroline supplied the information.

"It's a nice piece of rug-weaving," Quist stated. "That thunderbird appears to be done in genuine *bayeta*." He paused to explain: "That's the particular type of red wool the Navajos used in their best weaving. You see, the early rugs were largely woven from native wool—mostly white, grayish white, and some black. Then color commenced to creep into the designs. From Mexico, the Indians got *bayeta*, which had been imported originally from Turkey. Then when the soldiers were out here, the Indians got a certain amount of blue from uniforms—I'll leave it to you as to how they got the uniforms. Gradually, other colors were used when dyes became known on the reservations."

"My grief!" Lilith said. "You seem to know a lot about Indian rugs."

"They're an interesting subject," Quist smiled. "Especially that thunderbird design. I don't know as I ever saw a rug with that exact design woven into it before. That's a sort of divine symbol of the Indian's religion, meaning—oh, say, 'Sacred Bearer of Unlimited Happiness,' or something of the sort. The Indians, like most people, are touchy about their religion. What is mere superstition to us may signify something holy to a Navajo. I remember hearing a number of years ago of one weaver who depicted in her design a figure representing one of her gods—it was what is known as a *yei* blanket. As I heard it, she was

212

banished from the tribe, though nowadays you see *yei* blankets fairly often."

"Did you say 'she'?" Lilith asked.

Quist nodded, smiling. "Women are really more daring than men sometimes, you know."

Caroline frowned. "Now that you mention it," she said, "it seems as though Uncle Gid had some trouble getting that rug woven. Some tribesman on the reservation objected to the use of the design. I can't remember just what happened. Anyway, Uncle got it, as he got nearly everything else he went after." She looked depressed and after a moment announced she was going out on the gallery to watch the moon rise above the Sangre de Estebans.

Lilith said she'd go, too. The women got coats, and Quist accompanied them out to chairs, where they watched a huge ivory ball of a moon rise above the far mountain peaks. No one talked very much, and after a time Caroline said she guessed she would go to bed, added "good night" and went inside the house.

Quist stubbed out a cigarette on the sole of his boot and started to rise. Lilith said, in a low voice, "Wait," and he settled back in his chair.

The chairs were close together, situated in a shadowed stretch of the long gallery, though a couple of rectangles of yellow light glowed dimly from the front windows. The moon climbed higher above the Sangre de Estebans, its mellow

213

rays now cut off from the occupants of the gallery by the wide roof overhead. Back in the hills a coyote commenced a shrill yip-yipping. The sound was taken up by other beasts and increased in volume, suddenly ceasing as abruptly as it had started. Now and then voices drifted faintly up from the bunkhouse. A cricket chirped cheerfully at edge of the gallery.

Quist waited. Lilith said finally, "I don't think there's any need for putting it off any longer."

"Putting what off?" the man asked.

"Be honest, Mr. Quist. Your main object in coming out here was to question me about Gideon's affairs, wasn't it? And then you thought perhaps it was too soon after—after the funeral to ask me things. Isn't that correct?"

Quist said, "Well, it does sort of seem a trifle inconsiderate of me, but the sooner I can learn certain things, the sooner I may be able to clear up all this business. But it's not fair to you."

"You can forget my feelings. This is something that has to be done, sooner or later. I'd like to get it over with."

"I'm glad you feel that way." Quist still hesitated, momentarily at a loss where to start. "Perhaps if I'd paid more attention that night you came to the hotel—"

"And you were so sure I was wrong in my suspicions," Lilith cut in swiftly. "But you see, I knew better than you—"

"You had facts I didn't have."

"—that something was to happen. No, I didn't have facts. I just sensed that something terrible was going to happen. There's some sinister force working against the Thunderbird. I know it."

"I remember, that night," Quist said slowly, "you hinted that the danger to your husband might be someway involved in this matter of freight thieving. What did you mean by that?"

"I'm not sure. I only know that after that other wreck Gideon came home terribly angry one night. He refused to tell me what was wrong, but did say that from then on he was doing his best to prevent train wrecks. When I questioned him, he evaded my questions. What do you suppose he meant?"

Quist shook his head. "I've not got the faintest idea." He changed the subject: "Mrs. Harmon, your husband once had some trouble with Caroline Trent. Can you tell me what caused it?"

"I can, but I won't," Lilith replied. "I think that is something that concerns Caroline and is, to put it bluntly, none of my business. You'll have to ask her about that. I think it has nothing to do with the present business. I'll admit this much: I think Gideon was unfair to her."

"Did it concern money matters?"

"I don't think so."

"Did Gid ever tell you he planned to make a new will whereby Caroline would receive a better deal than she had in his first will?"

215

"Nothing of the sort was ever mentioned to me. Judge Harnsworth mentioned something of the kind only last Wednesday, but I could tell him nothing. Whatever Gideon left, I intend to see that Caroline receives a fair share of anything I get."

Quist nodded and went on, "Now I'm going to get personal. You can answer or not, as you see fit. I understand Gid met you in Denver. Can you give me the details of that meeting?"

Lilith hesitated. A minute passed. She commenced finally in a low voice: "Perhaps I'd better go back to a time before I knew Gideon Harmon. I'd lived in Denver since I was a child. My people weren't what is known as wealthy, but I was given a good education. We were well off, I suppose. Then Father lost his money and he and Mother both died. I had to go to work. The education I'd received hadn't fitted me for earning a living. I could sing and play the piano. I knew something about literature. For a girl in Denver, those days, such talents didn't go far in the matter of earning bread and butter."

She paused, then continued: "I made inquiries and found that waitresses were needed, and washwomen. I didn't think I'd be much good at anything of that sort. I had other offers, but they weren't the sort of thing I'd consider." She didn't say what the offers were, but Quist could guess. "I could sing, and when I had a chance to do that, I took it. No, I don't think I was a very good singer, but I was adequate for the sort of audiences I entertained. I was singing in a place called the Coronado Opera House when I met Gideon."

"I know the place," Quist said.

"That saves me explaining, then." Lilith's short laugh sounded a trifle brittle. "Gideon visited the Coronado one night, saw me, and came backstage. He came the following night, and on the third night—on the third night I promised to marry him. We were married the following morning and came back here."

"Do you know what took him to Denver in the first place?"

Lilith considered the question. "I don't know a great deal about it. He came there for a new saddle, or Hoddy Belvard did. I suppose it was partly for business, partly for pleasure—"

"Belvard was with him?"

Lilith nodded. "They were quite friendly those days, though later they had some argument about the money Belvard was paying for the property he'd bought from Gideon."

"Was Belvard at the Coronado with Gid?"

"If he was, I didn't see him. I didn't meet Belvard until the morning I married Gideon. Belvard was one of the witnesses; the minister's wife the other. I think Belvard thought Gideon was making a fool of himself over a woman much younger." She added, a little hopelessly, "I don't know, maybe it was the wrong thing to do."

"Didn't you love your husband?" Quist asked. And waited for the blow to fall.

"You've no right to ask that," Lilith flared. She half rose from the chair, then again sat down and became calm. "I said I'd answer your questions. I shall. Did I love my husband?" She paused as though considering the question thoroughly, then said in frank tones: "Love him? No, Mr. Quist, I didn't. I respected him, honored him, but I don't think it was love. We enjoyed each other's company. I think I made him a good wife. I know I tried to make him happy."

"I shouldn't have asked," Quist said awkwardly. "It was one of those questions that just pop out when you're not thinking."

"I don't blame you for wondering about it. Anyone would. Gideon was so much older than I. Maybe it was wrong to marry him, but when he asked me and I saw a chance for security—well, I took it. That may sound queer to you, but I was so tired of seeing those same faces before me, night after night, in the Coronado, and even being pawed, sometimes, by men who were half drunk. If you were a woman you'd understand. It was all cheap and tawdry. Of one thing, though, I'm certain: Gideon Harmon never regretted marrying me."

There was silence between them for some minutes after that. Finally Lilith asked, in what she endeavored to make light tones, "Is the questioning over?"

"I reckon it is," Quist nodded. "Maybe I asked things I shouldn't have, but I'm trying to cover every angle—"

"I'd gladly tell you more, if there were anything to tell. You're entitled to anything I have. I haven't forgotten how kind and considerate you were that night when you were asked to tell me my husband had—was dead." Impulsively one hand came across to rest on Quist's hand where it lay on the arm of the chair. He could feel Lilith's warm nearness. "It—it gives me a feeling of safety, just knowing you're trying to do something, Greg—" She stopped abruptly.

"Greg's all right with me," he said. "And—"

"After all, first names among friends—"

"—wasn't it Shakespeare who said, 'What's in a name?' Lilith, for instance. Wasn't Lilith supposed to be Adam's first wife before he met Eve?"

A ghost of a laugh escaped the girl's lips. "I never heard that before. All I ever heard was that the original Lilith was a witch who went around frightening children."

"I'm glad I'm grown up," Quist said dryly.

Lilith rose suddenly to her feet. "I must get to bed. Caroline will be wondering what's keeping me. I'll see you at breakfast, Greg."

"Good night, Lilith."

He doffed his Stetson, watched while she entered the house and closed the door, then he bent his steps toward the bunkhouse.

17. Shots in the Night

When he entered the bunkhouse Quist saw Garrity seated at a desk, working at some sort of account book. He'd been scribbling figures on a pad of writing paper, which he pushed to one side when Quist came in. He nodded shortly but didn't say anything. Palmer, Moody, and Judkins were engaged in a three-handed game of seven-up. Skillet Osborn was tinkering with the wick mechanism from a kerosene lamp. They spoke to Quist. The card players invited him to take a hand, but he refused with thanks and started to manufacture a cigarette as he sat down to watch the game.

Garrity rose abruptly to his feet and said, "I'd like to talk to you a minute, Quist—outside."

Quist eyed him a moment, then nodded, lighted his cigarette, and followed Garrity through the bunkhouse doorway. Garrity led the way down toward the corrals, out of earshot of the men in the bunkhouse. The night was brilliant with moonlight, and when Garrity stopped and turned around, Quist saw his face was working with emotion. He said quietly, "What's on your mind, Stark?"

Garrity replied nervously, "You told me a few days ago that you'd see I got a fair break when I got ready to talk."

"That still goes," Quist answered quietly. "I figured you were about ready to spill something."

"Dang it, you're right. I can't stand it any more. I came here—I've lived on the level—"

"Whoa! Not so fast, Stark. What's this all about? Now don't get excited. Just go ahead and talk easy. Is it something about Harmon's death?"

"And Blackmer's and that train wreck. That other wreck. Quist, I'll go crazy if I don't square myself." His tones held a note of hysteria.

"I'm giving you a chance to tell me," Quist said, even-toned.

"You'll send me to prison—maybe worse."

"That's to be seen, Stark. If you talk straight—"

"I'll talk straight. Here's something to show you I'm not lying. I'll tell you now that there's a scheme to wipe you out."

"Who's going to do it?"

"Voit—the Egg."

"When? How?" The words came swiftly from Quist's lips.

"The first chance he gets. If not tonight, then he'll shoot you from the rear some other time. Tonight I was to have held you in the open door of the bunkhouse where you'd make a good target—"

And that was as far as Garrity went.

From the brush, on past the corral, came the sharp crack of a Winchester. Quist dove for the earth and reached it even before Garrity reeled and fell. A second shot reached Garrity's

221

crumpled figure, but by this time Quist's forty-four had leaped from the shoulder holster and a stream of flame was spurting from its muzzle.

A third shot threw dust and gravel in Quist's face, momentarily blinding him, then he heard the rapid drumming of a pony's hoofs through the brush.

Men poured through the bunkhouse door. By the time the cowhands reached Quist he was shoving fresh cartridges into the cylinder of his six-shooter. Black powder smoke still drifted on the night air.

"What in blazes happened?" Moody demanded as he sprinted up. The other three men were voicing similar remarks.

"Come on, saddle up!" Quist snapped. "We've got to—" He stopped. "No, let it go. That hombre's got too big a start. Sounded like he was heading for Cenotaph, and he'd lose us, once he got there."

"But what happened?" Judkins asked.

"Somebody fired on us from the brush," Quist said shortly. He knelt at Garrity's side. "Go get some water. We can talk later."

Even while he was examining the unconscious Garrity, he heard Lilith's voice from the house and the reply of somebody near his side, but he didn't get what was said. By the light of the moon he was making a rapid examination of Garrity.

"Stark hit bad?" Osborn asked.

"Dang' bad," Quist said grimly. "Once in the body, once in the head."

"Is he going to die?"

"Probably."

Judkins came racing up with a bucket of water and a lantern. "You any idea who done it?" he asked.

"Cripes no," Quist grunted shortly.

"But Stark didn't have any enemies—"

"Maybe the slugs were meant for me."

Moody said belligerently, "Darn' funny you brought Stark out here and—"

"Don't make any more mistakes, Moody, like you fellows did last week," Quist said, hard-voiced. "It was Garrity asked me to come out here. I think he knew something about Harmon's death. He was just starting to say something when the shooting started. Now, you bustards shut up and don't bother me."

The men fell silent. There wasn't much Quist could do with Garrity's head. It looked bad. The man's breath was coming with difficulty. There was blood on his lips.

Quist looked up suddenly to see Lilith standing near. "Isn't Caroline out here? She's not in the house."

Quist swore under his breath and stood up. "She's not? I thought she'd gone to bed."

"So did I," Lilith frowned. "Is Stark hurt badly?"

"It's plenty bad," Quist replied. "But what about Caroline?" He saw now that Lilith had on a long coat over some sort of loose-fitting garment.

"There's Miss Trent now," Moody said suddenly.

They all looked around to see Caroline approaching from the far side of the corral. "Heavens, Caroline! Where ever have you been?" Lilith asked.

The girl was fully dressed in her riding clothes. Her face looked white. "I saw—saw him," she stammered through chattering teeth.

"All right, we'll hear that later," Quist said impatiently. "We've got to do something about Garrity and do it quick. I don't think he'll last until we can get a doctor out here. We'll have to take a long chance and take him to town. Lilith, give us all the blankets you can spare. Moody, you hitch up the lightest wagon you've got around here. I hate like the devil to move Garrity, but it's his only chance. Maybe if we can get him to Doc Lang . . ."

He left the words unfinished. Lilith was hurrying to the ranch house. There was a light in the kitchen there now, and the Mexican girl was standing in the open doorway. The other men had rushed to get out a wagon and harness and a pair of horses. Caroline started to follow Lilith, but Quist seized her arm. "Now," he said, "tell me what you were doing outside."

"I don't like your tone, Mr. Quist," the girl said angrily. "You act as though I'd had something to do with the shooting." Her anger had banished the girl's fright, which was what Quist had been striving for.

"Never mind my tone," he snapped. "I asked a question. Stark Garrity may be dying. There's been too much murderous lead spilled around here. I'm going to know why, if possible. Now talk up."

Caroline lifted her chin defiantly. "You're not the only one who wants to find out things. You haven't accomplished much, so far as I can see, Mr. Quist. I've as much right to try as you have—"

Quist's eyes widened. "You mean to tell me you were playing detective?"

"Why not?" Caroline demanded hotly.

Quist relaxed. "All right," he said wearily, "give me the story."

Caroline told him briefly what had happened. She'd gone to bed, but couldn't get to sleep, then had risen and sat at her open bedroom window. "I heard Lilith come in and go to her room. Then I thought—I wasn't really sure—I thought I saw a rider moving through the brush. If it was a rider I thought maybe I could follow him and see what he did. My riding clothes were handy, and I got dressed quickly and slipped through the window. Once I'd reached the brush I couldn't see nor hear anybody—"

"You little fool," Quist grated savagely. "You might have been shot."

"If a detective's always afraid of getting shot he'll never learn anything," Caroline said tartly. "I moved through the brush as quietly as I could, then stopped to listen. I saw you and Stark Garrity stop and talk. Then, not far from where I waited, the shots were fired. Then you started firing your gun—I guess it was you. I figured that was no time for me to put in an appearance, so I crouched down and waited for the shooting to stop. While I was waiting, the rider dashed past, not five yards from me, and I saw his face plainly for a moment in the moonlight—"

"Who was it?" Quist snapped.

"That man they call the Egg—Hugo Voit."

Quist drew a long breath. " 'Fools rush in,' " he commenced a quotation, then paused. "All right, Caroline, I'll admit you have accomplished something. Now we've got a witness to this last shooting. But don't ever take such a chance again, do you hear?"

The girl didn't answer, and Quist again bent by Garrity's side. Caroline stopped beside him, wet her handkerchief in the bucket of water and commenced to bathe the unconscious man's head. Quist said, "You'd better get back to bed, girl."

"You're going to town, aren't you?" Caroline asked. Quist nodded. "I might as well return now, too," Caroline went on. "I'll go gather up a few things. Have one of the men saddle my horse, please. I won't hold you up a minute. I promise."

Quist didn't reply. The wagon had been up to the house gathering blankets. More were brought from the bunkhouse and placed in the bed of the wagon when the horses were drawn to a stop not far from the spot where Garrity lay. Osborn saddled horses at Quist's request, then they lifted and placed Garrity on the thickly padded wagon bed and placed blankets on top of him.

By the time they were ready to start, Caroline and Lilith had arrived from the house. Quist said, "Moody, you drive the wagon. Judkins, you get in beside Garrity. Keep him from being thrown about as much as possible. Moody, you've really got to drive. Get to Doc Lang's as quick as the Lord will let you, regardless how much bumping around Garrity gets. It's our only chance. If we can deliver him to Doc alive, he might pull through."

The wagon was already moving out of the yard. Caroline was in the saddle. Quist put foot into the stirrup and swung up on his own horse. They called good-by to Lilith and swept off in pursuit of the already swiftly running wagon.

18. Man Hunt

It was about nine the following morning when Quist entered the Stopgap Restaurant. The breakfast rush was over, and the place was empty except for one man lingering over his coffee at the counter, not far from the entrance. Quist took a seat at a table in the far rear corner. Within a few minutes Caroline emerged from the kitchen in fresh gingham. She nodded to Quist. "I thought you might be in this morning," she said soberly, "and I saved some wheat-cake batter." She turned back to the kitchen again.

The man at the counter rose and rapped some money against his coffee cup. Caroline came out of the kitchen, received payment for the man's food, and stood watching him leave. When the door had closed she came over to Quist's table with some silverware. Quist said, eying her quizzically, "Where do I stand on your list this morning, Miss Detective?"

"If there ever was a list," Caroline said bitterly, "I think I'd tear it up. All this killing and shooting! What's wrong with men, anyway? Women don't act that way." Her voice softened. "You don't look as though you'd even gone to bed. What's happened? How's Stark Garrity doing?"

"He's still alive. Delirious. I've spent most of the night at Doc Lang's. Gathered a little sleep off

228

and on, waiting to see if Garrity would be able to talk. What do you know about him that you can, or will, tell me?"

"Very little. He came to work for Uncle Gid a number of years ago. He was a good foreman."

"Uh-huh. Has Pete Dewitt been in this morning?"

"Not yet. That's unusual, too."

"Pete's right busy. I saw him at Doc's about five this morning for a few minutes. He hasn't located Voit yet, though Voit was seen in town last evening about an hour before we arrived with Garrity. Now the man seems to have disappeared. Pete feels he's still in town someplace. Who's George around here?"

"George who?"

"I don't know. In his delirium Garrity was apparently trying to tell me something about somebody named George and a railroad wreck. It didn't seem to make sense."

"I don't make anything of it," Caroline said. "Does Dr. Lang think Garrity will live?"

"He doubts it. Doc Lang gave me the devil for moving Garrity last night. On the other hand Doc admits, considering the nature of Garrity's wounds, that Garrity wouldn't have lived until we could get Doc out to the Thunderbird. Taking Garrity in to Doc probably saved an hour or more in getting him medical attention. He was unconscious when I left, though now and then he'd rouse and babble a few words. Doc doesn't know if he'll regain clearheadedness or not before he dies, but he's staying close in case Garrity does."

Caroline shook her head and went to the kitchen, returning within a few minutes with coffee and wheat cakes. Quist started to eat, and Caroline brought him an extra supply of butter. She had started away when Quist caught her arm and said, "Sit down a minute. I've got questions to ask."

Caroline eyed him steadily a minute, then seated herself across the table. Quist said, savoring a mouthful of wheat cakes, "I've decided to start a list of my own. Yours will be the only name on it." He chuckled at the look in her eyes as she started to rise. "No, sit down. I'll try to be serious, though a breakfast like this should be enjoyed without serious thoughts. But I want to clear up certain matters. Why did you leave the Thunderbird when you were living there with your uncle?"

"I don't think it's any of your business," Caroline said tartly.

"Look, Caroline," Quist said tersely, "the Thunderbird Ranch and Gid Harmon are someway involved in a lot of killing that's taken place in these parts. I'm making that my business. A court of law could make you talk, you know. It might be pleasanter telling me about it." He took a swallow of coffee.

Caroline looked annoyed. "All right. I don't suppose it makes any great difference anyway. Uncle Gid wanted me to marry Hoddy Belvard."

Quist whistled softly. "So that's how it was. And you didn't like Belvard?"

"I had nothing in particular against him. He used to call on me when I lived at the Thunderbird and we took rides together. But I never dreamed of marrying him. And so I said 'No.' And Uncle Gid didn't like it. He had some idea of joining the Thunderbird with the HB-Connected and letting Belvard run the whole outfit—"

"Just a minute. Did Belvard approach you on the subject of marriage before he spoke to Harmon about it?"

Caroline shook her head. "It was Uncle Gid who told me first. He admitted he was surprised when Belvard spoke to him, but thought it would be a good match for me. The longer he dwelled on it, the more he commenced to think it his own idea. That's why he was so angry when I refused to accept Hoddy Belvard."

"And you quarreled?" he asked through a mouthful of food.

Caroline smiled dryly. "That's an understatement. I'm afraid I lost my temper and said things I shouldn't have."

"About what?" Quist asked, setting down his cup of coffee.

"The way Uncle Gid tried to dominate

everybody. He thought because he had money he could get anything he wanted. I couldn't see things his way, so I packed up and left the Thunderbird. I was heartbroken for a time, but with a little money my mother had left me I opened the Stopgap, and that kept me too busy to do any weeping."

"Didn't you and Gid ever make up?"

"Not really. He came in the Stopgap once and offered to buy the place if I'd return to the Thunderbird. I refused and he stomped out swearing."

"Then your trouble with Gid never had anything to do with Lilith?" He poised a forkful of wheat cake before his lips.

Caroline's eyes widened. "Heavens, no! Our quarrel took place long before he'd ever met Lilith."

"And you never went back to the Thunderbird again?"

"Of course I did. Uncle Gid sent Lilith in to ask me if I wouldn't come and stay at the ranch with them. Of course I refused, but Lilith and I became friends, and I used to ride out to see her now and then."

"Gid didn't object?" He chewed rapidly for a moment.

"Not at all, but he always managed to leave the house when I arrived. Maybe he didn't like to be reminded of our quarrel, or maybe, in view of the fact that he and Belvard weren't so friendly after a time, he hated to admit that perhaps I'd been right. We spoke, but that was about all."

"The day Gid Harmon was buried, you didn't arrive back from the cemetery with Lilith and Garrity. Why?"

Caroline looked startled. "You have checked up on me, haven't you? Well, I don't know as I'll tell you, Mr. Quist. You act as though you suspected me of—"

"Look, Caroline, do I have to remind you again that a court of law could make you talk?" Quist said patiently. "It's been remarked that you had time to leave the cemetery and ride to the Thunderbird the day Blackmer was killed."

"Why—I—never!" Caroline gasped. "I didn't ride in the direction of the Thunderbird at all—"

"Where did you go?" Quist persisted, lifting his coffee cup.

"Why, no place in particular. I just rode and rode—" The girl paused suddenly, then continued earnestly, "You probably won't believe this, after the way I've talked against Uncle Gid, but when I saw him being buried I started remembering all the kind things he'd done for me, and I just had to get away where—where nobody would see me cry. So I got my horse at the livery and—"

"Rode and rode and cried and cried," Quist finished.

"Something like that." The girl looked miserable.

Quist's lips twitched. "All right, brighten up. Wheat cakes or no wheat cakes, I won't ask for a place on your list if you're going to look like that."

The girl smiled, moist-eyed. "You believe me, then?"

"I haven't said I disbelieve you," he evaded, then laughed softly and took another mouthful of food. "You know"—carelessly—"I always did admire your shade of red hair. Probably that's why I recognized it so quickly when I found these on a chair at the Thunderbird." He took out his wallet, removed a folded cigarette paper, opened it and displayed the two strands of reddish hair. "It's my guess you were out to the Thunderbird the day Gid Harmon met his death."

Caroline stared at the hairs, then raised her eyes to meet Quist's gaze. "I suppose this is more suspicion piling up against me," she said in a tight voice.

"But you were out there that day," he persisted swiftly. For the moment his food lay untouched.

"Yes, I went out there that day," she admitted.

"Why?" he snapped.

"Do you know, Mr. Quist," the girl said coldly, "I don't like your attitude! I accepted a certain amount of domination from Uncle Gid—but I don't intend to have you bullying me. Oh yes, I know—a court of law can make me talk. Well, Mr. Quist, maybe it can and maybe it can't."

And looking at her determined chin, Quist himself commenced to experience doubts on the subject. He said mockingly, "Miss Trent, would you mind telling me just why you went to the Thunderbird that day?"

Caroline flushed and her lips tightened. "If I tell you, it is only because I've nothing at all to hide. And you may or may not believe me—just as you wish. I've told you my relations with Uncle Gid weren't always pleasant, when I was living at the Thunderbird. Well, one day he found that one of his tax receipts was missing. As I always took care of such things for him, he held me responsible. I said he hadn't given it to me; he insisted he had. There was quite an argument. I still don't remember him giving it to me. He may have just dropped it into a drawer where I kept some papers of his with some papers of mine. I've heard since that he got some sort of strongbox for his papers—"

"You found the receipt eventually?"

"The day before Uncle Gid died. I was going through some old letters and things—and there was his receipt. In view of the quarrel we'd had, I decided to take the receipt out to him the very next day. And that's what took me to the Thunderbird." She studied Quist for a moment, while he chewed meditatively. "You don't believe me, do you?"

"On the contrary. It's too simple not to be true. If you'd been lying, you'd have made up a much more involved tale."

"Thank you for your confidence," Caroline said sarcastically.

Quist chuckled good-naturedly. "Did anybody ever tell you you went around with a chip on your shoulder? Maybe Uncle Gid wasn't solely to blame for those arguments."

"I'm sorry, Mr. Quist. I've never stated he was solely to blame."

"Why has nobody ever mentioned before your being out there?"

"I don't know. I didn't think much about it. I thought perhaps either Lilith or Garrity had mentioned it. After the inquest it just slipped my mind."

"I suppose." Quist frowned and drained his coffee cup. Caroline went to refill it and sat down again. Quist said, when she had returned, "Who was at the Thunderbird when you arrived?"

"I didn't see anyone at first. Then, just as I dismounted before the gallery, Stark Garrity came out of the house and closed the door behind him. Come to think of it, he acted sort of queer that day. I asked where Lilith was, and he said she'd gone riding and didn't know just when she'd be back. He added that Uncle Gid had gone to Tanzburg to see Dr. Jorge."

"What time was this?"

Caroline considered. "I can't say exactly. Probably around four—maybe earlier, or later. I didn't pay much attention."

"Then what happened?" Quist was rolling a cigarette now.

"Garrity asked what I wanted. I told him I had a paper that belonged to Uncle Gid. Garrity said he'd give it to Lilith—"

"That was a slip of the tongue," Quist said quickly.

"What?" Caroline frowned.

"Ordinarily, Garrity would have said 'Gid'—not 'Lilith.' Unconsciously he was admitting that Gid was already dead. Go on, what happened next?"

"I said I'd wait a few minutes to see if Lilith returned. Garrity rather acted as though he didn't want me there, but I brushed past him and entered the house and sat down to wait. I may have waited five minutes or more, then I decided I'd better get back to the Stopgap for the supper hour. I gave Garrity the receipt, and he went out to my horse with me. And—I guess that's all. Next thing I knew, I heard Uncle Gid had committed—"

"Caroline," Quist interrupted, "think carefully now. How did that room look when you were there?"

"Look?" Caroline appeared surprised. "Why, just about the way it always does, I guess."

"Think hard. Were the chairs in their usual places? Had any of the rugs been moved? Or any of the furniture?"

237

"No-o," Caroline frowned. "I don't see—wait, there was something different. That big thunderbird rug wasn't on the wall."

"Did you see it at all?" Quist held the match poised before his cigarette.

"Yes, I remember now. It lay in a heap between that oak table and the wall, over near the window. Come to think of it, I remember mentioning it to Garrity, and he said Lilith had had it taken down—that there were moths getting in it—or she had been cleaning or something."

"That clinches it!" Quist exclaimed. He lighted his cigarette, drew deeply on the smoke, smiling triumphantly.

"I don't understand. Clinches what?"

"Caroline, you're a sweetheart! Things are a lot clearer now. Thank God for that lost tax receipt."

"Well, it's nice to be a sweetheart," and the color rose in Caroline's face, "but I still don't understand."

"You will in time. I just want to—" He paused as Pete Dewitt entered. "Any luck, Pete?"

"Not a bit," Pete said wearily. "I'm damned—excuse it, Car'line—if I can figure where the coyote is hiding out."

Caroline asked what coyote Pete was referring to, and rose to bring him a cup of coffee. When she came back to the table Pete thanked her and said, "Hugo Voit. That was a pretty nervy thing you did last night, Car'line, according to what

Greg says. I haven't had time to get in and tell you before. Yes,"—in answer to Quist's question—"I got the warrant for Voit's arrest. But where is he? We know he came to town last night, and he took a bed at that Cowmen's Rest joint up the street. We took his horse that was standing out in front of the place, so we know he didn't get away on that—"

Quist said, "Good Lord! You took his horse!"

Pete stared at Quist a minute, and a slow burn of crimson commenced to flow through his features. "Gawd! What a fool I am," he said hopelessly. "Of course, I should have left the horse where it was. Voit probably looked out a window, saw the horse was gone, and suspicioned we were already on his trail. And then he probably ducked out the back way."

"On some stolen horse," Quist said.

"I should be kicked from here to Kansas City," Pete said bitterly. "No, he won't get away on another horse. I don't think he will, leastwise. I figured he might try something of the sort, so I've deputized quite a crew. I've got a man at the end of every street leading out of town. At any rate he won't *ride* out of Cenotaph if he makes a getaway. And every man has orders to shoot to kill on sight, and not take chances."

"Quite a man hunt you've started," Quist commented.

"Started, yes, when maybe it's too late." Pete

looked downcast. "If I'd had an ounce of brains I could have him by this time. Maybe he did get away before daylight. Still, nobody's reported a stolen horse, and I've been moving around this town plenty, ever since you brought Garrity to Doc's last night. By the way, I stopped there on my way here. No, there's no change in Garrity. Mumbles something now and then, but he don't make any more sense than he did."

"We might try riding out to the HB-Connected," Quist proposed.

"I doubt it would do any good. Hoddy Belvard rode in to town about half an hour ago. I asked him about the Egg. Belvard says he hasn't seen Voit since last Saturday."

"I think," Quist said slowly, "Belvard's a liar."

"Want I should arrest him?" Pete asked quickly.

"No, let it ride as is for the present. But you remember, I told you Garrity mentioned a plot to rub me out, just before he was shot. Belvard was probably in on that, and I think Garrity was over to the HB-Connected yesterday. When Voit saw that Garrity didn't light me against the bunkhouse door last night, he realized Garrity wasn't going through with the plan. So he shot Garrity, hoping to kill off evidence. When the time comes we'll pick up Belvard, but if we arrested him now he'd just deny knowing anything about anything. And we might have a tough time proving he was wrong."

"Oh yes," Pete said, "I got a reply from Sheriff Egan at Tanzburg this morning. He hadn't replied before, as Dr. Jorge was out of town for a few days and just recently got back. Jorge says that Gid Harmon never called on him."

"That's one more bit of evidence, but I don't know what we'll do with it," Quist said slowly.

"And there's a telegram for you down to the station," Pete went on. "I wanted to take it, but the telegrapher didn't want to give it to me, so long as you're in town, so I didn't force matters."

Quist rose to his feet, followed by Pete. Caroline said, "That breakfast is on the Stopgap, Mr. Quist."

Quist said thanks, added, "You're still a sweetheart," and hurried from the restaurant, followed by Dewitt.

"That Caroline girl," Quist observed, "seems to have a will of her own."

"There's a lot of men around town," Pete said wryly, "including myself, who've never been able to persuade her to change it."

They strode on. Quist said suddenly, "I wonder . . ."

"What now?"

"When I was at Doc's, Garrity kept mumbling something about wrecks and somebody named George."

"Yeah, I heard him too."

"What about Dr. Jorge over at Tanzburg?"

"You mean the two names?"

241

"They sound alike."

Pete laughed shortly. "Ezra Jorge has the name of being a good veterinarian. And he's had some success with treating human ailments—sprains and the like."

"Do you know him?"

"Not very well. I've seen him once or twice. Last I heard he was spending much of his time at a small farm he owns, someplace north of Tanzburg, trying to work out a new cure for glanders in horses."

"It's about time somebody tried something else besides the usual kill-or-cure systems. That bleeding and purging has ruined more horses—"

Pete said suddenly, "Anything new, Luke?"

Luke Rutson was approaching from across the street. "Not a blasted thing, Pete." He nodded to Quist, then continued, "If Voit's still in town, he's sure well hid. There's been three trains through since midnight, but only one of those stopped, and we watched that careful. The boys went through that bunch of boxcars on the spur, t'other side of the station. He wa'n't in none of them. And there ain't nary a horse going to leave town 'thout it gets spotted. Every road out is covered."

"Might be he's hiding out on a roof someplace," Quist suggested.

"It could be," Rutson nodded. "But we've thought of that, and already investigated a lot of roofs he might have climbed to. We learned one thing. Saturday night when he was in town, he bought a box of forty-four ca'tridges at Perkins' General Store."

"Forty-fours, eh?" Quist said. He looked at Pete.

Pete said, "That makes it look like it was Voit that killed Blackmer and took your gun, out to the Thunderbird, last Thursday, Greg. I never knew him to carry anything but a forty-five."

"But you've got that forty-five now," Quist reminded. "Maybe Voit and I have something in common: we both like the same gun. And it proves Voit was in town Saturday night, even if we couldn't seem to find him."

"Perkins says it was late when Voit rode in. He was at the door of the store, just ready to close up. Voit got his ca'tridges, got on his horse, and rode out of town again."

The men talked a few minutes more, then Pete and Quist continued on to the station. Pete waited on the platform while Quist went inside. Within a few minutes Quist emerged from the building. Pete immediately saw that Quist had important news. "What is it?" the new sheriff asked.

For reply, Quist handed him the telegram, which read:

Have located mules north of Tanzburg. You better come fast loaded for bear.

CARSTAIRS.

19. A Running Fight

Dewitt frowned and looked up. "Who's Carstairs?"

"The T. N. & A. S. wrecking boss, working out of Puma Junction. He wanted to help running down those freight thieves. You see, the brakie who was killed in that last wreck was Carstairs' brother-in-law. I'd say, judging from the way that message is worded, that he'd located the thieves. . . . Say, didn't you say Doc Jorge had a farm north of Tanzburg?"

Dewitt nodded. "Maybe there is something in the similarity of those names we were talking about, Greg. Well, what's the next move?"

"I've got to get to Tanzburg. There's a freight comes through here at ten forty-seven. We can flag that down—"

"I'm going," Dewitt announced suddenly.

"You figure it's not worth while staying here to hunt for Voit?"

"I've done all that's possible. Luke Rutson can carry on in my place. He's got plenty help, in case they do run down Voit."

"I'd sure be pleased to have you, Pete."

"I'll be pleased to go. Remember, that wrecking job was done in Dawson County, so running down the thieves is part of my job. It looks like we'd have some riding ahead. How'd it be if I shoot a telegram to Sheriff Egan and have him round up some riders for us, so we'll be ready to go when we reach Tanzburg?"

"Now that's an idea, Pete. You'll justify your existence yet."

Pete scowled. "After the way I've let Voit slip through my hands, I'll only believe that when it's an accomplished fact, Greg." He consulted his watch. "We can get that freight at ten forty-seven, you say?"

Quist nodded. "It'll get us into Tanzburg around one this afternoon."

"Fine. I'll go send that message to Sheriff Egan, then give instructions to Rutson to handle things in Cenotaph while I'm gone."

He started toward the station. Quist joined him, with the remark, "I'll send a wire to Carstairs, too, to join us at Puma Junction. I know he'll want a hand in this."

At ten forty-seven, when the freight was flagged to a stop, the conductor was at first inclined to resent the lost time and carrying of passengers, but when he learned Gregory Quist's identity a quick change came over his manner. Quist and Dewitt settled on one of the cushioned seats running along the sides of the caboose, and the train again got under way. One brakeman was up in the cupola; another was fussing over the coffeepot on the small stove in the center of the caboose. The conductor told Dewitt and Quist to make themselves comfortable and returned to the papers on his desk where he'd been engrossed in making out his wheel report when the train was halted.

The brakeman at the stove asked Quist and Dewitt if they'd have coffee. Quist accepted, but Dewitt said something about using this opportunity to catch up on the sleep he'd failed to get the previous night. With which statement he stretched out on the seat and was almost instantly fast asleep. The brakie was curious as to the passengers' journey, but when Quist failed to display any inclination for conversation, the man took the hint and fell silent.

Quist rolled and smoked a cigarette. The train rocked along, mile after mile after mile, the trucks itemizing their monotonous *clickety-clack-click, clickety-clack-click* as they sped over the fast-retreating rails. The country on either side slipped by in an undulating, unbroken, blurred expanse of sand and sagebrush, grass and cacti. Occasionally, when the long freight train whipped around a curve, Quist had a brief glimpse of the distant Sangre de Esteban Mountains as they receded swiftly into hazy, purple remoteness.

It became stuffy in the caboose as the miles unrolled behind them, and the brakeman opened the rear door. Hot air, wind, dust, and cinders swirled through the interior of the car, fluttering the conductor's papers and bringing from that worthy a sharp expletive along with a sharper order. The door was again slammed shut.

Pete was snoring steadily now, his prone form rolling a trifle with each lurch of the speeding train. That, combined with the almost hypnotic quality of the *clickety-clack-click, clickety-clack-click* in Quist's ears, and the close atmosphere of the caboose, commenced to have its effect upon him: he started to grow drowsy, and was aroused only by something uttered by the brakeman at his observation post in the cupola.

The other brakeman called up, "What'd you say, Del?"

The voice again came down from the cupola: "It looks like we've got a 'bo aboard. I just caught a glimpse of a hat between the cars up ahead."

"Dangit! I thought we cleaned off those hoboes after we left Loboville."

"We might have picked up something when we stopped at Cenotaph, Charlie."

Charlie swore and started toward the rear door, muttering something that had to do with "kicking the breeches off any darned tramp that thought he could beat his way—"

He paused, feeling Quist's hand on his arm. Quist said, "Let me go up there and take a look. I've got an idea."

The brakie hesitated and glanced at Quist's boots. "Those high-heels won't be convenient for traveling that running board."

"That's my risk," Quist commenced shortly. "If—"

From the cupola came further words: "Yeah, there's a feller up ahead—fat man, but he's sure nimble on his pins."

"I'll take care of that," Quist said abruptly, pushing the brakie to one side and jerking open the door.

He stepped on the platform, reached to the iron-runged ladder, and swiftly climbed to the caboose roof.

The train was pulling on a long upgrade for the moment, and the engine far up ahead was puffing furiously. For an instant Quist braced himself on hands and knees, then, rising, made his way around the cupola, holding fast to the iron grips on the cupola roof. Far ahead, through brief breaks in the smoke, he could see stretching a long line of boxcars, rolling and jerking with the movement of the train.

Smoke and cinders swept back in a gale that obscured Quist's vision. Quickly he dropped flat on the running board, hoping to see beneath the smoke. For an instant the view cleared slightly, and there, several cars ahead, he sighted a pair of traveling feet, though the rest of the body was screened from view.

The feet reached the end of the car, leaped lightly across the intervening gap between cars; here the owner of the feet momentarily lost balance and crouched close to the swaying roof of the car. In that moment Greg Quist recognized the bulky egg-shaped form of Hugo Voit.

Quist raised his voice, shouting to Voit to halt. Whether or not Voit caught Quist's voice above the noise of the moving train is debatable. At any rate, something warned him: his head came around, there was a quick movement of his right hand. A slug whined perilously close to Quist's lean body.

Quist's gun was already out of its shoulder holster, its muzzle spurting flame and smoke, but accurate shooting was difficult from the roof of the jolting boxcar. Then smoke from the engine again swirled down, blotting both men from view.

Quist started forward, moving with as much caution as possible under the circumstances. The wind tore at his hat, and he jerked it more firmly on his head. Making all speed possible, he moved three cars nearer the front of the train on hands and knees, rising each time to leap across the space between cars.

Again the atmosphere cleared, but this time Voit was not to be seen; he was probably hiding someplace at the end of one of the cars. Gun in hand, Quist proceeded on, virtually feeling his way through thick gusts of smoke and cinders which were blown away from time to time, only to envelop him again.

Then, four cars ahead, he caught a flash of

crimson-orange flame and instinctively dropped flat, one hand clutching at the running board. He lost his grip, rolled to the edge of the roof, but managed to regain his balance and scramble back. The spot he had occupied but an instant before now displayed a clean gouge in the roof, where a leaden slug had splintered the wood.

A cloud of smoke billowed down, and some distance back, Quist heard Pete Dewitt's voice. On either side, blurred by the drifting smoke, a swiftly unrolling panorama of range country flashed past. Quist made his way forward through a sooty gray-black cloud that choked lungs and throat and nostrils. He reached the end of a car, glanced down. There was nothing to be seen except the jolting coupling and a confused view of swiftly vanishing ties. It was the same with the next half-dozen cars.

Once something came through the blinding veil of smoke and grazed slightly Quist's left cheekbone. He was never sure if it was a leaden slug or a large cinder. Abruptly the train struck another curve, winding to avoid the end of a long rocky ridge, and the smoke was whisked suddenly away.

There, not three car lengths ahead and running along the top walks, headed in the direction of the locomotive, was Hugo Voit. It was amazing, the speed at which his weighty form negotiated nimbly the running boards stretched along the tops of cars. The man's lightness of foot was almost unbelievable.

"Dang!" Quist grated. "If he can do that, so can I."

Flinging discretion to the winds, Quist started swiftly in pursuit of the fleeing Voit.

After a minute Voit glanced back and saw that Quist was gaining on him. Quickly leaping the gap between two cars, the man whirled, dropped to one knee and took careful aim, leveling his gun barrel across his left arm. A lance of fire spurted from the gun muzzle.

Still running in pursuit, Quist felt his own gun jerk in his hand and saw Voit sprawl sidewise at the edge of the boxcar roof. Even as he went down, Voit sent a shot winging viciously in Quist's direction. Something plucked at Quist's coat sleeve, and he knew the bullet had come close.

Voit was just struggling to his feet when Quist's next shot found its target. Voit sagged back, then as the train gave a sudden lurch he was whipped forward at the edge of the car. For a moment his hands clawed frantically at the wooden surface of the roof, before his tremendous weight carried him on, and he disappeared, plunging like a plummet into the space between his car and the one following, just as another cloud of smoke billowed down to envelop Quist.

Now, for the first time, he realized the train was losing motion as the brakes were applied.

Quist took a long breath, sat back on the top walk, and methodically commenced shoving fresh loads into his six-shooter. Pete Dewitt came bursting through the drifting smoke as the train stopped abruptly, coincident with the grinding of brakes and the hissing of steam.

Pete exclaimed, "What the hell!"

"It was Voit," Quist explained. "He fell between the cars a minute or so back."

"Alive?"

"I doubt it—now."

"I'll be darned. I woke up just as you were leaving. It took me a few moments to get awake—"

At that moment they were joined by the conductor and brakies, their features working with excitement. Quist gave brief details in response to their questioning. "I think," he added, "Voit must have been working his way up to the locomotive, with the intention of holding up the fireman and engineer and making them stop to let him off before Puma Junction was reached."

"He must have been hiding someplace near the station, at Cenotaph, when this train rolled in," Pete said. "He knew we had him trapped in town—"

"Well, let's go see what happened," Quist said.

They climbed down from the boxcar, followed by the conductor and the brakemen. Up near the engine, the fireman was calling back to learn why the conductor had had the train halted.

Some distance to the rear they came upon Voit's mangled body. The man had apparently been sucked beneath the wheels in his fall, and whether Quist's aim had reached a vital spot or whether the car wheels had killed Voit, Quist wasn't enough interested to determine. One of the brakemen ran back and procured a tarpaulin, and Voit's body was wrapped and carried to the caboose. While they were waiting for the tarpaulin, Quist and Dewitt searched along the tracks and finally found the six-shooter Voit had used. It appeared to be unharmed by the fall, and Quist instantly identified it as his own forty-four six-shooter which had disappeared the day Blackmer had been killed.

"This," Quist said, "pretty well ties Blackmer's murder to the Egg." He examined the cylinder; all loads had been exploded, but whether or not Voit had carried the hammer on an empty shell couldn't be determined, and the noise and confusion attendant upon the running train had made it virtually impossible to distinguish the sounds of shots. Quist stuck the gun in the waistband of his trousers with the remark that before long another gun might come in handy.

The journey was resumed, after a time, and the train was again running swiftly, to make up lost time, toward Puma Junction, with the grisly burden, wrapped in tarpaulin, stretched on the floor of the caboose.

At Puma Junction, Voit's body was removed from the train, Quist having previously gone through the clothing and removed such papers and other items as were found in the pockets. These he placed in his pocket for future scrutiny, after a brief survey had given him some idea of the nature of the papers, which were somewhat messy and required a bit of cleaning before they'd be in fit condition for a thorough examination.

Pete Dewitt had left the caboose long enough to send a telegram to Luke Rutson with news of Voit's death. And it was at Puma Junction that Carstairs and Deputy Steve Wilson joined Quist and Pete. Carstairs entered the caboose carrying two Winchesters. There was a six-shooter on his hip, and his face was grim. Quist introduced him to Dewitt, who already knew Wilson, and the men shook hands.

"Was that a body they just took off?" Wilson asked.

Quist told them of the fight with Voit. Carstairs said, "Geez! The action must have been hot for a few minutes."

Quist smiled thinly. "Any shivering I did wasn't from chilly weather." He indicated the two Winchesters Carstairs had toted in. "Are you aiming to use both those smoke-poles?"

"Figured maybe you'd like to have one," Carstairs replied. "I bought some extra ca'tridges, too. Same caliber as your six-shooter."

"Fine, thanks," Quist nodded. "Now, Carstairs, what about these mules? I want to know how you learned about 'em."

The train was traveling through open country by this time, with Tanzburg the next stop on the timetable. Carstairs commenced: "Well, it was sort of just luck, in a way. I'd taken time off from my work to sort of scout around, but I didn't learn nothing. Steve here, he was up against a blank wall, too, for all his riding."

"And I'd talked it over with Sheriff Egan," Deputy Wilson broke in, "and he'd done inquiring, here and there, but it was no go. Mules just didn't 'pear to exist in our neck of the range."

Carstairs continued his story: "Then who should blow in on me, last night, but Brother Ed—" He broke off to explain about Brother Ed: "Ed's one of these here itinerant preachers who goes riding about the country, preaching here and there wherever folks will listen. He ain't got no regular church, but buries and marries and baptizes wherever he happens to be. Up until last night I ain't seen Ed in nigh onto five years— he's been clear up north to Montana and other places."

Carstairs paused to stuff tobacco into a smelly brier, lighted it and puffed meditatively for a few moments. The train was running through mountainous terrain now, just passing through a steep-walled rock canyon, the sides of which seemed to hold and augment the steady *clickety-clack-click* of the trucks passing along the tracks.

"Anyway," Carstairs went on, "I was right glad to see Ed and hear about his travels. Seems that as he was riding south, heading for Tanzburg, one night he got lost and took a trail that led up a long winding canyon. It was quite late when he arrived at what he thought was a farm or a ranch. Well, there was quite a large number of hands around, and Ed thought they acted sort of suspicious. First he was told they couldn't put him up for the night, but Ed argued them out of that, so finally they let him sleep in a barn. Well, them goldarn mountain nightingales kept him awake all night long, and after the moon come up, Ed saw there was a big corral milling-full of animals—"

"Mules, eh?" Quist said interestedly.

"Mules," Carstairs nodded. "Well, Ed didn't think so much about that, thinking maybe there was farming done around there. But next morning at daylight he noticed several big barns. One of the doors was open, and inside the barn he saw what looked like a lot of crates and packing cases, which same struck him as mighty peculiar. And come daylight, Ed saw that the hands looked even rougher than they had at night, so he made plans to leave as soon as possible. They didn't offer him any breakfast and he didn't ask for any—just got on his horse and moseyed along."

"And your brother told you how to find this place?" Quist asked.

"He gave me pretty good directions. So I wired you and told Steve about it, and Steve sent a telegram to Sheriff Egan."

Dewitt said, "I wired Egan, too, asking that he round up a crew of fighters."

The train rocked along. Carstairs said suddenly, "Say, you remember the fireman from that last wreck—the one that was hit on the head and left to die?"

"Is he going to recover?" Quist asked.

Carstairs nodded. "They let him talk for a spell this morning when I went up to visit him. He didn't get a good look at the coyote that struck him, but from a distance the fellow looked like a fat man with quick little steps that moved easy across the sand."

Quist and Dewitt exchanged glances. "Sounds like Voit," Quist said. "That fireman's account has already been squared."

"And," Dewitt added, "that ties Voit in with the freight thieves, dang his hide!"

It was just a few minutes after one when the men alighted from the caboose at Tanzburg, which proved to be a town very similar in size and appearance to Cenotaph. Sheriff Max Egan, a small wiry man with an iron-gray goatee, met them at the station when they alighted.

"I got your wire, Pete," he said, "and have that crew ready you asked for." He shook hands gravely with Quist, saying, "I think we've got some good news for you, Mr. Quist."

Quist nodded. "I heard about the mules being located. Of course, maybe we're on the wrong track—"

"No, sirree!" Egan said. "Not this time. This is something Carstairs hasn't heard yet, neither. To make a long story short, four of those mules came in to Tanzburg this morning, drawing a wagon of goods—men's clothing and scotch whisky—though why anybody should drink scotch when he can get bourbon—" Egan spat a brown stream of tobacco juice. "Anyway, it was the scotch that got the fellow in trouble. He kept driving from saloon to saloon, trying to sell the stuff—and awful cheap too. So I just grabbed him and wanted to know why."

"Was it a brand called Glen Spey Scotch?" Quist asked.

"That's her. Black-and-yellow label, with red initials on the words. Well, come to find out the driver had already sold a lot of men's clothing to one of the clothing-store merchants here—and again awful cheap. Well, I never did believe in mistreating a suspect, so my knuckles wa'n't bad skinned up before this fellow that drove the mules decided it would be better to 'fess up he was peddling stolen goods. So I prompt arrested the clothing merchant for the receiving of same, and he did some talking, too, and this wa'n't the first time he'd bought goods from the fellow."

Egan paused to spit again. "The upshot of the matter is that it was freight goods, stolen from wrecks on the railroad—wrecks that was caused by the thieves in most cases, not only on the T. N. & A. S., but north of here as well. And you'll never guess who's at the head of the thieving."

"It wouldn't be Dr. Jorge, would it?" Quist asked.

Sheriff Egan's face dropped. "Sho', now, how'd you guess?"

"Suspicion's been pointing that way," Quist said quietly.

There were astonished exclamations from Carstairs and Deputy Wilson. "Why, it's only about three months back I had a lame shoulder, and Doc Jorge fixed me up fine," Wilson burst out.

"Doc Jorge fixed up lots of fellers that way," Egan nodded, "but he's a slick one, just the same. I tried to pick him up this morning, but somebody said they'd seen him riding out of town again, so I reckon he's returned to his hide-out. I knew he had a place, north of here, somewheres, where he went frequent, but he always give out he went there to work on a new cure for glanders and to do some experimenting with stock. And as he's right good treating such, I never doubted his word. Cripes! He always voted for me when I ran for—"

"Do you know where his place is?" Quist cut in.

"I'll take you and the boys there," Egan nodded, "and we'll round ourselves up a passel of sidewinders—"

"What I want to know," Wilson interrupted, "is where those wagon tracks disappeared to that day. Did you find out where the wagons got to?"

Egan nodded. "It's plumb simple when you know what happened. Those wagon tracks led to the east face of red buttes. Right now, we're west of those buttes. Jorge's place is at the end of a long canyon that reaches just this side of those buttes. From where he's situated, it's plumb simple to get to the top of the buttes. So what does he do? When wagons arrive with stolen freight, ropes are lowered and the freight pulled up. Then they pull the wagons and next the mules. Horses might object to that, but mules is tough critters—"

"I'll be danged!" Quist exclaimed. "And the thieves who do the work just scatter on their ponies and eventually work back to Jorge's place, leaving law officers nothing to follow except some hoofprints that fan out in all directions and some wagon tracks that vanish smack-dab against those red buttes."

"That's it." Egan nodded. "Jorge sort of heads the gang, but there's a hombre named Voit who runs things. Want to go get 'em?"

"The quicker the better," Quist nodded. "I killed Voit on the way here." He paused and gave details. "There's still work to be done."

"With Voit's killing, you made a good start. Let's go get a drink. No need putting off a nasty job any longer."

20. Freight Thieves' Finish

Across from the railroad depot a number of armed men—probably thirty of them—waited in the vicinity of the Semaphore Saloon. Along a lengthy reach of hitchrails, saddled cow ponies switched tails at buzzing flies. Egan led his companions to the saloon, pausing on the way to ask a lanky string bean of a man wearing a deputy's badge: "Did you get those four extra mounts, Wash?"

"They're ready to move, Max, when the riders are," Wash replied.

"All right. Go tell Marshal Griggs not to forget to feed the prisoners in the jail, if I don't return for a spell. And tell Griggs we might as well let that tramp in the corner cell board a few more days. You can't turn a man out on short notice in these times." And then to Quist and his companions of the caboose: "C'mon, we'll wet our gullets before we drift. It might prove a dusty ride."

Twenty minutes later the cavalcade of riders swept out of Tanzburg before the wondering, curious gaze of the town's citizenry. Egan, Quist, Dewitt, and Steve Wilson rode in front, the others being strung out behind, with those in the rear riding wide to avoid the dust of the leaders. Every rider in the group was well armed; about half of them carried rifles, in addition to their six-shooters.

The riders headed due north, riding in the very shadow of the Pihuela Range. The foothills rose gradually on the right until they'd blended with the rugged peaks, just beyond which were the red buttes. From time to time Egan checked landmarks to determine that they were traveling correctly.

"This feller that drove the load in to town," Egan confided to Quist, "give me right good directions for getting to Jorge's canyon—if he wa'n't lying. And I don't think he was; he's too dam' anxious to get off easy with a good word from me, once those scuts have been brought to trial." He spat a splashing brown stream and added grimly, "If there's anybody left to bring to trial. You know, I hate to take this action against Doc Jorge, always thought right well of him, but when a man runs counter to law—well, friendship ceases."

Now and then the procession of riders crossed a small cottonwood-lined stream, and the horses were watered. Then the men pushed on again. The sun had passed meridian sometime before and was dropping on its long westward journey. The shadows had commenced to lengthen when Sheriff Egan again called for a halt.

"The entrance to the canyon is hereabouts, someplace," he stated, checking certain land-marks. "I reckon it's just about over there"—

pointing to a narrow passage between two foothills. "Light, boys, and rest your saddles a mite. We still got a ride before us."

The deputy known as Wash produced beef-and-biscuit sandwiches. Canteens were half emptied. Quist had been scrutinizing the gravelly soil where here and there small tufts of grass sprang above the surface. He returned to where Egan was chewing on a chunk of beef and stated, "Four mules and a wagon have passed this way within the past twenty-four hours."

"Probably that hombre I arrested today. Well, that's added proof we're on the right trail," Egan said. "It's going to be dark when we get there, Mr. Quist. Would you rather ride in by daylight? If so, we can bed down for a spell and plan to arrive at dawn."

"How do your men feel about it?" Quist asked. "I'd like to hear your ideas."

"My men will follow whatever I choose."

Quist speculated, "We might have a better chance for a surprise at dawn. At the same time, if that fellow you arrested doesn't return when he should, the thieves will, maybe, be expecting trouble. I'm for going on now, before they get suspicious that something has gone wrong."

"Great minds irrigate the same ditches," Egan said dryly, and dyed a rich brown some leaves on a nearby sagebrush. "You and me think alike." He turned and called to the others, "All right, you hombres, no use letting your saddles get cooled off."

Five minutes later the riders were wending their way through the foothills of the Pihuelas. For a time they climbed steadily, then the trail dipped; a little later they were climbing again. The sun dropped; light lingered but a few minutes before darkness closed in. One by one stars winked into being overhead. From time to time Quist's ears caught the rustling of cottonwood leaves in the night breeze, though now it was difficult to see where he was headed. Only the shadowy figure of Sheriff Egan by his side told him he was on the right trail. Max Egan seemed to have the eyes of a cat—a small, steely-muscled tomcat.

Now and then a match glowed momentarily while one of the riders lighted a cigarette. Pete Dewitt, on Quist's left, said, "Greg, there doesn't seem any end to this ride. First thing we know we'll be coming out on the other side of these mountains."

"Not without cutting through those red buttes," Quist replied. "And you'll remember I never did find any pass through those cliffs."

After a time the stars paled and the sky became lighter and they knew the moon was up, though on this side of Pihuela Range it wasn't yet visible. The horses moved steadily on. There wasn't a great deal of conversation, and what there was was held in lowered tones. At regular intervals there ensued a loud splashing sound as Max Egan relieved his bulging cheeks of a quantity of tobacco-brown saliva.

The way commenced to drop, and after passing between two high ridges the riders found themselves dipping down through a high-walled canyon, which narrowed until not more than three horses could pass comfortably abreast. The rock-cluttered floor of the canyon picked up the sounds of horses' hoofs and flung them against the narrow canyon walls, from whence they were hurled back to the riders' ears, greatly magnified. Deeper and deeper the way penetrated into the mountains, twisting and turning. Then gradually commenced a long climb upward, with more turnings and bends.

Abruptly, on one of the canyon walls ahead, moonlight showed and the way rapidly grew wider, the walls on either side shrinking in height as the horses pushed up and up. There may have been an hour of this sort of going; perhaps less, but after a time Egan passed the word back for a halt to rest the panting horses. And then, after a ten-minute rest, the men pushed on once more.

Abruptly the riders emerged from the canyon to see a broad, moonlight-bathed, grassy slope rising before them, the slope appearing to terminate in a sort of tableland, or mesa, which reached clear to what Quist judged was the top of the red buttes. At any rate there was an almost horizontal line silhouetted against the night sky, and it was a simple matter to imagine stolen freight being hauled up from mule-drawn wagons below.

At a point near the top of the grassy slope was a cluster of buildings, from one of which lights showed. Sheriff Egan called for a halt. "I reckon we'd better spread out, men," he said, "and then we'll start to close in. When we get nearly there, I'll hail the house and call on the scuts to surrender. We've got to give 'em that much chance, anyway"—he spat a long brown stream that glistened in the moonlight—"though I'm hoping they won't listen to me."

And just at that moment there came a loud hee-hawing from a corral among the buildings. "Mules!" Egan said disgustedly, and spat again. Another mule took up the braying, and then another.

Suddenly the door of the house was flung open and a man stood framed against the light. "That you, Deke?" he bawled uncertainly.

"Dangit," Egan growled. "This starts something before I'm ready." He raised his voice, "No, it ain't Deke and Deke won't be back. I put him in a cell this morning. This is Max Egan. Is Doc Jorge there?"

The door was suddenly slammed shut. Lights in the house were quickly extinguished. Abruptly a window was flung up and a rifle barked, the slug whining high over the heads of the waiting riders.

Egan sighed. "This starts it. Spread out and unlimber some lead toward the point where that flash showed. Then gradually close in on the scuts and we'll—"

More fire burst from other windows of the house. Quist reached for the rifle in his saddle scabbard, jerked it to his shoulder and pulled trigger. Other men near him were firing now. The horses were closing in. Quist emptied the rifle and reloaded. A rider not far from him groaned with pain and toppled from the saddle.

"Get to the ground," Egan howled. "We're just sitting ducks out here in this moonlight. But keep pushing toward the house."

Lancelike streaks of orange fire spurted from various windows in the house. Pete swore suddenly. Quist said, "Did they get you?"

Dewitt displayed a bloody crease across the back of one hand. He said, "It stings, but that's all."

Bullets were cutting through the air like angry hornets. There came a swift drumming of hoofs, and Quist saw that Carstairs was again in the saddle, riding like mad in a wide arc to approach the house. A moment later Quist saw him disappear in a tall clump of brush a short distance from the house. He waited to see the flash of Carstairs' gunfire, but none came.

The staccato roar of the guns lifted to a crescendo. On Quist's left a horse went down, kicking wildly. Its rider, already on the earth, dropped the reins and dashed forward at a crouching run. The windows of the house displayed momentary bits of crimson fringe.

Quist's rifle emptied again. He thrust it into the boot on the saddle and, jerking his six-shooter from shoulder holster, moved swiftly nearer the house. After a moment his left hand plucked from the waistband of his trousers the six-shooter he'd recovered from Voit that day.

The air was heavy with the acrid odor of powder smoke by this time. And all through the din of firing, Sheriff Max Egan's sharp voice kept issuing commands to "close in, like you didn't care to live forever!" Several of his men were sprawled on the earth now, left behind as their comrades advanced, some leading their horses, some having left their mounts behind. What damage was being done to those in the house, there was no way of telling.

Egan's voice again sounded above the rattle of gunfire: "You, Doc Jorge, you'd better give up. We got you trapped—"

An abrupt increase of firing interrupted the words. Max Egan went down, gasping and choking.

Quist quickly reached the man's side. "You hurt bad, Max?"

The sheriff cursed and spat out a chew of tobacco. "Ain't hurt a-tall," he stated grouchily.

"One of them slugs come so close it startled me into swallowing my cud. I might have strangled to death."

He swayed as Quist helped him to his feet, and Quist saw that one arm dangled uselessly at the sheriff's side. "You're a poor liar, Max," Quist said. "Now you take it easy. I'll run things from here on."

"You go to hell," Egan snapped. "Ain't nothing wrong with this arm, 'cepting that I can't lift it. I still got an arm left." He retrieved his gun and sent three shots winging toward the house.

Quist shot his gaze quickly over the grassy slope. On either side men were firing and reloading, firing and reloading. They were nearer the house now, and even while Quist looked he saw a man pitch forward on his face.

A horseman came galloping from the direction of the house. Quist lifted his gun.

"Don't shoot!" the rider cried. "It's me—Carstairs."

He dismounted in a running stop, even as he pulled the horse to a halt. Egan demanded, "Where you been?"

"Doing something that needed doing," Carstairs said. "The way we're going, all the advantage lies with them in the house. But that will change in a few minutes."

"I asked, where you been?" Egan said again.

Carstairs explained. "I worked around to the

back of the house and got some dry brush which I stacked against the wall. Then I touched a match to it. You'll see them bustards making tracks out of there before long—"

"You set fire to the house?" Egan exclaimed.

"You've called it right."

Egan cursed his useless arm and grumbled, "I don't know as I hold with burning them coyotes out. Don't seem human—"

"It didn't seem human when they burned my brother-in-law in that caboose, neither," Carstairs said, hard-voiced, "after they shot him through the head."

Egan nodded. "Maybe I'll learn to keep my big mouth shut someday."

Even while he was speaking, a lurid glow of light rose at the rear of the house. Then came excited cries. The flames spread rapidly, and darting figures could now be seen plainly through windows lighted by tongues of flame.

Suddenly the door was flung open again and a man started out on the run. A dozen bullets cut him down before he had taken two steps. Another figure appeared and miraculously passed through the hail of lead that was directed toward him. He was heading in the direction of the horse corral.

"They'll be trying to get mounted," Egan bawled loudly. "Cut 'em off, men!"

At the house, figures were now leaping from windows to avoid the raging inferno that flamed inside the walls. A spot of orange fire appeared on the roof, disappeared, to be followed by twin tongues of fiery light. In an instant the whole roof was ablaze, lighting brilliantly the surrounding landscape. The flames crackled and roared, almost drowning out the barking of the guns.

Quist was again in the saddle, riding toward the house. A man on foot suddenly appeared on either side of him, trying to drag him from the saddle. He shot one and struck the other across the face with his six-shooter. The grasping hands fell away.

By this time two of the bandits had succeeded in reaching the horse corral, but both were cut down by a hail of flying lead. Running men were silhouetted an instant against the light from the flaming house, then were seen to fall forward and lie without movement. A horse and rider went crashing to earth, the horse screaming madly with pain, its hoofs wildly flailing the air. The drum of gunfire went on.

Suddenly cries for mercy and offers to surrender penetrated the din. The horsemen closed in, the firing of guns started to fall off. Only the house continued to blaze furiously.

Five minutes later a circle of riders had surrounded a group of terrified freight thieves, who stood shivering with their arms high in the air, some of them begging not to be shot.

Egan had hauled himself back on his horse and

with one arm hanging loosely at his side pushed between the riders. "Anything been seen of Doc Jorge—" he stated, then, as his eyes fell on a bulky-waisted, middle-aged man in shirt sleeves, Egan continued bitterly, "Doc, you blasted fool!"

"Admitted," Doc Jorge replied. "I pushed my luck too far for once." He looked pale, but was keeping his nerve in direct contrast to some of his companions who were now on their knees begging for mercy. "Yep, I can see now I didn't show any sense, Max—hey, looks like you got a hurt in that arm. Somebody get me some water and rags. I can fix that in a jiffy."

Quist spoke to Dewitt, and the two went on a tour of inspection of the other buildings. They passed a corral full of mules and another corral holding saddle horses. There were several wagons about. In one of the buildings they found a pulley mechanism and heavy ropes. In the barns they saw, piled nearly to the rafters, packing cases and crates of stolen merchandise—clothing, machinery, liquors and wines, tobacco, household goods, canned food—there seemed no end to the variety of merchandise the freight thieves had looted from wrecked railroad cars.

By the time Quist and Dewitt returned to the spot where they had left Egan and the others, the burning house was practically finished. Several men were given such aid as was possible to relieve their wounds; other men were beyond help.

Quist and Dewitt found Sheriff Egan sitting by himself, against one of the corrals, nursing his wounded arm, which had by now been cleaned and bandaged, and furiously chewing tobacco. The rest of the men stood some way off, with the prisoners.

"Find what you expected to find?" Egan asked, getting to his feet.

Quist nodded. "Those barns are packed with loot."

"I'll have the boys hitch up some wagons and haul it to Tanzburg. You won't have to bother with it."

"Thanks. How'd we come through?"

"One of our boys was killed outright. We got several wounded, but none what you'd call serious. As to them danged freight thieves, there's about a third of 'em left to be brought to trial—and if I had my way, they'd all be hung—all except Doc Jorge. I feel sort of sorry for him. I guess he wa'n't too much to blame. He's working on the wounded right now."

Quist said, hard-voiced, "There's an account that Jorge will have to settle."

"Nobody's denyin' that—not even Doc himself," Egan said quickly. "Trouble was, he needed money to carry on experiments in curing stock of their ailments. He'd bought a bunch of mules to work on, mules being tougher than horses, and kept 'em up here. Got 'em from up north someplace. That's why we never saw 'em come through Tanzburg. But his money ran out, and when Voit came to him with a proposition for robbing freight cars, Doc Jorge fell in with the plan—figuring he'd only do it once to get some money. You know how that goes. Once he was in, he couldn't get out. Voit wouldn't let him. Though Doc swears he never knew there was any killing of train crews, or that wrecks were deliberately plotted to happen. And I believe him." The sheriff spat a thin brown streak.

The light from the glowing embers of the house was dying away now. Quist said, "Where'd he meet Voit?"

"Now that's a queer thing too," Egan said slowly. "Voit was Doc Jorge's half brother. Voit looked him up when he came down this way."

"From where?"

"Doc doesn't know for sure, but he suspects that Voit had been mixed into a lot of dirty work, train robbing and so on, up in the northern states—Voit and Belvard, they came to this country at the same time."

"Belvard was mixed into the freight thieving, I suppose," Dewitt put in.

"I don't know as he was," Egan replied. "Doc never saw Belvard, but Voit told him Belvard was playing for big stakes over near Cenotaph, but he never told Doc what they were exactly. Voit used to stay at Belvard's ranch most of the time and take liquor there when they'd robbed a freight train."

"And so we've got to get Belvard on some other charge," Quist said tiredly.

"Looks that way," Egan nodded, and spat again. "Though you'd think those crooks would have had a right good thing here. Jorge got around to other towns, made contacts to find what sort of merchandise dealers would buy, and then he'd deliver at mighty low prices. Mostly, he didn't sell stuff in Tanzburg, but there's two fellers there have been buying from him right along. One I arrested this morning—I guess, by this time, I mean yesterday morning—and the other I'll get when I go back."

"The T. N. & A. S. owes you a lot, Max," Quist said. "I'm going to see that it's not forgotten. Pete and I both appreciate your help."

"Forget it. For that matter, there's some other lines that are indebted to you, Mr. Quist. Your road isn't the only one that was robbed." He added with a scowl and another splashing of brown saliva, "After all, this was being carried on right in my own county. I couldn't stand for that, you know."

"And you didn't," Pete said.

The three men talked awhile longer, then Pete and Quist decided to get an early start back to Tanzburg, leaving the cleaning up and freighting job to Egan and his men. Quist looked up Carstairs, returned his rifle, and said he'd see him again some time. Then he and Pete procured fresh horses from the corral and loped away from Doc Jorge's place, intent now on reaching Cenotaph as soon as possible.

It was nearing eleven in the morning when Quist and Dewitt reached Tanzburg. Quist at once sent a long telegram to Jay Fletcher, the division superintendent, advising him of the rounding up of the freight thieves and giving fairly generous details regarding the accomplishment. Nor did he forget to make mention of the help given him by Sheriffs Dewitt and Egan and Deputy Sheriff Steve Wilson. That done, there was nothing to do except sit around and wait for the next train going to Cenotaph.

It was after suppertime when they dismounted from the train at Cenotaph. Luke Rutson was there to meet them, and congratulated Quist on the outcome of his fight with Voit.

"I made the mistake," Rutson said apologetically, "of telling the boys you'd got Voit, so the news is all over town. I don't suppose it makes any difference, does it?"

"I reckon not," Quist said. "I wonder if Belvard knows about it."

"I was talking to him in the Sundown," Rutson nodded. "I was some surprised when Belvard said it's a good thing Voit's finished—that he'd never trusted him and so on."

"I'm sort of surprised myself," Quist said dryly.

"Anything else happened, Luke?" Dewitt asked.

"Nothing to speak of. Judge Harnsworth intends to read Gid Harmon's will tomorrow. Mrs. Harmon was in to see about it, and the Judge asked me to let you know. Harnsworth added that it couldn't be put off any longer."

"Where'll he read it?" Quist asked.

"At his office. Mrs. Harmon will be in town—"

Quist swung on Dewitt. "Tell the Judge to invite me, too, and ask him to have Belvard there. He can drop a hint that the will may concern Belvard. Can you fix it, Pete?"

"I reckon so."

"And you might as well count yourself in on the deal. It may prove interesting. C'mon, let's find some restaurant that's still open, before we hit the hay—wait a minute, I want to see if there are any telegrams for me."

Dewitt followed Quist into the station. Two telegrams were waiting for Quist. The first was rather lengthy, and he read it through, then stuffed it into a coat pocket. The other was from the division superintendent, Jay Fletcher, in reply to the one Quist had sent from Tanzburg. It read:

Your good news lifted a load from my mind. Men you mentioned will be rewarded, but don't know how to show you my personal appreciation. As special

277

investigator you are now free to follow other pursuits, which I imagine concerns the lovely Lilith. May I offer to stand as best man at the wedding?

JAY.

Quist laughed shortly and showed the message to Dewitt.

Dewitt read it through and, smiling, raised his eyes to meet Quist's. "Do I offer my congratulations, now, Greg?"

"You'd better save 'em for a spell," Quist said shortly. "Nobody's yet convinced me I'm the marrying kind." His topaz eyes twinkled suddenly. "Besides, I haven't talked to the girl about it—yet."

A man pushed through the doorway of the station, glanced around, then approached Dewitt and Quist. "Mr. Quist?" he asked.

Quist nodded. "What's on your mind?"

"Doc Lang sent me to find you, if I could. Stark Garrity is due to regain consciousness pretty quick, and he may not last long. Doc said you wanted to talk to him."

Quist whirled toward the station doorway. "Right now, there's nothing I want more." He called back over his shoulder: "I'll see you, later, Pete. Adios!"

21. A Direct Accusation

Quist was freshly shaven and wore a clean white shirt and new bandanna when he stepped into the Stopgap for breakfast the following morning. There were still several customers at the long counter, but Caroline found time to smile and ask: "Stack of wheats, mister?"

"With ham and lots of coffee."

The breakfasters thinned out while Quist ate. Finally the last one had left. Caroline cleaned dishes from the counter and tables, then said, "I don't want to hurry you, but I've got to leave right soon."

"I know that, too. I'll be ready when you are."

"Are you going to Judge Harnsworth's?"

"I've got to see that you get there safely. Pete been in yet?"

"He finished about ten minutes before you came in." The girl paused, then, "I heard Stark Garrity died last night." She looked narrowly at Quist.

Quist said, "So I understand."

"Weren't you there?"

Quist admitted he was there.

"Did he—did Garrity throw any light on Uncle Gid's death?" the girl asked hesitatingly.

"Can you think of any reason why he should?" Quist asked.

Caroline reddened a bit angrily. "Why ask me a

question like that? It's almost as if—as if—" She paused, helpless.

Quist chuckled. "That's one thing I like about you—you flare up so easy. Yes, Garrity did fill in one or two details I'd only suspected before."

"What were they?"

"You'll hear in plenty of time. Mr. Hoddy Belvard will be at the Judge's, too, and he'll have to hear, and I don't like to repeat my stories."

"Hoddy Belvard!" Caroline's eyes widened. "What will he be doing there?"

"That," Quist assured Caroline, "is something I'm not quite sure of. Come on, grab your bib and tucker and we'll be on our way."

Caroline glanced down at the brown plaid gingham dress, smoothed her hair. "I don't need a hat, and it's too warm for a coat," she said. "I'm ready when you are." She stepped back into the kitchen a moment, then reappeared, ready for the street.

When they arrived at Eli Harnsworth's office, on the northeast corner of Waco Street, at Main, the Judge hadn't yet put in an appearance. Pete Dewitt was already standing on the sidewalk in front of the building which advertised on its broad front window Harnsworth's name with, below, the words Attorney at Law. The office was situated directly across from the courthouse, which was convenient for the Judge such times as he officiated in his position as justice of the peace.

Caroline and Quist spoke to Pete. Pete asked a question concerning Garrity's death, but Quist put him off with, "I'll tell you later. Here comes Belvard."

Belvard came jogging up on his pony, alighted at the hitchrack, flipped his reins over the tie rail, and strode around to the sidewalk, doffing his Stetson to Caroline and nodding to the two men.

"I suppose you're waiting to hear Gid Harmon's will read," he said. "I don't know why Judge Harnsworth requested me to be present. I feel quite sure Harmon hasn't made me one of his beneficiaries, unless"—a hopeful gleam appeared in Belvard's eyes—"Gid decided to cancel the debt I still owe on my outfit. We were good friends once, despite our slight differences the past year or so."

"I don't suppose you care to state what those differences were about," Quist said quietly.

"I don't know why I shouldn't." Belvard shrugged his shoulders. "Though it was a purely personal matter. You see, I'd fallen behind a bit in the payments I was to make to Gid, but I'd finally made him see that everything would be all right. . . . By the way, Quist, I hear you killed the Egg, yesterday—sorry, Miss Trent, that's a blunt way to mention it."

"No need to apologize to me," Caroline said tartly. "The news is pretty well known in

Cenotaph by now. Mr. Quist may not care to have the matter brought up—"

"There's nothing much to bring up," Quist interrupted. "It was my job, in the first place. In the second, it was Voit's life or mine. Why are you interested, Belvard?"

"I'm not, particularly," Belvard said carelessly. "I was just wondering if you found anything on him that might show he was responsible for Gid Harmon's death."

"Such as what?" Quist said bluntly.

"I've not the least idea. You're a detective. You know what to look for in such cases. Not that I care, one way or the other. Voit worked for me, but I never liked him. I told him long ago that I was ready to dispense with his services, but he kept hanging on—until last week. Then he suddenly pulled out without a word. Just what was the trouble between you and Voit, Quist?"

"I don't like bad eggs," Quist said shortly.

"Here's Harnsworth now," Dewitt said suddenly.

Judge Harnsworth, a tall, portly man in his sixties, with a somewhat pompous manner and metal-rimmed eyeglasses, came striding along the sidewalk. "Ah, waiting I see," he said in a reedy voice. "Sorry if I've kept you—Mrs. Harmon not here yet? Well, we'll go inside, anyway."

He opened the door to his office and ushered his guests into a large room with a desk at the rear wall. In one corner was a safe. There were a couple of pictures on the walls, and a framed diploma; a case filled with calfbound volumes took up the greater part of another wall. There were several straight-backed chairs scattered about the big room, and a swivel chair stood at the desk. The floor was covered with a threadbare green carpet. Windows in one wall and in the front of the building allowed light to enter.

"Sit down, Caroline—gentlemen," Harnsworth said. "Mrs. Harmon should be here any minute— ah, here she is now."

Lilith had entered and again closed the door behind her. She was in riding togs—divided skirt, flannel shirt open at the throat, high-heeled boots, and Stetson hat. With her handkerchief she was brushing dust from her clothing as she entered. Quist looked at her and thought he had never seen a lovelier woman.

Lilith swept the room with her smile, though its warmth was tempered somewhat by the cool nod she accorded Belvard. "Hello, Greg, Pete. Caroline, I love your hair done on top of your head that way. I'm sorry if I'm late, Judge Harnsworth. It's such a lovely morning, I guess I didn't ride as fast as I should have."

"You were well worth waiting for, Mrs. Harmon," Harnsworth said gallantly. "We really haven't been in here but a minute. If you'll all sit down now—please." He turned and busied himself with the knob of the ancient iron safe in the corner.

His guests seated themselves in a semicircle before the desk, Quist at the Judge's left, Belvard on the extreme right of Harnsworth. Lilith seated herself next to Quist, then came Caroline and Pete.

Harnsworth returned to his desk with a paper in his hand and sat down. He cleared his throat and said in a thin reedy tone, entirely devoid of any emotion: "You have been brought here to hear the reading of the last will and testament of Gideon Harmon." His voice became more human for a moment: "So far as we know to the contrary, this is Gideon's last will. If there ever existed any other will, it has not come to light. There are a few other beneficiaries aside from those present, but they come in for relatively small amounts, such as remembrances to members of Gideon's Thunderbird crew and a few friends in Cenotaph, which will be paid in due course."

"Is there any particular reason for my being here?" Belvard asked.

Harnsworth hesitated and looked appealingly at Quist. Finally he said, "You are here at Mr. Quist's request."

Belvard stiffened. "What's the idea, Quist?"

"You'll understand before long. This business involves the murder of Gid Harmon, as you've probably guessed, now—"

"Good Lord!" Belvard exclaimed. "I had nothing to do with that. I have a perfect alibi for the day he died. You know that."

"I know nothing of the sort," Quist said coldly. "You just imagine you have an alibi. I've done considerable investigating and found certain clues. Stark Garrity told me some things before he died that explained things I'd hitherto only suspected."

Lilith exclaimed, "Greg! Was it Garrity who killed my husband?"

"That's it!" Belvard said eagerly. "It was Garrity! But you can't tie me up with Garrity's doings, Quist. I never had anything to do with him. Even our crews didn't mix—scarcely spoke—"

"I make no accusations against the cowhands of the Thunderbird or HB-Connected," Quist cut in. "As to you and Garrity, that's a different matter. No, Belvard, you didn't kill Harmon, but you know who was responsible for his death."

"That's a lie!" Belvard sprang furiously to his feet.

Quist said wearily to Dewitt, "Pete, you'll have to keep him quiet, I guess."

Pete drew his six-shooter and growled, "Sit down, Belvard, and listen." Belvard sat down, his features working angrily.

"Look here, Greg," Lilith smiled, "I saw quite a bit of Mr. Belvard when he used to visit Gideon at

285

the ranch. Maybe they did have their differences, but I can't believe Mr. Belvard had anything to do with the death of my husband."

"You know better than that, Lilith," Quist smiled thinly. "Of course he had something to do with Gid's death—and nobody knows that better than you do."

"I?" Lilith sprang to her feet, looking bewildered. "Don't talk ridiculously, Greg. How should I know?"

"Because you killed him," Quist stated quietly.

22. Conclusion

For just an instant there was silence, then Caroline's "Lilith!" rang through the room, the tone sounding both pained and surprised. Pete Dewitt's eyes were bulging from their sockets. Quist said sharply, "Don't get careless, Pete."

Here Judge Harnsworth's stammering voice cut in: "This is no time for levity, Mr. Quist."

"Really, Greg," Lilith said coolly, "I must agree with the Judge. Garrity must have told you a whopper to make you believe I did anything like that. I can't understand—"

"You can and you do," Quist stated.

"Judge Harnsworth," Lilith interrupted, "I must protest this business—"

"Mrs. Harmon is right," Harnsworth said righteously. "Quist—"

"Mrs. Harmon," Quist said coldly, "is guilty as the dickens. And you are going to listen while I prove that statement. If Lilith and Belvard prefer, we can place 'em in cells right now, or they can listen, too. Just as they see fit."

Lilith directed a chilly smile in Belvard's direction. "After all, it might be amusing to hear what's been cooked up concerning us. I'd prefer that to being taken to a cell, wouldn't you?"

Belvard said sullenly, "I don't know what else we can do."

Lilith laughed confidently. "Go ahead, Greg Quist. This is certain to be funny. I'll enjoy hearing your apology later."

Quist started again: "Belvard came to this country a number of years back and made a partial payment to Gid Harmon for the ranch now known as the HB-Connected. Probably he never planned to complete the payments, but Harmon had insisted on retaining the deed until full payment was made, so Belvard tried to arrange a marriage with Harmon's niece, Caroline, in the hope that the Thunderbird would be left to Caroline, along with everything else Harmon owned. That idea too failed, though it did bring about a quarrel between Harmon and Caroline—"

"This is a pack of lies—" Belvard commenced, but at a look from Dewitt he fell silent. An amused smile played about Lilith's red lips, but she said nothing.

"So," Quist went on, "Belvard conceived another plan. One way or another, he prevailed upon Harmon to go to Denver with him, and there he introduced Harmon to Lilith. Harmon fell in love with her, they were married, and he brought her back to the Thunderbird—"

"My grief, Greg," Lilith cut in, "I've never denied any of that, though I do deny that Hoddy introduced us and planned—"

"About a year ago"—Quist ignored the interruption—"Harmon learned that Lilith and

Belvard were meeting very frequently. He thought his Thunderbird luck had deserted him, he took to drinking, he quarreled with Belvard on Main Street, shook his fist in Belvard's face and made certain threats. From then on, Belvard and Lilith met secretly. Harmon suspected this and, to trap them, announced he was leaving on a trip to Tanzburg. Instead of that, he hid in the brush, not far from the ranch, and followed Lilith one morning when she rode past. Lilith met Belvard on the trail, and the two of them went to an old cabin of Harmon's, up in the foothills—"

Lilith asked, her eyes flashing, "Do you realize exactly what you are insinuating, Mr. Gregory Quist?"

"Facts will back up my statements," Quist said coldly.

Lilith appealed to Harnsworth, her features crimson: "Judge Harnsworth, must I sit here and—"

"I'm telling you to sit there," Quist snapped, and Lilith fell silent, while Quist went on: "Belvard and Lilith saw Harmon approaching the cabin, and Belvard sneaked out through the rear window, where the horses had been tethered in the brush, so as not to be seen by any chance passer-by, while Lilith remained in the cabin, in an effort to convince Harmon she was there alone. It didn't work, as Harmon must already have seen the hoofprints where Belvard's horse joined Lilith's pony. I imagine Harmon started from the cabin to find and shoot Belvard. Apparently he drew his gun, or maybe it was already drawn. Lilith tried to prevent this. There was a scuffle. Lilith seized Harmon's wrist, bent it back. Maybe she pressed the trigger. At any rate the gun was exploded against Harmon's body. As Lilith released Harmon, he fired another shot—perhaps at Lilith, I don't know. But Pete has that bullet, which I dug from the floor—"

"Now wait a minute, Quist," Harnsworth protested. "Harmon was a pretty powerful man. Are you going to maintain that Lilith had the strength to bend his wrist back?"

"Exactly," Quist nodded. "Harmon's wrist showed the marks of her fingernails—and don't forget that Harmon's right wrist had been sprained and was weak. Neither was he as young as he once was, while Lilith is a healthy young woman and, I'd say, fairly strong." He glanced at Lilith as though for confirmation, but the woman just stared wide-eyed at him. "So that was the situation," Quist said. "Belvard knew he'd be suspected of a hand in Harmon's death, so he and Lilith planned to call it suicide, or at least throw suspicion in another direction, as they weren't sure they could make a suicide theory stick with the authorities."

Quist paused to reach for cigarette papers and tobacco, and rolled a cigarette while he talked: "To make it appear like suicide, there should be but one cartridge exploded in the gun. Harmon's gun had been fired twice, so Belvard substituted one of his own cartridges in the cylinder of the weapon. Then, between them, they hoisted Harmon's body across the saddle of his horse. Belvard set out for Cenotaph to establish an alibi, while Lilith mounted her own pony and led Harmon's horse, carrying the dead body, back to the Thunderbird Ranch."

"Very, very interesting," Lilith purred coolly. "You almost make it sound believable, Greg. I must say—"

The scratching of Quist's match interrupted the words. Quist took a deep drag, blew out the smoke and said, "Now Stark Garrity comes into the picture. Stark had been one of Belvard's gang of bandits up north one time—"

"I never had anything to do with bandits!" Belvard raised one hand in protest. "You—"

That was as far as he had got when Dewitt rapped him across the knuckles with the barrel of a six-shooter and told him to shut up. Quist picked up the story again:

"Garrity had killed a man and was still wanted by the law. That was the club Belvard had to hold over him. Garrity had broken away from Belvard and come to the Thunderbird, where he worked faithfully for Harmon until Belvard came into the picture. I suspect that Garrity had fallen in love with Lilith too. At any rate, when she arrived at the Thunderbird with Harmon's body it was Garrity who helped her take it inside the house, while she told him of the plan to make the death look like suicide. Even against such honest impulses as he had, Garrity promised to help her. And then, unexpectedly, Caroline arrived at the house to bring an old tax receipt—"

"Greg!" Caroline looked horrified. "Was Uncle Gid there when I entered the house?"

Quist nodded. "The body was lying on the floor between the table and the wall. There was no time to carry it to another room. While Garrity stalled you off at the front door, Lilith jerked that scarlet thunderbird rug off the wall and flung it over the body, effectually concealing it. Then she hid in one of the back rooms; when you entered the house she was nowhere in sight. After a short time you departed—"

"Lilith," Caroline wailed, "this can't be true. Tell us it isn't." But Lilith had no reply now. She was staring at Quist like one hypnotized. Belvard gulped but didn't say anything.

"After Caroline departed," Quist continued, "they placed the body nearer the center of the room. It was then they noticed Harmon's hat was missing, and Lilith quickly got another to take its place, though a really smart person would have picked one with the sweatband stained."

Belvard exploded suddenly, "Dang the luck!" and as suddenly fell silent again.

"Not luck, poor planning," Quist smiled thinly "But you had the nerve for a bold stroke anyway." He explained: "Belvard would have an alibi when the suicide was announced, but Lilith didn't. It was known that I was coming to Cenotaph, and Lilith came to me with a cock-and-bull story about her husband's life being threatened and asked me to take a job protecting him. That gave her an alibi, as she was with me when news of Harmon's death arrived. Later she tried to confuse me still more with a note she claimed she had found in one of Harmon's pockets, and which was signed with a red thunderbird. That was pure poppycock, of course, but it did give me cause for thought until I saw a bottle of red ink and plenty of that same blue-lined paper in the bunkhouse. Lilith also hinted that Harmon's death was linked with the doings of the freight thieves, to throw me still farther off the scent—"

"I suppose," Belvard snarled, "that I had something to do with the freight thieves."

"Not much. That was mostly Voit's doings, but he was in your employ and you got some of the profits. Oh yes, Doc Jorge talked some—" He broke off to say to Lilith, "It was a bold stroke, all right, but you overdid it, lady." Her dark eyes showed a flicker of interest, and Quist explained, "You knew I had some reputation as a detective, but you knew too much about that reputation. No one would be likely to remember as much as you claimed to remember about me, so I knew somebody who was familiar with my work had done some coaching. I realized now it was Belvard. And, Lilith, there was just enough truth in various things you told me to make your story plausible. You're a smart actress, with just the right amount of nervousness in your manner—and maybe that was genuine because of the game you were playing—to make me think you were concerned about Harmon's welfare. But when you knew so much about my so-called exploits, lady, I became almighty suspicious."

Quist drew on his cigarette. "There were other things that made me mistrust the setup: Garrity's burning of saddles to destroy bloodstains; in fact Lilith's horse had been cleaned the night she came to Cenotaph, so I wouldn't see mud on the hoofs—oh yes, I checked that at the livery—the cleaning of Harmon's horse's hoofs at—"

"You tawny-headed devil!" Lilith exclaimed suddenly. She bit her lips at the involuntary outburst; her dark eyes flashed sparks.

"Now we're getting somewhere," Quist smiled at the woman. "The day before Harmon was buried, Lilith, you heard that he might have drawn a new will. That gave fresh cause for thought. The original will gave you practically everything. The thought of a new will in Harmon's handwriting worried you. You wanted to see it. So did I. I started for the ranch, ostensibly to return a horse

I'd borrowed. Garrity learned I'd taken the horse from the livery. Through Garrity you arranged for Voit to go to the Thunderbird and get that second will. Voit got there before I did, but John Blackmer had trailed Voit and caught him red-handed. Voit killed Blackmer, then saw me approaching. He hid, knocked me unconscious, then left after an attempt to frame me for Blackmer's murder."

"This is terrible!" Harnsworth exclaimed fervently. "What is happening in these parts? It's a disgrace to the good name of Cenotaph."

Quist stubbed out his cigarette and went on: "Garrity didn't like the way things were going. Last Sunday he rode out to meet Belvard and Voit, to tell them he intended to leave the country. They laughed at his fears and rode with him most of his trip back to the Thunderbird. From a short distance off they saw me arriving there and worked out a plan to kill me, to which Garrity reluctantly consented. Garrity was to place me where I'd make a clear target for Voit's gun. But that night Garrity again lost his nerve. When Voit, hidden in the brush, saw that Garrity hadn't carried out the plan, he shot Garrity, hoping to prevent a revelation of their schemes. Luckily, Garrity lived long enough to tell me these things—"

Belvard interrupted suddenly, his face white, "All right, you've got us. But you can't touch me. I never killed anybody."

Lilith laughed scornfully. "Hoddy, keep your chin up. We're not licked yet. We may go to trial, but they'll never convict *me*. I'll swear Harmon's death was an accident, as it was. The gun went off by chance during the struggle. But I'm his widow, and with the money he left me I'll hire better lawyers than—"

Quist interposed, "Just a moment, Lilith." He drew from a pocket a bloodstained, soiled sheet of paper and handed it to Harnsworth. "I think this will stand up in court, Judge. I took it from Voit's body day before yesterday. I think he was holding it so as to control Belvard and Lilith. It's messed up some, but readable."

Harnsworth accepted the paper, adjusted his glasses, commenced to read. Abruptly he glanced up. "Why—why, this is a holograph will, signed and dated by Gideon Harmon. It supersedes the first will. Aside from a few beneficiaries, the bulk of the estate goes to Gid Harmon's niece, Caroline Trent—"

"Are you saying that *I'm* left out?" Lilith demanded.

The Judge shook his head. "Gideon was smart enough to make it legal by leaving his widow, Lilith Harmon, the sum of one dollar"—quoting from the holograph will—" 'because of her infidelity.' "

Angry spots of crimson darkened Lilith's cheekbones. "The fool!" she stormed. "Did he

296

think that would prevent my getting his money?" Her short laugh was brittle. "Where there's a will there's a way—to break it. And I think Gid Harmon's widow will get her just dues. Once a court of law—"

"You won't take it to a court of law, Lilith," Quist interrupted. "I've had one of the railroad's special investigators doing a little sleuthing up in Denver, and just last night I received a reply to certain questions. The old doorman at the Coronado Opera House remembers you very well, Lilith, and he remembers the night a man of Belvard's description took Harmon around backstage to meet you, when you were Lilith Farrell."

"I don't deny my stage name was Lilith Farrell," the woman said coolly. "It was printed that way on the opera-house program."

Quist said with grudging admiration, "You've been a good actress all the way through, Lilith, but you can't outface facts. You see, that old doorman also remembered that a man named Farrell— Whitney Farrell—had once married you, and that Whitney Farrell fitted the description my investigator had for Hoddy Belvard—the name he took when he came here to defraud Gid Harmon, while you waited in Denver. And my investigator went back through the records and found a copy of your marriage license. So, Lilith, you're still Mrs. Whitney Farrell, and you can be charged with bigamy, unless you can produce divorce papers. And you're not Harmon's widow. Your plan for getting Harmon's wealth has fallen flat as a pancake. Nor have I forgotten Whitney Farrell, leader of the old Hole-in-the-Rock bandits, who slipped through my fingers a good many years ago—"

"All right, we're licked." Lilith was plainly shaken, but still defiant. She threw a quick glance at her husband, Whitney Farrell, now known as Hoddy Belvard. The man was slumped in his chair, his face ashen gray with fear. Lilith laughed scornfully. "Pull yourself together, Hoddy. We're not convicted yet."

Something of the woman's courage seemed to pass into the man. He straightened in his chair, managed a weak smile. "I'm with you, Lilith, no matter what happens." Their eyes met, something unrecognized by the others passed between them.

Lilith turned to Caroline, took her hand. "I hope I haven't disappointed you too much, honey. You're a good kid, and I'm counting on you to help me."

She rose from her chair, holding the attention of the others, and Caroline, confused, moist-eyed, started to rise with her. And in that moment Lilith gave Caroline a shove that sent her stumbling across Pete Dewitt's lap, knocking the six-shooter from Pete's hand.

At the same instant Belvard came to his feet, his

gun out, covering the others. "Don't move, Quist, or I'll plug you. Good work, Lilith. We still make a team. Get some rope and we'll tie these people up until we can get away."

Dewitt was swearing under his breath, trying to untangle himself from Caroline, who was struggling to her feet.

"You, Dewitt, get your hands high," Belvard ordered. "Not you, Quist. I don't want your hands near that shoulder holster. Keep 'em down. Better still, put 'em in your pockets where I can watch 'em."

Quist laughed softly, stuck his hands in his coat pockets, and shot twice through the cloth. "Lucky I carried that extra gun this morning," he was saying.

Belvard sagged at the waistline, the impact of Quist's heavy forty-four slugs bringing about an involuntary pressure of his trigger finger. His six-shooter roared just as Lilith sprang tigerishly toward Quist. Abruptly she paused in mid-step, stiffened, then slumped to the floor, even as Belvard pitched forward on his face.

Powder smoke swirled through the room. Quist quickly smothered the fire smoldering about the hole in his pocket and knelt by Lilith's side. He looked up after a minute and saw Dewitt crouched over Belvard's body. The eyes of the two men met, and each gave the other a short nod.

Harnsworth was the first to speak. His thin reedy voice piped out, "Good God!"

Dewitt strode over and glanced down at Lilith. "What a woman!" he muttered.

Quite suddenly Quist realized that Caroline was sobbing on his shoulder. "She was too darn—darn beautiful to die," Caroline wailed through her tears.

And then there was a sudden rush of people into Judge Harnsworth's office. . . .

After the excitement had died down, and there was no one left in the office except Caroline, Quist, and the Judge, Harnsworth spoke:

"Now that this is over," Harnsworth sighed, "maybe we can return to peaceful pursuits. I suppose you two each have your plans."

"I don't know about Caroline," Quist smiled, "but my sole ambition right now is to get a place on Caroline's list."

And he knew by the look in her eyes that he'd have no trouble achieving that ambition, even though he asked to be placed first.

(Allan) William Colt MacDonald was born in Detroit, Michigan, in 1891. His formal education concluded after his first three months of high school when he went to work as a lathe operator for Dodge Brothers' Motor Company. His first commercial writing consisted of advertising copy and articles for trade publications. While working in the advertising industry, MacDonald began contributing stories of varying lengths to pulp magazines and his first novel, a Western story, was published by Clayton House in *Ace-high Magazine* in 1925. MacDonald later commented that when this first novel appeared in book form as *Restless Guns* in 1929, 'I quit my job cold.' From the time of that decision on, MacDonald's career became a long string of successes in pulp magazines, hardcover books, films, and eventually original and reprint paperback editions. The Three Mesquiteers, MacDonald's most famous characters, were introduced in 1933 in *Law of the Forty-fives*. His other most famous character creation was Gregory Quist, a railroad detective. Some of MacDonald's finest work occurs outside his series, especially the well researched *Stir Up the Dust* which was published first in a British edition in 1950 and *The Mad Marshal* in 1958. MacDonald's only son, Wallace, recalled how much fun his father had writing Western fiction. It is an apt observation since countless readers have enjoyed his stories now for nearly three quarters of a century.

Center Point Publishing
600 Brooks Road • PO Box 1
Thorndike ME 04986-0001 USA

(207) 568-3717

US & Canada:
1 800 929-9108
www.centerpointlargeprint.com